THE LAST KNIGHT

by
CLAIRE LUANA
&
JESIKAH SUNDIN

forest tales
Publishing and Photography

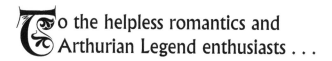o the helpless romantics and Arthurian Legend enthusiasts . . .

This swoony faerie tale is for you!

Glossary & Definitions

Aghanravel	(AH-gan-ra-vell) a fictional city in in the Glens of Antrim along Lough Neagh, province of Ulster, Northern Ireland. Home to the fictional Clann Allán.
Breton	(breh-tun) People from Brittany (a region in France) or who speak the Celtic language of Brittany (similar to Cornish).
Britannia	(breh-tan-knee-uh) A Roman province that incorporated all areas of the island of Britain south of Caledonia (what is mostly Scotland). This term is still used to this day.
Briton	(Bri-ten) the people who inhabited the island of Britain before the Anglo-Saxon invasion and who spoke Brittonic languages known today as Welsh, Cornish, and Breton. During the mid-medieval period, they inhabited most of the west coastline of Britain, even up into parts of Scotland.
Caerleon	(Car-LEE-un) A city in Southern Wales. Known as the mighty Roman "City of the Legion" and where King Arthur is historically believed to have held court.
Clann / Clan	(Kl-an) A tribe of close-knit and/or interrelated people, spelled "clann" in Ireland and "clan" everywhere else.

Dál nAraidi — (Dahl-en-ah-ride-ee) a Cruithne kingdom, or possibly a confederation of Cruithne clanns in the medieval era, located in Northeastern Ireland around Lough Neagh.

Druid — (Drew-id) a person in ancient Celtic cultures who belonged to one of the highest-ranking professional classes. While some were religious leaders, many were also legal authorities, presided as judges, bards (aka lore keepers and historians), medical professionals, and political advisors. In neo-pagan circles, druids are considered nature magicians as well.

Fiann / Fianna — (FEE-an / FEE-an-uh) In Irish mythology, they were small war bands, typically semi-independent. In history, they were usually young warrior nobles / war bands who didn't own land of their own or hadn't yet come into their inheritance.

Fionnabhair — (FEE-oh-nuh-var) the Irish cognate of the Welsh name Gwenhwyfar or Gwenevere, meaning "white fay" or "white enchantress"

Fomorians (aka Fomhórach / Fomhóraigh) — (Foe-more-ee-ahn) They are known as the "people/tribes (children) of the goddess Domnu," a supernatural race and the enemies of the Túatha dé Danann, the first settlers of Ireland. Though many from both clanns intermarry. The Formorians are typically portrayed as orcish-like giants with water-monster features. Children born of Formorians and Túatha dé are considered extremely beautiful.

Grail — (Gr-ALE) From the Old French "graal" which means crater, dish. Grail's were common serving dishes. The idea of a "cup" or "chalice" is from the 13th-14th century.

Gwenevere	(Gwin-iv-eer) the English spelling of Gwen-hwyfar, Welsh name for "white fay" or "white enchantress"
Lough Insholin	(Lock Inch-uh-oh-lin) means "Lake of the O'Lynn Island," for the Ó Fhloinn family, or O'Lynn, who hailed originally from Londonderry, Ulster, and eventually took over most of Antrim.
Lough Neagh	(Lock Nay) A large lake in the province of Ulster, Northern Ireland.
Ogham	(Ome) the ancient 20-letter rune alphabet of Britain and Ireland, used primarily by druids. Also used as divination runes in neo-pagan magic.
Otherworld	(Uh-thur-werld) also known as Tír na nÓg in Irish mythology, it is the realm of the gods and the dead
Pendragon	(Pen-drah-gun) the title given to the King of Briton during and after Roman occupation through the medieval period, primarily held by a king in Wales. Also known as the Head Dragon.
Sídhe	(Shay) The faerie people of Irish mythology (Túatha dé Danann) who lived beneath the hills (gateway to the Otherworld).
The Morrígan	(More-ree-ghon) the Celtic goddess of war and fate, the Great Phantom (Fay) Queen, often interpreted as a triple sister goddess. Also known as the "Crow of Battle" or the "Carrion Crow" and can shapeshift into a crow. Some scholars believe Morgan la Fay / Morgana stemmed from The Morrígan.

Tintagel	(Tin-TAH-jell) City in North Cornwall, where Arthur was conceived.
Túatha dé Danann	(Too-ah day don-an) is translated as "people/ tribes (children) of the goddess Danu" and were a supernatural race in Irish mythology who lived in the Otherworld, but who interacted with humans in the mortal realms. They are also known as the first settlers of Ireland. Often called "faeries" and "elves." Though Irish, the mythological figures appear throughout the Celtic/Gaelic world.
Uí Tuírtri	(Oo-EE tour-tree) A clann of Northern Ireland, descending from one of the three Collas, primarily ruled by the O'Lynn chiefs.
Ulster	(Ohl-stir) Province in Northern Ireland

"Then it is better, sir, to love

whom one cannot have?"

"Probably better," Lancelot said.

"Certainly safer."

John Steinbeck

The Acts of King Arthur and His Noble Knights

Chapter One

Arthur

The runestones clattered to a stop. Their long, rounded forms remained shadowed in the cave's flickering light. Arthur leaned forward to examine the carved marks on the wood, even though the Ogham language would elude him.

Merlin crouched down, sweeping his gray woolen robes out over the rough cave floor. The druid pressed two fingers to his lips and then grunted softly to himself.

Arthur stilled his hands at his side. The urge to test Excalibur once again was almost too powerful to resist. But no, a hundredth try wouldn't yield a different result. The sword wouldn't pull from its jeweled scabbard, no matter how hard he tried. Excalibur was stuck.

"Úath." Merlin touched the Ogham rune and peered up at Arthur. "Hawthorn. The faerie tree." He touched another wooden rune. "Straif."

"Blackthorn," Arthur said. "I do know that one."

Merlin dipped his head. "Then you probably already know that this rune is often associated with The Morrígan."

Arthur blew out a breath. "Morgana?" he asked.

A dark storm cloud crossed Merlin's ageless tan face at the mention of his wayward pupil. "This magic has the smell of fae all over it. If not Morgana, one of her older sisters. Perhaps Elaine."

Arthur swore under his breath. "So, there's a faerie curse on Excalibur?"

"Yes," the druid replied simply. The gold in his hazel eyes glinted from both torchlight and magic. Part mortal and part incubus, Merlin's cambion blood possessed a rare gift to divine glimpses into the future. Though not in a trance, Merlin's pupils narrowed with magic as the lines around his eyes relaxed. "Though," the druid said, blinking, "this curse is worse than I feared."

"We suspected a curse when the angry missive arrived, demanding Lancelot's head. But you say it's worse? I'm not sure what's worse than offending three unhinged sídhe heirs of the Túatha dé Danann."

"There's a second curse. I suspect a gift from the second sister, Morgause."

Arthur's blood turned cold within him. "Tell me."

"I fear Caerleon itself is also cursed."

"The keep?" Arthur asked, horror welling within him. He had claimed enemies a plenty in his four years on the throne without a stuck sword and a cursed fortress to contend with.

"Not the keep. The land itself. If you remain

king, Briton will begin to wither as the land's life-force slowly drains away."

Arthur seized the tankard of ale Merlin had poured him and hurled it into the fireplace. The copper vessel ricocheted against the fireplace's back wall and then bounced across the floor before rolling to a stop against Merlin's booted foot.

Merlin was unmoved by Arthur's outburst. The tall druid simply bent over and picked up the dented tankard, setting it on a nearby table.

A flush of embarrassment flooded Arthur. He and Merlin had been through much during Arthur's rise to power, and the man knew all of him—every shining hope and shadowed fear. Still, it was no excuse. Arthur was king of Caerleon—the famed Roman "City of the Legion" of centuries past—and overking of the Kingdom of Gwent. Kings did not lose control over every piece of bad news.

"Finished?" Merlin asked, raising a dark eyebrow.

"Are you?" Arthur asked, raising one of his own.

Merlin barked a laugh. "Shall we move to the good news?"

"There's good news?" Arthur loosed a shaky breath. "Are you trying to kill me, druid? Tell me."

Crouching on his cave's stone floor once again, Merlin pointed to another rune. "Fearn—Alder, the warrior's shield." Touching another wooden rune, he said, "Úr. Heather, for healing and the Otherworld. Interesting . . ." Merlin indicated another rune with a side glance Arthur's way. "Ébhadh. It symbolizes conflict resolution. See how the Ébhadh partially lies atop Óir, the spindle tree?"

Arthur met the Merlin's inquisitive stare with a quick nod.

"The solution to your problem will come in the form of something small, perhaps delicate, but that wields an unexpected mighty strength."

Merlin left Arthur to ponder his revelations and crossed the room to a dark, smoky corner, where a set of shelves bore numerous items of questionable origin. Before the Lady of the Lake had declared Arthur the Pendragon and gifted him Excalibur—and, thus, sovereignty as king over Caerleon as well as all of Briton—he had been fascinated by Merlin's craft and spent many a wondrous hour flipping through cracking tomes, smelling bundles of dried sage, and peering into jars of pickled crickets. These days, he hardly had time to say hello to his old friend, let alone ponder the mysteries of the unknown.

The druid returned with a flat silver bowl, placing the common grail dish on the table between them. He filled the bowl with a pitcher of water and the droplets tinkled against the metal. "All magic can be undone. Every curse has a cure. It is just a matter of finding the right one."

"If you can't find a solution, no one can," Arthur said, watching as Merlin positioned crystals in a rainbow of colors around the bowl.

"How is Lancelot faring?" Merlin glided his hand over the bowl in sweeping passes. To Arthur's untrained eye, Merlin's movements seemed to match the tattoos carved onto the shaved sides of the druid's head.

"He's as ornery as a stallion with a pebble in his

shoe," Arthur said. "It doesn't help that Percival and Galahad refuse to give him a moment's peace. Their jests have been merciless."

"They find a potential war with the sídhe fae to be humorous?" Merlin asked, leaning over the bowl.

"They're knights. And bored ones at that. So, the prospect of war may not be humorous, but they and their fellow soldiers find the prospect of battle exciting. And more so, they're men. The fact that Lancelot's betrothed caught him in bed with not one, but two kitchen maids . . ." Arthur sighed. He loved Lancelot like a brother, but he had half a mind to let Morgana and her sisters unleash their wrath upon him. How could the man have been so stupid?

"I blame myself," Merlin said. "I knew how dangerous it was to deal with the fae. But when Morgana came to me, wanting to be my apprentice as her older sisters had once been . . . Well, I let her flattery carry away my better judgment."

"We share the blame, my friend. Despite seeing Lancelot flirt his way into the beds of half the women in my court, I thought that his feelings for Morgana were different. He knows better than most not to trifle with the Túatha dé Danann. I should have trusted my instinct. Forbade their union."

"Morgana was desperately in love with that fool man and has been since before her magic manifested. And for a time, I believed Lancelot felt the same. If you had tried to keep them from each other, we'd be scrying for a cure to a different curse."

"Damned if we did. Damned if we didn't." Arthur ran his fingers through his short hair.

"That is the way of love, Your Majesty," Merlin said as the gold around his hazel eyes glowed unnaturally bright. "Ah, here we go. I found something. Give me a moment."

Arthur paced the length of the cave, eating up the distance across the plush carpet with his long strides. He wasn't sure why his friend preferred to live in this cave, deep beneath the grounds of Arthur's keep. But, at least, he had relented when Arthur offered to donate a few furnishings.

Growing even more restless, Arthur found his fingers straying to Excalibur's jeweled hilt. What kind of king couldn't draw his own sword? What kind of king was poison to his own kingdom? He shook his head, sending up a prayer to the gods that Merlin could find a way out of this.

"Yes, there is an answer!" Merlin shouted, his eyes wide. "I've seen something. More like, someone."

"Someone?" Arthur whirled around, hurrying back over to the bowl. The dish was empty, but for the still water and their own reflections. Once again, Merlin's magic eluded him.

"A knight. A fifth knight of Caerleon. He is the key to unlocking the curse." Natural light returned to Merlin's eyes as he pulled out of his trance and looked at Arthur. "The Alder rune now makes clearer sense to me. At first, I thought Fearn signified Lancelot, but no—"

"Who is this man?" Arthur asked, relief welling in him. His kingdom needed more noble-titled warriors anyway, but his other duties had prevented him from ordering a proper search. Perhaps this cure could be a solution to two different problems.

"I cannot see his face in my vision."

"How will we find him then? He could be any-where in Briton."

"You must host a great tourney. Announce that you seek the strongest men in the land to fight for you. He will be there. And his blood will unlock the sword."

"A tourney. You're sure?" Arthur asked.

"The future is never certain. But I see this fate more clearly than most. If you hold the tourney, the warrior will come. Alder is not only the warrior shield but also unlocks the faerie realms."

"And this warrior's blood will heal the land as well? The second curse?"

Merlin frowned. "This is less clear to me. But I see that this fifth knight will help you find the Oth-erworld's Grail. And the fae's legendary bowl has the power to heal as well as break all enchantments."

Arthur groaned. "The fae's Grail? It's a legend. My father wasted years of his rule searching for it. If I must rely on finding the Blessed Grail, I fear all is lost."

"Excalibur was a legend as well, yet the Sword of Light *blessedly* hangs at your side," Merlin pointed out.

"Blessedly stuck in its scabbard," Arthur grum-bled. Disappointment welled in him. He needed a solution, not a quest over a myth shrouded in mist.

"You will have something your father never had. This fifth knight is the key. Five is a sacred number, representing the elements of this world—air, water, fire, earth, and aether. Together, you will have a chance."

Arthur gnawed the inside of his lip, then gave a reluctant nod.

"Or, you can give up now and hand your kingdom over to Morgana and her sisters." Merlin's hazel eyes flashed.

Arthur bristled at Merlin's slight, drawing himself up to his full height. "A tourney and a fifth knight, you say. Very well. We will have both. We *will* restore my sword and my kingdom and show the sídhe faerie court that Arthur Pendragon is not so easily bested."

Chapter Two

Fionnabhair

I tossed a bag of gold at the man's mud-splattered boots, wishing I could knock his teeth out with the coins instead. "Here is yer blood money."

Donal O'Lynn looked up from the apple he was cutting with a curved hunting knife, his dark eyes hinting at mirth. "Why Princess Fionnabhair Allán, in the flesh. To what do I owe this rare pleasure?"

Around the tent, Donal's warriors chuckled at their clann leader's slight. They all knew why I was here, and why I travelled alone. Though the men's laughter was light, their hands hadn't strayed from the hilts of their swords. They clearly viewed me as a threat, which was perfectly fine with me. I was one.

My fingers curled into fists when Donal tossed a delicate slice of apple into his worm-rotted mouth.

"Don't waste my time O'Lynn." I spat the name of the Uí Tuírtri Clann chieftain, the sworn enemy of my own family and clann. "I'm here for my father and sister. There's enough gold in here to ransom them twice over, just to ensure ye cooperate."

Donal took a huge bite from the uncut area of his apple, chewing slowly, savoring his ill-gotten victory over Clann Allán.

I didn't shy away from his gaze, taking in his long braid, the notch out of his left earlobe, the curving golden torc circling his throat. The slight twist in his proud posture that betrayed a pain—a wound to his right side or hip perhaps. I tucked all the information away. Details were what made a man. Details were how you found his weaknesses. And skies help me, I would find this man's weakness.

"Why don't ye sit and sup with me." Donal motioned to a small table nestled into the corner of his war tent. The hide walls reeked of sweat and blood, though far too clean to have seen battle. Donal tilted his head, a gesture meant to appear polite. But I knew otherwise. "Ye must have journeyed far," he said, "all the way from the glens of Antrim. Beautiful country. I'm partial to yer fertile land myself."

"I don't sup with snakes," I hissed. "Ye have yer money. I travelled alone. Now I want my family."

"So impatient." The corner of his lip curled in a smile that didn't reach his eyes. "Fine. We will negotiate yer way. Take yer money and go. Brin and Aideen Allán are not for sale today. Not for gold anyway."

I ground my teeth to keep my anger in check. I had spent the past month galloping through the province of Ulster and into Túatha de Londonderry, promising the moon to half the Dál nAraidi clanns, anything to raise sufficient funds to ransom my father and sister. I was sore, I was tired, and I had promised my sister or myself as a bride to a dozen different chieftain's sons. And now the fool man *didn't want gold?*

"Do not toy with me," I said. "I am not in the mood."

"Neither am I," Donal stood. "I'm afraid I enjoy having a king of Tara in my prison far too much. My men have not tired of yer sister's company, either. Keeping the men of Clann Uí Tuírtri happy is a matter of pride."

My sword was halfway out of its scabbard before I knew it. But O'Lynn's men were just as fast, and I found myself frozen, with the points of six swords leveled at me. Fury writhed in my veins, my blood deafening in my ears. For him to suggest that my sister had been defiled by his soldiers . . .

"Relax, Allán," he sneered. "I jest. No need to die today."

"What makes ye think I would be the one dying?" I countered.

"Ye've prowess in battle, I'll give ye that, lass. I saw yer little warrior band on the field at Ballymena, right before I took yer father. Impressive. But even ye cannot defeat seven men in hand-to-hand combat."

"I'll take my chances." I flexed my fingers on the hilt of my sword. I suspected he was right, though I would never admit it. I had sparred with four before, during endless drills with the warriors in my fiann— one of three female and male mixed war bands in Northern Ireland. But yes, seven was too many.

"Stand down," Donal snapped at his men, who quickly complied. "My men can't be killing ye today, because I have need of ye yet, lass. I told ye I would not take yer gold, but there is something I would trade for yer family."

I sheathed my sword, furrowing my brow. "I'm listening."

"Will ye sit?" He motioned to the table again.

My nerves gnawed at my gut, but I nodded stiffly. Perching on the edge of a wooden chair, I thunked my helm onto the crudely fashioned, hewn table. The bleached white antlers on my helm clawed toward Donal.

He pushed my helm aside, feigning disgust. "Ye're nothing like her, ye know."

"Who?" I asked.

"Yer sister. She's quite compelling." Donal speared a hunk of cheese with his knife, sliding the piece into his mouth.

I stifled a grimace. His praise of my sister was no surprise, nor his cutting comparison of us. Aideen's physical beauty—auburn curls, honey-gold skin, and brown doe-like eyes—paled in comparison to her compassionate heart and her clever wit. She was beloved throughout the clann territories by young and old. And where Aideen was the warmth of autumn, I was the ice of winter—white-blonde hair, silver eyes, skin smooth and white as fresh cream. My father, Brin, praised us both, boasting how a chieftain needed the warmth of his hearth and the cold of his steel. Some days, I believed him.

"Mistreat my sister and yer life will be forfeit," I

finally replied as my fingers played against a point on one of my helm's antlers.

Donal flashed a toothy smile.

"Tell me of this deal ye speak of," I continued. "The hour grows late."

"There is a king across the Irish Sea—"

"In Briton?" I asked.

"Indeed. A king in Caerleon, Wales, by the name of Arthur Pendragon. And he has something I want. A sword."

"I fail to see how yer problem interests me." What was he on about? A sword in Briton? There were plenty of swords right here in Ireland. Was there no end to the greed of men?

"I have received word that Arthur Pendragon is hosting a tourney. To choose a new knight."

"I wish ye the best in earning the position." I knew I walked a dangerous line, but I couldn't help the bitter reply. O'Lynn thought to make light of my family's imprisonment, so I would make light of him.

"But it's ye, fair warrior, who will be winning the role. *Ye will* compete in the tourney. *Ye will* win. *Ye will* steal his sword and bring it to me. When I have the sword they call Excalibur in my hands, yer father and sister will go free."

I let out a disbelieving laugh. "Ye expect me to sail to Briton, win a tournament, *become a knight*, and steal a king's sword? I believe ye have taken too many hilts to the head, O'Lynn."

Donal leaned over the table, his smell of sweat and ale washing over her. "What I *have* is the upper hand. While ye have two choices. Do this for me, bring me Excalibur, and yer family goes free. Or refuse, and yer family becomes permanent guests here in Lough Insholin."

"And risk facing a king of Tara's warriors?"

"Clann Allán will be too busy fighting amongst themselves for a dead king's throne. Why do ye think my demand that ye attend me alone was an easy request?" He leaned forward and lowered his voice, as if we shared a knowing secret. "For how long did ye raise money? How many chieftains refused their sons in marriage to either princess of Allán?"

Blood drained from my face as the truth of his words sank in. Last winter a neighboring clann nearly vanished from the goddess's green earth in a battle over title and land. I was loathe to agree but, at this moment, Donal O'Lynn could set the terms. He could order me to steal the faerie queen's slippers, and I would have to do so to restore my father's rightful place in Aghanravel, home of Clann Allán. I supposed fighting in a tournament wasn't the worst task he could have set before me.

"And if I do this, ye will let my father and sister go free?"

"Yes."

"And while ye wait for yer precious sword, not a hair on their heads will be harmed?"

"Of course."

"They will be fed and clothed generously, protected as one of yer own clann?"

Donal put a hand on his leather breastplate, over his heart. "I swear it as Chieftain of Clann Uí Tuírtri. Their captivity will be as gentle as springtime."

I narrowed my eyes at him, my mind working the puzzle, turning each piece over to find a trick, an angle. "Why do ye want this sword?"

"Does my answer change yers?" Donal asked, stabbing another chunk of cheese. When I didn't answer, he continued, almost bored. "Suffice it to say, this sword, called Excalibur, has special value, both to me and a new acquaintance of mine."

I didn't like his demand . . . but what was to like about this situation? I sighed. It seemed I wouldn't be sleeping in my own bed for some time yet. Nor my family in theirs. "Ye will pay my expenses," I said. "My passage to Wales, entry in the tourney."

Donal stood, bending over to retrieve the bag of gold I had deposited before his great chair. He tossed the coins onto the table in front of me, as I had to him just minutes earlier. Large, calloused hands gripped the back of my chair as he leaned over my shoulder. "I would say ye have gold a plenty, lass."

My skin crawled at his nearness, his breath on my neck. It was all I could do not to pull a knife and slide the blade into his ribs.

"Now best get riding. The tournament starts in one week."

Interlude

Morgana

The crow soared above the war camp, a scatter of movement far below her. Cool spring air brushed against her dark feathers with every beat of her wings. Pregnant clouds gathered on the horizon, shadowing the moors of Ulster. She would need to find his tent before the storm rolled over the landscape. Her trained black eye peered past the numerous fires dotting the encampment, sliding over humans busy with their tasks. There it was. A large hide tent.

She released a loud caw and crows in nearby trees burst into flight, their wings like black leaves swirled by a furious Samhain wind. They circled around her, swarming in looping lines and knots in the sky. Distracted by the ominous sight, the guards failed to notice when she flew past and slipped into their chieftain's tent.

Donal O'Lynn's sharp gaze fell upon her as she

landed with a flutter of wings before his crude black-thorn tree throne. A slow smile teased his cruel lips as he watched her magic summon the shadows of his makeshift court. Darkness and thousands of whispers—the desperate, greedy prayers of men at war—swirled around her, fueling her transformation from crow to a faerie queen and druid priestess.

"Morgana," Donal said, tipping his head in deference. His gaze crawled over her body as he lifted his eyes to finally meet hers.

"You have pleased me, mortal." She glided past him to a decanter of ale and poured herself a goblet. But rather than enjoy a sip, she turned and held the cup to his mouth. "Drink."

His hawk-eyes never left hers as he drank long and deep. His Adam's apple bobbed as he swallowed.

Morgana spoke. "The witch now sails the Irish Sea for Wales."

"Witch?" He laughed, as if she spoke lies. How fickle the mortal mind, quick to judge and quick to forget. She was fae. Lies never graced her tongue.

"Shhh . . ." Morgana caressed his stubbled cheek with one long, sharp nail. "Since the beginning of time, men have slaughtered their brethren in wars for what *she* offers. I have bathed in their bloodshed and fed on their fear. I know the signs."

Donal licked his lips. "I far prefer what *ye* offer."

"Of course you do." She leaned in and pressed her lips to his, satisfied when the hard lines of his muscles trembled beneath her touch. Men were weak. And Donal O'Lynn was weaker than most. "Mmm . . . you taste of power," she murmured. *My power*, she thought.

Donal's eyes riveted onto her once more, expectant. "Then tell me, why do ye desire to wrest power from this King Arthur?"

She pulled away—seductively—enjoying as the man before her fought his animal urges to claim her now before she flew away. A knowing smile curved her lips as she called once more to the shadows and whispered prayers, ignoring his question. Let him wonder. Let him yearn for the answer until he was driven mad with longing, as the weak often are. She had learned much in her time with Lancelot, most of all that when it came to human men, she would never again surrender her power.

Or her heart.

Darkness rushed around her. But, before she returned to her crow form, she said, "Do not fail me and you will be king."

"Of where?" Donal rasped. "Ulster or Briton?"

But she said nothing, for her powers of human speech were gone. The crow regarded the human male with one beady eye. He smelled of ambition, lust, and blood. It would do.

The magic welled up in her and she crowed, loud and triumphant. Then she took flight from the hide tent and joined the black-feathered murder darkening the sky.

Chapter Three

Lancelot

Lancelot had been taking his breakfast early this past month. Early meant enjoying his trout and stewed figs with a side of solitude. This morning, however, he would not be so lucky.

"Good morning crabapple," Percival said brightly from the end of the table, where he crouched over a heaping plate of food. The lad was trying and failing to keep the mischievous grin from his face. It seemed the only thing he was never without.

"I told you not to call me *that*," Lancelot growled as he sat down at the other end of the table. It was too early for Percival's shenanigans.

Galahad grunted from his seat next to Percival, where he was wiping his trencher clean with a chunk of honeyed rye bread. "At least he doesn't call you 'chipmunk.'"

Lancelot struggled to keep a smile off his face at that nickname. Of all Percival's ridiculous pet names for them, calling Galahad "chipmunk" had to be the best. The Norse man was built like a well-muscled oak tree. "I keep telling you to just crush his windpipe in your fist," Lancelot said to Galahad while waving down a servant for a goblet of ale and a trencher of food. "That'd teach the lad a lesson."

"I don't think our king would like that much," Galahad retorted.

"I wouldn't like what?" Arthur asked, striding in, pulling his gloves off. It seemed their king had already visited the Round Table—the Roman amphitheater grounds—to prepare for this morning's tournament. Did the man ever sleep?

"Galahad crushing the life from me, ye ken," Percival said sweetly, batting his flaxen eyelashes. The knight was far too pretty for his own good, with straight chin-length copper hair that brushed at his pale square jaw. And he had only just turned eighteen. Lancelot sighed. Had he been so . . . obnoxiously cheerful at that age? He didn't think so.

Arthur stood with arms crossed and a sideways look directed at Percival. "Indeed, if Galahad ended you, it would deprive me the pleasure of doing so myself. Is there a reason you're in my chair?"

Galahad let out a deep booming laugh as Percival scrambled out of Arthur's chair and into one across from the large knight. "Wanted to see what it felt like, Yer Majesty," Percival said with a sheepish grin and clumsy half-bow from his chair.

"And?" Arthur asked, raising an eyebrow. His tone was light, but Lancelot could see the tension in the set of his king's muscular shoulders. He was worried about the tournament today. It was too important to go awry.

"A wee too serious," Percival remarked, stuffing his last piece of sausage into his mouth, adding, "Yer Majesty."

Arthur nodded sagely. "A serious ass needs a serious chair."

The knights burst out laughing, and even the servant who placed a trencher in front of Lancelot was struggling to keep a smile from his face.

Lancelot grinned at Arthur as he dug into his meal of venison sausage, trout, creamed barley, and stewed figs. When Arthur had become king, a part of Lancelot had worried that his ascension would change things between them, that his friend would become distant and unreachable. He was the only family Lancelot had, even if just sworn blood brothers. His concern hadn't been warranted, however. For the most part, Arthur was one of them—a fellow warrior noble. Or at least, he tried to be.

"Keeping your own counsel?" Arthur nodded toward Lancelot, who sat all the way at the other end of the table.

"Trying to keep away from those two." Lancelot nodded back at Percival and Galahad.

"All in good fun—" Percival began, but Arthur cut him off.

"The tourney grounds are readied," he said. "We've at least three dozen knights signed up to compete, some hailing from as far as Northern Ireland and Normandy."

Lancelot nodded, grateful for Arthur's change of

subject. And then his mood soured as he thought of the last few weeks. He shouldn't need his king's protection from Percival and Galahad's barbs. Lancelot was Arthur's second-in-command, leader over all of Arthur's soldiers. But these past few days, he had not been himself.

Their king continued to speak about the tournament's details, but Lancelot only half listened, chewing his breakfast mechanically. How had things gone so wrong and so quickly? Lancelot had always loved the pleasures of men and women, and men and women loved to pleasure him. Dalliances had never felt like a curse.

Not until Morgana.

There had been something about Merlin's apprentice, Arthur's half-sister—from the first time Lancelot had laid eyes on her, she had fascinated him. Her beauty was ethereal and otherworldly, from the long ebony hair glinting auburn in the sun, to her discerning violet eyes, to the curve of her hips and breasts, arresting even in the simple gowns she wore while working in Merlin's cave. Raised by the Lady of the Lake, Lancelot was no stranger to magic. But Morgana's faerie power sang to him. A forbidden fruit that had to be tasted.

And taste her he did—all over the keep.

Heavens above, he grew hard just remembering the heat and desperation of their coupling. Nails raking down his back, teeth digging into the flesh of his shoulder. When she had suggested they marry, nuptials had seemed a novel idea. He was twenty-five after all, old enough to have sons several times over.

And the passion—he couldn't imagine a time when he wouldn't want that fire in his life. Almost as soon as he had agreed, he realized his mistake. There was a wildness in her eyes that unsettled him more than he cared to admit, and she grew jealous, deeply jealous, like he was now a thing that she owned, not a man with a life and a path of his own. But he didn't know how to extricate himself from the match. Arthur seemed keen on the idea of strengthening his alliance with the Túatha dé Danann beyond his own blood ties; what king wouldn't want the might of faerie behind his reign?

And so, Lancelot indulged in what he knew best: a distraction from his coming nuptials. He hadn't sought out the two maids—he wasn't *that* fool a man—but when they had offered themselves to him . . . well, he hadn't said no either.

Morgana had torn into the room like a black thundercloud, and he feared for the girls, believing she would kill them in her rage. He had feared for himself too, if he were honest. Before him stood a black sídhe druidess, crackling with power and venom and vengeance. Pointing a finger at him, she spat a curse. A curse that sounded more like prophecy.

"If this is your wish," she had sneered, gesturing to the two girls. "Then this is your lot. Never again will you know the pureness of love that flows between one man and one woman. There will be a woman, a Gwenevere pure like the white of driven snow. You will long for her with all your heart. Perhaps she will love you too. But, if you join as man and woman, she will not only bring your downfall, but the downfall of all you love." Her violet eyes slitted in triumph. "Briton. And my half-brother, Arthur." And with those cruel words ringing in the air, she had vaporized into a crow and flown through the opened window and into the moonless night's chill.

The two girls had run sobbing from the room, clutching their clothes to their naked bodies. Lancelot sat, stunned, sheets draped around him as he digested Morgana's words, turning each one over in his mind while trying to find a way in which his life hadn't been irreparably changed. She had said he would love a "Gwenevere." The name was a legend in Wales, a nearly long-forgotten Cymry word for a white enchantress, a white sídhe fae. Well, he knew no such woman. Even when he had lived with his elemental foster mother, they had encountered no such creatures. He had heaved a shaky breath. Morgana's curse was meaningless.

"Lancelot?" Arthur was looking at him from the other end of the table. "You've paled as white as a ghost."

Lancelot shoved his thoughts away and summoned a carefree smile. "Just wondering if we'll indeed find a new knight today," he said, redirecting to a safer topic.

"Merlin seems certain of it," Arthur replied quickly. "We must all keep our eyes open. Amongst the competitors is a man who can break these wretched curses."

Lancelot nodded, guilt flooding through him. He had never been worthy of Arthur's friendship. He remembered clearly the day he had arrived in

Caerleon at the age of fourteen, his foster mother, the Lady of the Lake, by his side. Uther was to foster and train him in the ways of war and men, as the prince Lancelot was born to become. He was old to begin such training, and Uther welcomed him with the same care he gave most of his subjects—thinly veiled interest. His foster mother departed in a misty vapor and left him to his own devices, and to the cruelty that followed for being fae-raised. The second time a mother figure had left him as an offering—or burden—for another to take in.

It was a time when Lancelot didn't understand the ways of men after being raised by faeries. His fellow soldiers had been quick to teach him—taking turns either ignoring his presence or picking on him until he bruised and bled. He was an exiled prince, a title with no power, a man with no living biological parents. No kin that he could claim as his own. He had drifted through Caerleon, desperate for connection and finding little.

Until Arthur. Until his friend made Lancelot his blood oath brother during a village feast and claimed him before all. Uther regarded Lancelot as another son soon after.

But how had Lancelot repaid him? With curses. Arthur's current struggles were all Lancelot's fault. After Morgana had left his room, she had flown to Arthur to demand Lancelot's head for his betrayal. Arthur's refusal to give in to her demands invited the wrath of Morgana's two fae sisters upon Briton. The kingdoms of Wales already questioned Arthur's claim to the Pendragon title without their suffering for his decision to defend Lancelot. And then there was the third curse. The one for Lancelot alone. He knew he should have told Arthur, but he couldn't bring himself to add to his friend's worries. Lancelot would handle this one himself. As long as he stayed away from any stray Gweneveres, everything would be fine.

Chapter Four

Fionna

My mood teetered between anoyance and awe as I surveyed the strangely round amphitheater from atop my mare. Wide grassy berms stepped down toward the enormous field below, where competitors swarmed like ants. I squinted as the sun glinted off a particularly bright set of armor. I snorted. A set that clean had never seen battle.

I straightened my own leather armor, wishing the plates and guards didn't hang quite so loose. The ride across the Irish Sea and into the Severn Sea to the port of Cardiff, Wales had been nothing short of hell. Despite fair weather, my stomach had not taken kindly to the undulating waves or the rocking boat. I had passed a full three days at sea by spending equal times vomiting over the side and cursing Donal O'Lynn for setting me on this foolish quest. By the time I sighted land, I was weak from hunger and sick to my core. Two days of rest had restored my strength. Still, my agony had given birth to several creative ways to kill the man. I prayed to the sister goddesses that I would have every chance to use them.

But now I was here, and there was nowhere to go but forward. I clicked my tongue, urging my horse, Zephyr, down toward the field. The mare tossed her head, blowing out a snort that sounded skeptical. "I don't know why we're here either girl," I muttered, patting Zephy's dappled gray coat. I was grateful I had one ally here, at least.

Back home, clannsmen often snickered at my mount's Greco-Roman name. But when a cleric had visited from the Holy Roman Church and uttered the old god's name for the wind, I had known it fit her perfectly. My mare galloped light-footed, as though across clouds . . . the name was a far better moniker than the one my father had originally gifted her—Bolg Liath—Irish for "grey belly."

A riot of colorful pennants fluttered above a gathering crowd. The people were clothed in fine velvets and silks, the garments trimmed in pearls and threads of gold. Everything about this land spoke of plenty. I considered my own attire of rough hand-spun linens, animal furs and hides, and worn, oak gall-stained leather armor. They looked crude in comparison.

On my ride from Cardiff's seaport to Caerleon, my head had swiveled to take in the rolling green hills, golden fields, and tidy lime-washed villages bounded by neat stone hedgerows. A warm sun had shone down upon me from an azure sky, glittering off the crystal-clear rivers I had passed. Flocks of quail scattered before herds of red deer, who had hardly remarked my passage. My admiration made me feel slightly guilty, as I compared this verdant land to Northern Ulster's wind-swept shores and craggy mores. Of course, I still preferred my home. Perhaps the thought of stepping foot on that cursed boat once more had made Briton look so appealing.

As I neared the amphitheater's tourney green, I donned my stag helm. Few of the other competitors wore helmets yet, but I imagined those warriors were men. I doubted women could compete here. Briton was not as enlightened as her Celtic cousins across the Irish Sea when approving of female warriors—perhaps even women, regardless of station or occupation. Well, it was an easy problem to solve with my helm. Some men grew funny about fighting a woman. I would just as soon be treated like all the rest.

I slid off Zephyr and led her through a maze of swinging practice swords and chatting contestants, toward a bright tent slashed in the red and gold of Caerleon. Outside the tent, a wooden scoreboard towered above the crowd on tall legs. Painted placards, announcing the participants' colors and crests, hung from numerous wooden pegs. I tied up Zephyr and ducked inside.

Two men, clad in black leather armor and red cloaks, turned as I entered. I nearly stumbled, glad that my helm disguised the blush heating my cheeks. Perhaps it wasn't only the fair land of Wales that overflowed with abundance. Her men, it seemed, also put those of my homeland to shame.

The two before me couldn't have been more different. The man on the left possessed black chin-length hair curling about his head like a halo, and blue eyes as piercing as ice. Dark stubble shadowed his olive skin, framing a mouth with full pouting lips that didn't seem entirely fair on a man. Where the dark-haired man was tall and well-muscled, the man on the right towered over even him, with thickly muscled arms crossed over his well-sculpted chest. His blond hair was pulled into a messy top-knot, slightly darker than the honey-gold of his neatly-trimmed beard—a similar fashion to the Norse men in nearby Danish settlements.

I found myself wishing I had something to drink.

"Here for the tourney?" the dark-haired man asked. His voice was deep and smooth as silk, and he carried himself with an air of authority that was instantly recognizable. This man was in charge here. Perhaps only second to the king.

I nodded.

The taller man clapped his fellow on his shoulder. "Told you not to fret like a nursemaid. Things always turn out."

A look of annoyance crossed the other man's face. "You're in luck. A Northern Lord's son dropped out of the tourney. We're in need of another competitor."

"Good," I said, lowering my voice in a manner I hoped was convincing.

The big man walked behind the table and took up a quill. "Name?"

I thought fast. "Er, Finn Allán. Of Clann Allán. In Ulster, Ireland."

The man raised an eyebrow, turning his already handsome face truly devastating. *Steady Fionna*, I cautioned myself. I was here to get the sword and get out. I could ill afford any distractions, even such handsome ones.

"All the way from Ulster, eh?" He wrote my name down. "Nice to meet you Finn. I'm Sir Galijorheledanik of Swansea, but call me Galahad. And this is Sir Lancelot du Lac."

"Throwing out your long name now, are we?" the dark-haired man, Lancelot, dryly quipped.

"Fretting like a nursemaid *and* jealous." Galahad grinned and turned my way. "Sir Lancelot feels inadequate and needs to prove the size of his—"

"Don't we all," I interjected, hoping I sounded as ridiculous as these men. This earned me a large grin and a wink from the Norse man.

Lancelot placed hands on his narrow hips and was looking at me with his head cocked to the side. "Speaking of size, you're awfully small. You sure you're up to the task? The first bout is a four-man melee, followed by three more rounds of hand-to-hand combat. There are real warriors out there who've seen battle."

"I'm sure," I said, bristling. "I'm sure I've fought in more battles than many of yer so-called warriors."

Lancelot and Galahad exchanged an amused look. "Why don't you take off that helmet, so we can get a real look at you, boy," Lancelot said. "The tournament is to first blood only, but that doesn't mean men aren't injured. I would hate to send a green lad out there to be ripped apart."

I backed up a step, trying not to panic. "Ye wrote my name down. That means I'm in, doesn't it?"

Lancelot took a step toward me. "Yes, but the king's law—"

"Then I'll see ye on the field," I said and swiveled on my heel, striding from the tent with Galahad's booming laughter trailing behind me.

I stalked toward the practice ground, my heart hammering in my throat. I felt uneasy in this new place, surrounded by these strangers, like my skin was on too tight. I prayed to the sister goddesses of war and fate that I could shake off the feeling before my time to fight.

Aideen's heart-shaped face swam to my mind, and I let out a deep breath, centering myself. I knew why I was here, and I knew what I had to do. I had held a sword from the age of four and had fought with a fiann since my first blood coursed. These pampered men wouldn't know what hit them.

Thirty-two men competed in the tournament that day. Well, thirty-one men and one woman. The first round was comprised of eight groups of four warriors, who would compete in a melee-style battle. I was in the last group and watched with interest as the other men fought before me, taking in the details, weapons, and fighting styles of each competitor. I would be pitted one-on-one with some of these men in future rounds. It would serve me to learn what I could.

Nevertheless, I found my eye wandering to the throne dais where King Arthur Pendragon surveyed the tourney. Even from a distance, I could see that the man was handsome—his short brown hair bounded by a circlet of gold oak leaves, his aquiline profile commanding in the morning sun. A sword hung from his narrow hips, decorated by a ruby atop the pommel. Excalibur. I set my jaw. That sword would be mine.

The two warrior nobles from the tent flanked Arthur in the stands, along with another I hadn't seen yet, a handsome young man with copper hair and an exuberant attitude. Arthur and his knights of Caerleon, the virile guardians of this realm.

The winner of the tournament, if deemed worthy, would join these proud men as the fifth knight to defend this land. The thought made me uneasy. Deceit wasn't in my nature. As far as I knew, these men had done nothing to warrant O'Lynn's ire, at least not to justify stealing a priceless relic like Excalibur.

I cast aside my sentimentality with a vicious shove. Excalibur was merely one sword. Little good the blade did while hanging on this pompous king's hip. In my hands, this blade would save my sister and father and keep our clann from civil war. I would take Excalibur and flee this land. It mattered not whether these men were young or old, handsome or vile, honorable or cruel. I would take what was mine and never see them again.

It was with that thought that I stepped into the ring, saluting my three opponents with the blade of my sword. The pommel's worn grip soothed me, lulling my raging nerves.

As the first man came at me, a beast in brown armor trimmed in gold, a grim smile broke across my face. I was ready.

Chapter Five

Galahad

Galahad liked rooting for an underdog, and so watching the little warrior in the stag helm thoroughly trounce the competition pleased him greatly. His good cheer only increased as Lancelot's eyes grew wider and more disbelieving. His brother-in-arms let out a muffled exclamation as the boy—Finn was his name—vaulted over his opponent and landed a blow on the man's undefended left flank. Sometimes he thought Lancelot forgot that others existed in the world who were also good with a sword. It didn't hurt for him to be reminded.

Arthur appeared impressed as well. His king leaned forward, forearms resting on the rail, his forehead wrinkled. "Where did you say that fighter was from?"

"Ulster, Ireland," Galahad said. "Seems your reputation is spreading far and wide."

Merlin had joined them atop the platform and

watched with fingers tented before him, still as a statue. The druid unnerved Galahad, with his gold-ringed eyes and whispered words. But Arthur trusted him, and so by extension, Galahad did too.

"Do you sense anything about the competitors?" Arthur slid a glance to Merlin.

The druid nodded his head up and down slowly. "There is something. A presence here that pulls to me . . . that is *other*. Hard to say where *it* comes from."

Galahad idly spun a ring on his right index finger, pondering what a strange twist of fate had brought him here to sup with kings and druids and the sídhe. He hadn't believed Excalibur was cursed, not until he tried to pull the sword from the scabbard himself. Infernal faeries. What did this mean for Arthur's sovereignty as king over the land?

Savoring the reminder of simpler times, Galahad ran his thumb along the smooth silver of the ring. His father, a blacksmith in Swansea, made each of his eight children such a ring, swearing this token would always lead them home. The ring's constant presence brought Galahad comfort, especially when his fate seemed too strange. Galahad spun the silver ring and gnawed the inside of his lip as he thought of his mother's incurable optimism, even when she served soup thinned with water and stale bread. Her happiness was infectious and he grew up never realizing how poor they were in a large Danish seaport town that boasted several blacksmiths.

Percival jogged up the steps to the platform, pulling Galahad from his thoughts. The young warrior's pale brow furrowed. "I'm back from the surgery tent.

The chirurgeon says that Lord Iwan is bleeding profusely and won't be able to fight in the upcoming round."

The next moment, the crowd roared, drowning out what Arthur had opened his mouth to say.

Galahad looked down on the field below. Finn had drawn first blood with a slicing blow across his opponent's meaty thigh. Their match was over.

"He fights like a wee banshee," Percival remarked. "Watch out lads, we may soon be joined by the world's smallest warrior."

"Lord Iwan would have fought this man?" Arthur asked, nodding to where the stag-helmed warrior stood before taking a long drink of ale. "Could the loser of Lord Iwan's round fight instead?"

Percival shook his head. "He was injured in their bout as well."

"What about one of the other competitors?" Lancelot suggested.

"Someone already defeated?" Percival shook his head. "Nae, that wouldn't be verra sporting."

There were supposed to be two more man-to-man matches before the victors of those would face off in a final battle. "I'll fight him," Galahad said. "His fighting style is unusual. It would be good practice."

Lancelot snorted, but Arthur nodded, gratitude flickering across his king's leaf-green gaze. Lancelot and Percival seemed to sometimes forget that a knight's job was to be of service to his king. That meant making your king's life easier, not more difficult.

Galahad stood and stretched, his back popping.

He patted his stomach, now taut from the afternoon's meal, though still rippling with muscle. "Wish I would have eaten a bit less," he remarked.

Percival laughed. "Gives him a fighting chance, aye?"

"Get your armor on," Arthur said. "We'll delay by an hour."

Galahad hummed a jaunty tune as he walked onto the green grass of the tourney round. He enjoyed sparring with the other knights, but he knew each of their patterns by now. With Percival, the key was to be leisurely, fighting and striking until the lad grew impatient and opened himself up with a wild attack. Lancelot, who was a superior fighter when his heart was engaged, seemed so sure of his superiority that he often missed training. Often, after sparring for hours, he would begin to tire, his sword-arm growing heavy and his breath labored.

It was Arthur he enjoyed sparring with the most. Arthur was careful, disciplined, and skilled. His king watched and analyzed and executed. The only weakness of Arthur's he had discovered was caution. Openings that a more daring fighter would have seized passed Arthur by. His king needed to learn to take risks. Galahad tried to always be there with that painful yet cheerful reminder.

The little warrior Finn was waiting in the fighting

ring, his helmet still on. He was swinging a sword in one hand and an axe in the other with a coordinated precision that often eluded even the most seasoned of fighters.

Finn turned and saw him approaching, his tenor voice muffled behind his helm. "I was hoping they'd send Lancelot."

Galahad chuckled, tightening his shield on his left arm. "I think he might be a touch afraid of you."

"Good," Finn said.

Galahad imagined his teeth bared in challenge.

"You sure are hungry, boy," Galahad said with a shake of his head. Had he been that eager for a fight, when he was growing into manhood? "Plenty of years to prove yourself."

"Why wait," Finn roared, and then lunged at Galahad.

Galahad brought his sword up in an instant and parried Finn's attack. The force of the boy's blow startled him. The fighter was strong, his thin short sword reverberating against Galahad's longsword. And fast. Galahad retreated against the force of Finn's assault. An axe and blade arced toward him in quick succession. The boy's style—to surge forward in a furious assault, and with unexpected strength—set his opponent on the defensive until he made an inevitable mistake. Well, that was enough of that.

Galahad roared and swung his shield at the boy, taking advantage of the significant height and weight he had on the other fighter.

Finn moved impossibly fast, rolling away from his blow. Galahad advanced with sword and shield.

He then struck in fast succession much as Finn had, but with terrible force. The boy withstood the assault with quivering muscle. Each strike was met with a pounding of metal on metal, metal on wood.

Galahad found himself grinning. This boy was *good*. In the distance, a part of Galahad registered the cheers and hazzahs from the other knights, but his focus remained on Finn. It had to.

Finn came at him, throwing axe raised. With a loud cry, he buried the blade into Galahad's shield. Galahad's muscles bunched as he wrenched the shield back, pulling the axe handle from the boy's grip. Finn's silver eyes widened. A noticeable response despite his helm. Then the lad's gaze riveted to the weapon he had lost. Galahad tossed the axed shield across the ring, priming to battle with only his sword. This would remain a fair fight.

Finn rewarded Galahad's honorable act by lashing out with his boot and connecting with the side of Galahad's knee. Pain exploded up his leg. His knee buckled. But he wasn't going down without returning the favor. He toppled forward. Catching Finn around the waist, he dragged the fighter to the ground, half on top of the man.

Finn growled and jerked his sword's pommel toward Galahad's head.

Galahad's hand shot out and caught Finn's wrist. So small. Yet so deadly. He bashed the lad's hand against the ground again and again until the boy's grip loosened and the sword tumbled from his fingers.

Finn thrashed beneath Galahad like a wild thing.

His small form remained enveloped by Galahad's bulk despite his efforts. The boy was skilled with a sword, but man-to-man, there was no way he could match Galahad in raw strength.

"Yield," Galahad growled, bringing his sword against Finn's throat.

"Ye yield," Finn replied, his voice as deadly as the grave.

A sharp prick nicked Galahad's neck. He peered sideways and blinked. Once. Twice. Finn had somehow managed to free a dagger, which was now leveled at the thick trunk of Galahad's neck.

Galahad started to laugh, the booming sound bubbling forth from deep within. "Good show Finn," he said, and then pushed off the ground to free the other warrior beneath him. He offered a hand to help the boy up, but Finn ignored it, scrambling to his feet.

Sweat dripped into Galahad's eyes as he shook his head. *What a strange man.* "A draw!" he called out, turning to the stands where Arthur gaped, eyes round and mouth parted. Galahad's booming voice carried over the crowd's low hum, spectators who were no doubt scandalized by how Sir Galahad had been nearly beaten by an upstart. Galahad didn't mind the prospect of losing so much. He had found his new sparring partner. "Your Majesty, the match should be declared a draw."

"A draw it is," Arthur announced as he stood and raised outstretched hands to quiet the crowd. "Finn Allán of Ulster will advance to the final round."

Galahad sheathed his sword and retrieved his

shield, pulling Finn's throwing axe from where the blade was buried in the surface. He flipped the axe over in his hand and offered the weapon to Finn, handle first. "Good fight," he said with a smile.

Finn took the offered weapon silently, staring at Galahad in seeming contemplation.

Without another word, Galahad turned and strode back toward the armory tent.

It was only when Galahad was past the crowds and peering faces that he let his smile slip. A strange feeling had arisen in him when he gazed into Finn's furious silver eyes. There was something strange about that warrior. Was this the *other* Merlin felt? Though Galahad didn't believe in premonitions, his skin prickled with gooseflesh as a sudden feeling came over him—a feeling that somehow, this tiny, stag-headed warrior was the key to all their futures.

Chapter Six

Arthur

Arthur had watched in disbelief as Galahad, the strongest man he had ever known, was was nearly bested by a fighter the size of a scrawny stable boy.

He had declared the match a draw as his friend had requested, before turning to Merlin.

The druid leaned forward, his fingers tight on the rail. His gold-ringed gaze followed the fighter like a hawk watching a mouse. "My king, I think we have found him," Merlin said. "The fifth knight. The one I saw."

"Are you certain?" Arthur asked, his hand straying to Excalibur. He tamped down the tendrils of hope growing within him—what if Merlin was wrong? What if the tournament was a failure, if the knight who could break the curse wasn't here? But what if the druid was right?

How Arthur longed to draw his sword, to hear

the clear ring of steel, to once again behold the faerie runes running down its length, urging the holder to "take me up, cast me away." He knew his loyal knights and friends did not question his right to rule, or his claim to the throne. But the sovereignty goddess' gift of Excalibur had made him, unquestionably, king of this land. If word of the sword's rebellion got out . . . Arthur wasn't sure how long he could fight off his challengers.

"I am never certain," Merlin replied, "but I do have a feeling. This is a path we must walk down longer."

"Then let us walk it," Arthur said. "Percival, will you summon the man of Ulster? I would like to speak to him."

Percival leaped from his seat and bounded down the stairs toward the man. Arthur suppressed a smile. Percival's youthful exuberance was equal parts endearing and annoying. Sometimes Arthur felt decades older than those around him. He tried to focus on the positive.

Arthur glanced at Lancelot beside him, whose blue eyes were narrowed. He didn't like how withdrawn his friend had been lately while he stewed in a world of his own thoughts.

"Ask him to take off his helm," Lancelot murmured for Arthur's ears alone.

"Why?" Arthur turned back toward the fighter who was summiting the stairs behind Percival. "We have never made such demands before."

"The king's law," Lancelot said.

"There is no such law."

"Sure there is," Lancelot said. "If you are king, your word *is* law."

"Finn Allán of Ulster," Percival said, announcing the warrior.

The short man bowed slightly, a fist over his heart. "Yer Majesty."

Not a low bow, Arthur noted. Some kings might be insulted by such a slight. Arthur was just amused. This fighter lacked respect for him. So why was he here?

"Take off your helm and let us see you," Arthur commanded.

Lancelot leaned forward slightly in interest.

Finn hesitated. "I would rather be judged for the skill of my blade than the look of my face," he said. His voice was slightly accented, but clear and hard.

"Are you refusing me?" Arthur slid a glance Lancelot's way. What was the boy hiding? Was he disfigured? And did Lancelot know something?

"I'm asking ye to let me win my final bout and prove myself worthy."

Arthur's eyebrows furrowed as he nibbled the inside of his lip. "Why do you want to be a knight of Caerleon?"

A split-second pause as Finn seemed to consider. "The truth, not what you think I desire to hear."

"Becoming a knight is the best way to help my family," Finn said.

Arthur nodded. "An admirable reason. Very well Finn, you will have one last chance to prove yourself worthy of knighthood."

Merlin leaned over, grasping Arthur's wrist tightly. He whispered in Arthur's ear: "Fight him yourself."

Arthur looked at the druid sharply. "What?"

"Take his measure yourself," Merlin said quietly.

Arthur examined Merlin's face for some explanation, and found none. The druid was as enigmatic as ever. But, he had learned to trust the man.

Clearing his throat, Arthur stood. "I shall be your opponent for your last bout. Make yourself ready. The match shall begin within the next candle mark."

Finn seemed momentarily taken aback but covered his slip in reaction well. Then, he dipped his head in a slight bow and turned, stalking off the platform.

"You should have made him take his helmet off," Lancelot protested.

"What do I care?" Arthur snapped, his patience at Lancelot wearing thin. "He could have the head of a donkey and I will knight him, if doing so means saving this kingdom." He took a breath, steadying himself. "Besides, you're pretty enough for three knights." He gave Lancelot a playful slap on the cheek before heading off the platform to retrieve his armor.

Percival's laugh followed him down the steps.

It had been years since Arthur had fought in a tourney. Despite the dire circumstances, he found his steps light as a smile played across his face.

The little warrior was in the corner of the ring and turned toward Arthur as he strode into the round. Arthur found the lack of deference strangely refreshing. The man from Ulster didn't scrape and bow or even kneel to him. This was the part of being king he least liked—the endless parade of supplicants and nobles, trying either to win his favor or to gain a favor.

"Not going to fight with yer fancy sword?" Finn nodded from Excalibur, still strapped to Arthur's hip, toward the simple blade Arthur held in his hand. Arthur stifled a grimace as his mood dropped like an anchor. All right, maybe the man's impertinence wasn't entirely refreshing.

"Excalibur is an enchanted blade," he replied with a slight shrug. "Such a weapon wouldn't be fair for a tourney."

"Then why won't ye take your sacred blade off?"

"Why won't you take off your helm?" Arthur countered.

Finn nodded at that, as if to give the point to Arthur.

Galahad had returned to the raised dais, and now waved a flagon of ale, calling out in a cheerful voice, "Are you going to yammer all day like old women or are you going to fight?"

It was all the encouragement Finn needed, for the man came at Arthur with a shout.

Arthur had watched Finn fight in several bouts now, including the fight against Galahad. So, he was ready. He countered Finn's furious strokes with parries and blows of his own. Their feet shuffled around the ring in a warrior's dance.

The fighting stretched on, each of them trying and testing, fighting and falling back.

Arthur panted. Sweat poured down his face. His muscles burned and shook from the exertion. Still, he was surprised to find that he had meant his earlier comment. Finn could have the head of a donkey, and Arthur would still be happy to have him as a knight. Even if he wasn't the man foretold by Merlin to break the curse. He could always use another soldier. But, if Finn *was* the man who would free Excalibur . . . Arthur had to know. Time to end this fight.

And, so, he took a page out of Finn's book. The warrior came at him with a particularly vicious swing. Arthur met it with his own blade. The two swords locked together. Finn strained against his sword, gritting his teeth while struggling to shove Arthur off.

Arthur pulled out a wicked little dagger sheathed behind his back and, in one lithe motion, he sliced across Finn's forearm. "First blood," Arthur declared.

The fighter's eyes went wide. "Did ye just . . . steal my trick?" he asked, breaking away from Arthur, his sword tip drooping toward the ground.

"Never let history say how we're not adaptable here in the mighty City of the Legion." Arthur grinned and, with a surreptitious motion, wiped the dagger's blade across Excalibur's leather grip.

The effect was instantaneous. Searing light blasted from Excalibur, sending streaks of silver over the gathered crowd. Arthur threw up his arm to ward off the onslaught.

Finn stumbled away from him as the crowd shouted in surprise—many pointing, a few running from the stands in fear.

But as suddenly as the magic had begun, the light died, leaving Excalibur quiet and dim at Arthur's side. Hope bloomed in his chest and he gripped the sword with a murmured prayer to the old gods.

His sword yielded.

Arthur pulled Excalibur from its scabbard, the sword ringing out in a single pealing note. The Sword of Light was as beautiful and deadly as the first day the Lady of the Lake had bequeathed the blade to him. He wanted to fall to the grass and weep in relief.

Around him, the crowd stood in hushed awe.

But Finn stood back warily.

Arthur scrambled for an explanation for the sudden burst of magic. Only his knights and Merlin knew that anything had been wrong with Excalibur. And he intended to keep it that way.

"I held this tournament to find a fifth knight! A fighter worthy to join my inner-circle of warrior nobles." Arthur called out. His deep voice resounded throughout the amphitheater. "And now we have found one. Excalibur itself has recognized the divine calling of this man. You all were witness to its magic, blessing his service to our land. You have seen him fight bravely and valiantly today. Caerleon is fortunate indeed to have such a worthy warrior to defend her, as well as all of Briton." His path was clear now. Though from a foreign land, Finn was Caerleon's— and his—only hope.

"So kneel, Finn Allán," Arthur said.

Finn did as he was told, his stag helm lowering before Arthur.

"Do you, Finn Allán of Ulster, swear fealty to me as your king, to follow me into battle and protect the land I govern?"

The stag helm lifted and silver eyes met his. "I do swear my fealty and my sword arm, My King."

"Then I, Arthur Pendragon, son of Uther Pendragon, king of Caerleon, overking in the Kingdom of Gwent, and High King of Briton, hereby deem thee knight." Arthur tapped his sword on the man's shoulders. A thin tendril of violet light left Excalibur and touched Finn's shoulders with each tap, and Arthur relaxed. The sword recognized Finn as belonging to his inner circle.

"Now rise, Sir Finn Allán, knight of Caerleon," Arthur said with confidence. But deep within, he wondered what sort of man he had just yoked to his kingdom.

Chapter Seven

Fionna

King Arthur Pendragon was not what I had expected. I tried to shake my unease. His words—the phantom feeling of his enchanted blade—settled upon my shoulders like a stonweight.

The crowd stood around the amphitheater, clapping and stomping their feet in jubilee. This unsettled me too. I hadn't expected to be welcomed. To be celebrated. In truth, I didn't know what I had expected.

Arthur addressed the crowd. "Join us for a feast in the Great Hall! We will make merry and show our newest knight a true Caerleon welcome!"

The hazzahs and hollers grew deafening, most likely at the prospect of free food and ale.

The king laid a friendly hand on my shoulder. "I am eager to become acquainted with you Finn, and I know my men are too." His touch sent tingles down my spine, and I nodded, unable to resist eyeing him sideways through the slit in my helm. Even with sweat beading on his tan brow, his helmet under his arm, he looked every inch a king. A square jaw and proud nose sprinkled with a light dusting of freckles, vibrant green eyes that spoke of a man of both wisdom and kindness, despite his youth. He had to be no more than twenty-two, yet he carried himself with the confidence of a white-haired ruler. And his smile . . . which he was turning on me right now. Lush lips, straight white teeth. Happiness transformed his face from handsome to knee-wobbling. A hay-loft smile, Aideen would have called it.

"A man who was blessed with such a grin can expect to enjoy a trip to the hayloft," I could almost hear my younger sister explain with a sly giggle. I swallowed back the ache tightening my throat. Was my sister safe? My father?

It was as if Arthur could hear my thoughts. Well, thankfully not *all* of my thoughts. "You spoke of your family. I should like to hear of them, and your life in Ulster," the king said. "I suspect you have a story to tell."

You have no idea, I thought darkly. I managed another nod.

"Ah, Percival," Arthur said, as the copper-haired young man vaulted over the railing of their viewing platform and down onto the ground before us. "Sir Percival of Caer Benic, the newest of my knights. Well, not anymore," Arthur corrected himself with a rueful laugh.

"The role of newest knight comes with all the shit jobs, Finn," Percival said with a wide grin. "I for one, am pleased to pass the torch. Welcome to Caer-leon, lad."

"There aren't any shit jobs," Arthur frowned, but his expression wasn't serious.

"Not for the king," Percival shot back.

To my surprise, Arthur just grinned. "One of the perks, my boy," he said, clapping the other man on the shoulder. Arthur's familiarity with his knights surprised me. Dál nAraidi clann chieftains were often close with their warriors, but I had expected a king of Briton to be aloof, to set himself apart. Arthur and his sword-brothers seemed—like friends.

"Will you show Finn to an extra room, so he can bathe and change? Then bring him to the feast?" Arthur asked Percival. "Hope that's not too much of a shit task for you."

"Nae, a job is far superior when there's ale at the end," Percival said, winking at me. "I think I can manage."

With a dip of his head, Arthur strode off, and I found myself walking beside Percival up to the wooden keep that was Arthur's main fortress.

Percival had the lanky build of youth, though his shoulders were broad under his leather jerkin, and he wore the sword on his hip with practiced ease. He'd fill out nicely in a year or two, I thought. His rich brown eyes were mirthful, framed by long copper lashes that would make any maiden jealous. I groaned inside, realizing that I was staring again. What was it about these men that addled my brain so?

The memory of Galahad's weight upon me set my cheeks flaming and a low heat coursing through my body. Never before in a fight had I ever seen a man as anything other than an opponent, a man to kill. But in that moment, my body had betrayed me. Every inch of me had wished that only night air separated us. My senses rebelled as if I could actually taste the salt and honey of his golden skin. The memory mortified me. A split second in battle made all the difference, and I had let the sweet daydream fill my mind. He had almost beaten me. Where would that leave my father? My sister? In my mind's eye, I seized myself by the scruff of my neck and shook—hard. No more slips.

From the amphitheater grounds, we followed a meandering path toward the keep, surrounded by chatting nobles and competitors. Arthur's fortress was a thing of beauty, hewn from dark timber that shone with brilliant red oak hues in the afternoon sun. I could almost envision the Romans establishing this military location, as I had been told by an overly-friendly warrior between bouts. The Pendragon banner—a red cloth trimmed in gold with an ornate dragon for the High King of Briton—fluttered from the keep's high timbered walls. The fortress sat atop a steep grass-covered hill, making the keep nicely defensible, and also a nuisance to climb toward.

The muscles in my legs burned as fatigue from the day's exertions settled bone deep. The high adrenaline from today was quickly draining from me, leaving a growing, empty pit within. I needed to eat, then sleep, then eat some more.

"I'll get ye a room in the East Wing, that's where Arthur and the rest of us knights sleep," Percival explained. "Ye can bathe and change before the feast."

My stomach clenched. I knew I was avoiding the inevitable, but I didn't want to face *that* moment—the very moment when my helmet came off and they all gaped slack-jawed as if I possessed three heads. Most men didn't take kindly to losing to a woman, and I didn't know enough about these four warriors to judge what their reaction would be. I would reveal my face after I had fortified myself with food. And ale. Lots of ale.

"I would like to go straight to the feast," I said, clearing my dry throat. "I'm starving."

A look of uncertainty crossed Percival's face, but then he shrugged. "If ye want to be covered in sweat and dirt. Yer choice, lad."

"Thanks," I said. "I'll bathe tonight," I added, finding that I didn't want him to think me a total savage. But then I caught myself. What did it matter what this man thought? I would bathe in blood if doing so meant I could steal the sword and escape alive. I had only one objective. Excalibur.

We crossed over the fortress's sparkling moat and into the keep's main courtyard, which brimmed with people in colorful dresses and coats. I craned my neck to take in three soaring towers and all the tidy rows of inner buildings constructed in cob and black timber fashion. Latticed windows scintillated in the warm sunlight and I squinted my eyes. I had never seen a structure so grand.

"Ye will like being a warrior noble here, Finn," Percival said with an air of infectious enthusiasm. "Food is excellent, the other knights are good men, and Arthur is a fair ruler. And women love braw knights," he said to me with a waggle of his ginger eyebrows. "If ye can steal one away from Lancelot, that is. The lot of them seem to be twisted around his cock, if ye ken my meaning."

"Yer meaning is quite plain," I said drolly. It didn't surprise me to hear that Lancelot was successful with women. The man was the most striking in the entire striking bunch. His blue eyes alone were remarkable, somehow filled with both fire and ice.

"Did I hear mention of my cock?" Lancelot jogged up behind them, falling into step beside me as we approached the Great Hall.

"No one is interested in yer cock," I retorted, prickling at his presence.

"You would be surprised." Lancelot slid me a smile and winked.

I focused on the ground moving beneath my feet. Did he just . . . flirt? Did he know I was a woman? Or did he sway toward men? Regardless, Lancelot made me uneasy, no matter how handsome he was. Several times during the tourney, I had caught his stare. While others on the throne dais appeared surprised by my show, the slight furrow of Lancelot's dark brows and the way his lips pinched suggested his disapproval. Of me personally or my prowess on the green? I knew not, and not knowing made him suspect as well.

The dark knight seemed more relaxed now, more at ease. I peered back up and wished I hadn't. He had loosened the buckles of his armor, revealing a glimpse of the broad plane of his chest through the low-cut neckline of his tunic. A finger of pale sunlight caressed his exposed olive skin and corded muscle. I swallowed thickly. Again. I really needed that ale.

We passed into the raucous Great Hall and I gawked at the sight. Two huge wrought iron chandeliers hung from arched vaulted ceilings, coated in wax drippings, while colored glass on the Hall's far end let in a kaleidoscope of rainbow hues. Dozens of long wooden tables flanked the room, their polished surfaces covered by an array of edibles. My entire clann could fit in this room. And be fed by this feast. I revised my assessment of Arthur's wealth and status. Caerleon was a rich city indeed.

I drew in a shaky breath and slowed my steps as my gaze locked onto the colored-glass windows once more. Windows could be stained? Or were they gems?

"A coronation gift for Arthur from the Túatha dé Danann," Lancelot said. "Presented by my foster mother."

"Beautiful," I breathed. "Faerie made, then?"

"The light glows more brightly in the presence of fae, so I was told."

I barely registered Lancelot's words. Rainbow beams of light held me captive as the air fairly vibrated with a magic that sang to my blood. For a moment, I was transported away from today and my troubles. It was as if I knew this place, though nothing could be further from the truth. My pulse thrummed loud in my chest, my lips parted with a wonder I could not explain. And I forgot—forgot about the knights at my side and the helmet upon my head until *he* shadowed my mood.

Lancelot stepped in front of my path—his ice-blue eyes flashing, his strong jaw set. "Do you wear that helmet to sleep Finn? Because you're a knight now, so the helm should be removed before standing before our king."

And before I could get my hands up to ward him off, he pounced, seizing an antler and jerking the helm from my head.

Cool air rushed in about me as my long white-blonde braids tumbled down over my shoulder. I took in a startled hiss of breath to smother the string of curses that threatened to bubble forth. Then, I squared my shoulders and drew myself up to full height, taking a perverse pleasure at the stunned expression on his face. Nothing for it. The deed was done. My secret was out.

Chapter Eight

Lancelot

Lancelot wasn't sure what he had expected under the crown of Finn's antlers, but not this. A woman. King Arthur Pendragon knighted a woman.

Even Percival, never without a jest or a jab, was rendered mute, his mouth slackened in shock.

It was a peculiar sensation, the current of emotions flooding through him. Already the surprise was wearing off, bleeding into something deep and low and hot. For what a woman she was—this stranger they had tied their lives to.

As if carved from marble, she had a face hewn of elegant lines and angles. Faint brows formed the trails of two shooting stars. White-blonde hair, plaited with black-stained leather in a cord of braids, bunched and draped over her shoulders. Her eyes glimmered like waterfall mist, her skin as pure and unblemished as an untouched snowdrift. She shone with a cold fire that called to him, a wild song that kindled an answering blaze within him, startling in its intensity.

Fear seized his heart with a gauntleted grip as Morgana's words echoed loudly in his mind. *There will be a woman, a Gwenevere pure like the white of driven snow. You will long for her with all your heart. Perhaps she will love you too, but if you two join as man and woman, she will bring not only your downfall, but the downfall of all you love. Caerleon. And Arthur.*

He had shrugged off the curse, dismissed her words as scorned nonsense. He knew no Gwenevere, no white enchantress pure as the driven snow. Or he hadn't . . . *then.*

"Sir Lancelot du Lac," she said, holding her chin at a haughty angle. "Is something amiss?"

Her words were a challenge, a dare. One he could not meet. For now, he saw the game she had played, saw how she had thoroughly out-maneuvered them. Arthur had made her a knight before the entire kingdom—an unmarried woman holding a noble title reserved only for men. No less, she had earned the spot. Gods help him, this woman outfought every competitor. She matched Galahad and Arthur blow for blow. Now they were too far down this road to turn back.

"Yer a lass!" Percival laughed, his arms akimbo. "A bonnie one at that too."

Perhaps Lancelot would have been delighted, too, had things been different. There were worse fates than to live and train beside a gorgeous woman. But Percival didn't know what this meant for Lancelot. For all of them. Didn't understand the danger she posed.

Arthur and Galahad chose that moment to stroll into the Great Hall. Arthur had removed his armor and once again donned his fine woolen tunic. His cheeks were flushed, a handsome smile on his face, almost boyish.

The smile disarmed Lancelot further, recalling memories of him and Arthur training with the soldiers, before Arthur's father had died at the hands of Saxons and Arthur's mother had declared never to remarry before disappearing into the Otherworld. When Arthur was a mere prince and not a King.

Seeing Arthur happy should warm the stone cockles of Lancelot's cursed heart. Especially as Morgana's vengeance had fallen over them all like a heavy cloak. At times, he felt as though he were drowning in his guilt and shame—but never as much so as right now.

Lancelot forced himself to watch when Arthur and Galahad noticed Finn—no, not Finn—who knew what her name really was. Arthur and Galahad saw her face first, for how could one not notice her ethereal beauty? Their eyes trailed down to the dull leather armor, the boots covered in dust, the sword at her hip. Brows scrunched, lips dipping into frowns, as they took in the helmet hanging limply in Lancelot's hand. And then the widening of eyes, the inhaled hiss of breath.

Arthur took a step back as though struck by an invisible blow.

Galahad, however, let out a bark of shocked

laughter, one big hand slapping his thigh.

"Finn's a lass," Percival proclaimed, a giddy twinkle in the lad's eyes.

"Yer Majesty," the woman said, lowering her plaited head. "I meant no disrespect. I wished only to be treated as an equal. To be given a fair chance."

"And you thought deception the only way to get it?" Arthur's voice was cold.

Lancelot could see his mind working, the thoughts flying behind his carefully-schooled features. "You thought we would not treat you fairly as you were?"

"Would ye have?" Her head snapped up and she met his eyes with a challenge that burned bright and clean.

Arthur looked away with a muttered curse. Uncertainty was an unfamiliar look on their king.

Merlin chose that moment to stroll into the Great Hall, hands buried in his charcoal gray robe, his hood shadowing his rugged face. When he caught sight of the woman, he stilled. The golden-ring around his ageless hazel eyes glowed and his pupils appeared almost reptilian. The druid's incubus blood was reacting to something *other*—but only Lancelot knew the magic Merlin sensed, the magic the color windows sensed too. The unspoken confirmation was nearly Lancelot's undoing. His muscles tightened with the need to rage, to destroy, to know her cold fire intimately.

"We're drawing attention," Galahad rumbled. "Perhaps we should continue this discussion at our seats?"

Lancelot looked about, trying to calm his rapid

pulse. It was true. The nobles, villagers, and warriors already seated were craning their necks to inspect the knot of knights.

Arthur nodded curtly and turned on his heel, stalking up toward the head table.

The woman marched after him, after grabbing her helm from Lancelot's grip.

He followed after her, head down to discreetly examine her armored form. She must be long and lean beneath the mass of buckles and leather but, with the benefit of his new knowledge, he could see a semblance of feminine curve there, waiting to be uncovered. How had he not seen her for what she was? Lancelot cursed under his breath as his cock began to stir beneath his breeches.

Arthur settled into the ornate chair in the center spot of honor, motioning for the woman to sit next to him. Lancelot took the spot to her right, forgiving Arthur for giving Lancelot's usual seat away. No doubt Arthur wished to question her. And Lancelot wished to listen.

Galahad and Percival filled in the chairs on Arthur's other side, Merlin settling in the empty seat next to Lancelot.

Arthur stood and hastily declared the feast begun, before dropping into his chair and turning to the woman with slitted eyes. "Who are you?"

"Fionnabhair Allán, oldest daughter of Brin Allán, chieftain of Aghanravel and a king of Tara," she said proudly, without flinching away from Arthur's fury. "Though call me Fionna." She leaned back in her seat and tilted her head toward Arthur. "I kept the truth of my sex hidden, but the rest is true. I hail from Ulster. I'm here to be yer knight."

"You will understand if it's hard for me to believe what you offer as truth," Arthur countered.

"Then believe the strength of my sword arm and the cut of my blade." Her cheeks flushed with Arthur's challenge, her eyes aglow.

Fionnabhair, Fionna. The name was honey sweet on Lancelot's tongue. His soul blazed hotter with her confession, as if recognizing the presence of a worthy conquest. An equal. Lancelot thought he might be sick.

Fionna continued, pointing a finger at Arthur like she possessed the audacity to poke the High King of Briton in the chest. "Ye said ye wanted the best in the land to be your fifth knight. Well, I am the best in two lands. So, which is it, King Arthur? Do ye want the best, or do ye want a *man*?"

The muscles of Arthur's jaw worked as he met Fionna's furious words, tension chilling the air like ice.

It was Percival who cracked the hoarfrost growing between them, the blessed fool boy. "We actually want the best *looking*, Fionna," he said, gesturing from his toes to his head with a crooked grin. "Obviously."

Arthur let out a strained burst of laughter, shaking his head.

Galahad reached out and mock-cuffed Percival across the ear, which Percival tried to avoid, resulting in a short tussle that found Percival's head locked under Galahad's sizable bicep.

But the challenge had passed, along with much of the tension. And when a servant appeared with a tray heavy-laden with wine goblets, everyone grabbed one gratefully.

Lancelot looked sideways at Merlin, who was watching Fionna with barefaced interest.

"You couldn't have foreseen this, druid?" Lancelot gave a false laugh, and reached for a golden-brown leg from a platter of chicken to appear natural.

"The Fates do seem to have a sense of humor," Merlin remarked, shifting the weight of his all-seeing gaze onto Lancelot. "Through I fear a dark one at that."

Lancelot tried not to shrink from the man, ignoring the feelings of unease that skittered like spiders across his skin. Merlin unnerved him when his cambion blood was at work. He saw too much. Sometimes Lancelot swore the druid saw the truth of his curse—knew the danger Lancelot now posed to Arthur and Caerleon—saw the damage he could yet do. Or perhaps he saw too little. Because he hadn't seen this—hadn't seen that their fifth knight would be a woman or the danger this revelation brought their brotherhood.

Doubt and fear warred inside Lancelot. He took a savage bite off the chicken leg, but the richly spiced meat tasted like sawdust in his mouth.

Should he tell Arthur the truth of Morgana's curse? No. He closed his eyes against the thought. He couldn't. Couldn't admit to letting him down one more time. What if Arthur sent him away, to keep his kingdom safe? Lancelot couldn't bear it. Arthur was his brother, this fortress his home. They grew up together when Uther agreed to foster him when he had reached the strange in-between age of boyhood and manhood. Perhaps he could try to convince Arthur to send her away, since a woman ranking within their knighthood was a terrible idea. But Arthur had already knighted her . . .

Another thought occurred to him. Perhaps he was overreacting. Certainly, he was attracted to Fionna. *But I don't love her*, he scolded himself. Perhaps Fionna wasn't the one Morgana had foretold. A Gwenevere was a creature of legend—a white fay, an enchantress from bardic tales and nothing more. Fionna was remarkable for her fighting prowess and beautiful, yes. But magic? He had seen no sign of magic beyond the glowing light streaming though the rainbow-hued windows. But that could have merely been a bright afternoon sun playing tricks on his mind. And he would recognize magic. After all, he was raised on the Isle of Man, among druid priestesses and sídhe fae.

Lancelot looked down to where Fionna sat, Arthur and Galahad and Percival all leaning into her like flowers tilting toward the morning sun.

"Are all women in Ulster such fierce warriors?" Galahad was asking.

"Many," Fionna replied, pausing. "But I am one of the best."

Perhaps she wasn't the woman. And even if so, the curse would only fall over Caerleon if he joined with her as man and woman. He could restrain himself. He shifted in his seat to hide evidence to the contrary. Relief welled in Lancelot, and he tore off a chunk of chicken with gusto. Yes, he would simply resist her. How hard could that be?

Chapter Nine

Percival

Percival always enjoyed a good feast, but that night's festivities were the best by far. Fionnabhair Allán was the most interesting thing to have happened to Caerleon for quite some time. She was akin to a maiden in a bardic faerie tale come to life, if that maiden could stick an axe through a man's eyeball without a second's thought. He hadn't even known that women came in this fierce and formidable variety. Was there no end to the surprising delights they possessed?

As the night wound on, the ale settled into Arthur and Galahad's blood. They appeared to have relaxed in Fionna's presence, chatting with her almost amiably. As it turned out, she was a princess, a king of Tara's daughter. No wonder she put Arthur to task so effortlessly.

Percival glanced to the head table's opposite end, where Lancelot sat brooding. Lancelot had a stick shoved firmly up his arse ever since Morgana. Percival resisted the urge to throw a grape at him. Before the disastrous business with Merlin's apprentice, Lancelot had been his favorite sword-brother, the most likely to join Percival in a prank or laugh. The most likely to flirt with him too. He never knew if those moments were in jest or earnest. Strangely, he found he hadn't minded either way. But those memories of Lancelot were fading. Each day, it grew harder to remember that carefree version of his friend.

With a bored sigh, Percival slouched over the table, resting his chin in one hand while the other picked at a splinter in the wood. The Great Hall had emptied hours earlier—or at least, it felt like hours—and he shivered in the night air. The fires in both grand hearths had cooled to barely glowing embers.

Galahad loosed a jaw-cracking yawn.

Fionna released an answering one, though she covered her mouth with leather-clad arm. "Perhaps I should retire," she said, before pausing. "Is there a particular room I should—"

"There's a spare room next to mine," Galahad leaned in, running a finger slowly around the rim of his empty goblet.

Percival narrowed his eyes. Galahad and Fionna were a ridiculously impractical match. Fionna was half his size. Galahad would probably crush the woman to death if he tried to bed her. Not to mention, Fionna seemed more inclined to crush a man's skull than lie with him.

"There's an available room in the North Wing," Arthur said. "I'll have the servants prepare the chamber for you."

Percival suppressed a groan. He saw what Arthur was doing—keeping Fionna far away from the knights' rooms in the East Wing. Where was the fun in that?

"I'll show her the way, lads," Percival offered, pushing his chair away from the scraps of food and empty goblets. Might as well find out exactly where her chamber was located.

Arthur hesitated.

"Ah, let him," Galahad crooned. "It's not like he's any danger to her, what with his vow and all." With a cheerful wink, he grinned at Percival and then raised his empty goblet in a mocking toast.

Fionna looked away from Percival's spitting glare and focused on Arthur, who was now pinching the bridge of his nose with his fingers. "I don't care one way or the other," she said. "Rest assured, no one is going in my room but me."

"Fine," Arthur muttered. His shoulders slumped as he leaned the back of his head onto his ebony wood chair, his glassy stare somehow burning holes through the rafters. After a few strained seconds, silent save the echoing clop of Fionna's boots, Arthur rolled his head toward Percival. "Stop by my study when you're done?"

Percival nodded before bouncing out of his chair after Fionna. Despite her shorter legs, she moved quite quickly. He had wanted to escort her, but now he found his nerves raw and ragged at the prospect. *Humor. Disarm her with humor*, he thought.

"I don't need a wet nurse to watch over me,"

Fionna snapped when Percival caught up.

"Good," Percival practically chirped in response. "Because ye would go awful hungry." He squeezed his pectorals, raising an eyebrow at her.

She rolled her eyes.

"I suppose ye dinnae need me to tell ye then . . ." Percival trailed off.

Fionna pursed her wine-flushed lips. "Tell me *what?*"

"That the North Wing is that way, lass." He cocked his thumb over his shoulder, toward a passageway they had breezed past just a few moments prior.

Fionna stopped in her tracks, whirling on him. Percival's blood thundered through his veins. Merciful gods, she was as intimidating as she was beautiful. And he couldn't stop looking at her mouth.

"Why are ye *now* telling me this?"

"Ye seemed so certain of yer course. I hated to correct you, is all."

She let out an exasperated hiss, before muttering under her breath, "Well, isn't that the story of my life." She pasted on a fake smile and inclined her head. "Sir Percival, please, do me the honor of leading the way."

Percival thrust out his elbow, offering her his arm. "Sir Fionnabhair, 'twould be my pleasure."

She ignored his gesture, and so he let his proffered arm drop, falling into step beside her instead.

"Sir Fionnabhair," she murmured. "Sounds odd."

"I'm actually not sure if there's a different name for a female knight. Madam Fionnabhair? Lady Fionnabhair?" he mused. "Maybe one of Arthur's books has an answer. What do they call women warriors in Ulster?"

"Warriors." Her face set like stone. Then the lines around her eyes softened slightly, like a bright afternoon fading to twilight. "What did Galahad mean? About yer vow?"

"Ye caught that, did ye?" Percival shoved his hands into his pockets. Well, he supposed his embarrassing secret would come out sooner or later. "I made a vow of chastity. Until I'm wed."

A surprised cough escaped Fionna's lips.

"Subtle," he said, willing his galloping heart to slow down to normal speed. She was just a woman. He talked to women all the time. When guttered after imbibing too much ale? Well, then he just talked endlessly.

"It's . . ." she searched for the words. "Not what most young men in Ulster would choose, anyway. Are things so different here?"

"Just for me."

She cocked an eyebrow at him, and when her silver eyes met his, a jolt of energy coursed through him. Faint, but unmistakable. He struggled to keep the shock from his face.

"Have ye not heard of the Blessed Grail?" he asked.

She shook her head.

"The land is fertile so long as the Grail serves a sovereign-blessed king. In the North, the Grail Maiden sups with the gods of Albion while she waits for the rightful king to arrive, using the fae bowl to serve her guests."

"Grail Maiden?"

"Yes, an earth goddess. Most men think the Grail is a myth, but it's not. My father, the last Fisher King, was the keeper of the Blessed Grail. When he died, the vessel disappeared." Percival slid her a half-smile.

"Do you know the location of this . . . sacred vessel?" she asked.

"No one knows for certain. Though it's possible the Grail Maiden guards the sacred vessel in the *in-between* until the Fisher King's heir can ask the Grail whom it serves. Ye see, my father died when I was young, when a neighboring clann lord lay siege to Caer Benic. But, because my father's blood flows through my veins, I have a connection to the Grail. I can sense . . . clues. Pieces of the puzzle that will help my king find the hidden location someday, even if partway to the Otherworld."

"Truly?" Fionna's face softened with his long-winded story, as if she cherished each word he uttered in his barely sober state. "What does the connection feel like?"

Like you, he wanted to say. *It feels like when you looked at me just now.* But he swallowed the words, not wanting to frighten her. "Hard to describe, really. A tingle. A knowing."

"Sure. But what does that have to do with you remaining . . . *chaste*?" She said the word as if it were a communicable disease.

"According to my father, the connection is lost if we dinnae remain pure of heart. And body. A holy virgin for a holy vessel. The bond of marriage purifies any coupling, of course."

"Oh, of course," she remarked tartly.

"Perhaps things are not so . . . proper in Ireland?" Percival grinned. He pointed left and they turned into a narrow hallway, heading toward a block of rooms in the North Wing.

"Perhaps," Fionna replied, arching an eyebrow. "This whole world feels strange to me."

"Wales was strange to me too, at first," Percival admitted. "When my father died in battle, my mother took me far from the world of men and raised me deep in Galloway Forest."

"You're Scoti?"

"Aye."

"I could tell you were Gael, though I considered ye a fellow Irishman until now."

"My family is of Pict heritage, long before the Kingdom of Alba formed." Percival flashed her a waggish smile. "Why else would I be so braw and fierce?" Fionna groaned and he laughed before continuing. "Arthur and Lancelot were the first men I ever remember seeing since I was a lad of six. I left at age fifteen against my mother's wishes, but Caerleon called to me."

"And yet now . . . this feels as true as home?"

"It's all of our home. Caerleon. Each other. Most of the knights had strange childhoods. Except Galahad that is, his father is a blacksmith, and he one of many mouths fed under their roof. That's pretty normal."

"He doesn't sound Norse."

Percival shrugged. "He was squired at a young

age by a Welsh Lord in Gŵyr and raised in a manor."

"I see." Fionna tilted her head. "What do ye mean by strange upbringings?"

"Well, Lancelot was raised by a faerie." Percival lifted his shoulder in a slight shrug. "Vivien, Lady of the Lake, druid priestess on the Isle of Man. Have ye heard of her?"

Fionna's face remained blank.

"She provides protection over Briton. She's also the one who gifted Arthur with Excalibur, making him the Pendragon, High King of Briton. Though, the scattered kingdoms have yet to unite under his rule."

"Is Lancelot part fae, then?"

"No, Lancelot is the exiled Prince of Benoic, from the Kingdom of France. His father, King Ban, was murdered by his rival and his mother fled for her life. The Lady of the Lake fostered Lancelot when his mother left him as an offering to the goddess for safe keeping. He joined Uther's court for military train-ing around the age of thirteen. He and Arthur have been inseparable ever since."

Fionna considered this, pausing. "Lancelot . . . a prince?" She turned to him, her brows knitted in a scowl. "He doesn't seem to like me very much."

Percival pasted a shocked look on his face, his hand to his breast. "Whatever do ye mean, lass . . ."

A half smile curved Fionna's lip, and Percival counted that a win. He thought of how to best ex-plain the situation to Fionna. When the faerie sisters, Elaine and Morgause, had first cursed Arthur and Caerleon, Arthur had sworn the knights to secrecy, not wanting word of his weakness to reach his enemies. But Fionna was a knight. She was one of them now. Didn't that bring her within their circle of confidence? Percival chewed on his lip. Curse his ale-addled brain and tongue that acted as though attached to a bard.

What to do?

He had found out the hard way that kings were funny about secrets and their pride. It had been a *year* since Percival had jokingly shared with several court ladies how Arthur didn't always wear small clothes under his breeches, and Arthur still turned scarlet at the mention of it. Best to receive Arthur's approval before airing all their dirty laundry to Fionna. But she was still waiting for an answer. Gods, he had been quiet too long! She must think him strange, especially after his rambling divulgences. He scrambled for an explanation.

"Lancelot had a bad experience with a woman," he practically blurted. "He's still recovering. Dinnae take his winning personality personally."

She nodded, her face unreadable. They were reaching the end of the hallway now.

"This is the biggest room in the North Wing. I hope it's to yer liking."

Fionna nodded her thanks and pushed through the door, closing it gently behind her.

Percival stood before her door, alone, with only her memory hanging in the torchlit hall. He found he meant it. He did hope she liked her time here. Because he wanted her to stay.

Chapter Ten

Arthur

Arthur didn't like being backed into a corner. And Princess Fionnabhair Allán had thoroughly and completely put him in one. The mood in his study was strangely subdued. The knights should have been cheerful, even jubilant, after the day's excitement—tourney, feast, finding a fifth. But instead, each man seemed lost in thought. Lancelot stood by the hearth, staring into the flames; Galahad fixed on some distant point out the dark latticed window. Merlin was always enigmatic, so the look of quiet contemplation on his still form wasn't quite so unsettling to Arthur.

It was if something had shifted this night in the bedrock of their lives, tilting their course in an entirely new direction. Toward a path Arthur couldn't see down. And *that* made him most nervous of all.

Percival appeared in the doorway, a flush on his cheeks that seemed to breathe life into all of them.

"Sorry I'm late, had to show our new knight all the perks of her new station, ye ken." He flashed his incorrigible Percival grin.

"She slammed the door in your face, didn't she?" Galahad asked.

"That she did, lads." Percival ducked his head in a nod before falling into an upholstered chair before the fire, one leg slung over the arm.

Arthur strode to the fireplace and leaned against the stone mantle, opposite of Lancelot, and sighed. His eyes were scratchy with fatigue and he had the start of a headache from all the ale, but he needed to talk this out, or he would never find peace tonight.

"What are we going to do about Fionna?" Arthur asked.

The room was silent, but for a pop of a log on the fire.

Arthur shifted uncomfortably. "I'll be the first to admit that her fighting skills are impressive. But we can't have a *female* knight. Caerleon will be the laughingstock of Briton!" The British kings from other chiefdoms and kingdoms already thought him strange enough, what with his kingship bestowed by a magic sword and a cambion druid for his chief advisor. Would anyone take him seriously if he fought with a woman by his side?

"Perhaps next time we shouldn't knight anyone before we see their face," Lancelot grumbled, not looking up from the flames.

Arthur's annoyance flared. "Thank you for that enlightening suggestion," he snapped. He needed his second-in-command back, not this moody shadow. A similar moody shadow he sported when he had first arrived in Caerleon a decade ago. Lately, it seemed like the man wasn't even here, his haunted gaze a thousand miles away. But where? What private hell was his friend lost in? And how could he bring him back?

"Female knights may be a novelty in Briton, but in Ulster, women warriors are commonplace," Merlin remarked.

"The Norse and Saxons too," Galahad rumbled. "Our shield-maidens fight alongside the men. They're just as good at killing as their husbands, brothers, and fathers."

Arthur frowned. That was true. Norse and Saxon war bands, his enemies to the east, were filled with men and women alike. But . . . asking women to fight was not done in Briton. Women were to be cared for, protected. They were the land's life-givers, the fair sex cherished for birthing strong warriors and kings for Britannia. Though Arthur had to relent. Fionna didn't need his physical protection.

"We all agree her fighting prowess isn't a concern, yes?" Galahad said.

The knights nodded.

"And perhaps the nobles will talk behind our backs, but we've never cared what those pompous arses thought," Galahad continued. "You've always done the unexpected, Your Majesty. Keep them guessing."

Arthur nodded in appreciation. That was true. But this cut to the heart of his concern, the one he was loathe to voice. It wasn't so much Fionna's femaleness that concerned him, it was her—Fionna-ness. The moment his gaze riveted onto her ethereal beauty and warrior's build, he had wanted her. She was a portrait of contrasts, hard against soft, dark against light. Even dirty and sweaty, wearing leather armor and a scowl upon her face, she had stolen the breath from his lungs, had set the blood racing through his veins. Sitting next to her at the feast had been like being in his body for the first time—newly aware of each sensation. His stomach, flipping nervously; his skin, feeling alive and energized as if by a lightning storm. His cock, hard and insistent. Fionna was a tonic far more potent than wine—the stubborn set of her jaw, her earthy scent of heather and moss, the lilting accent of her words challenging him as an equal. She had swept over him, sending his head spinning. He didn't know if he could focus with Fionna around, be dispassionate and fair and decisive. And that scared him more than even a faerie curse.

And then there were his other knights. He had seen their eyes following Fionna like drowning men seeking air. They all wanted her. Four stags—one doe—there was only one way this situation would end. The stags would tear each other apart trying to get to her. He had trouble enough with Morgana trying to destroy his inner circle and his kingdom, in some twisted effort to repair what Uther had done to her father and their mother. He didn't need the trouble Fionna brought, too. Fionna could tear them apart without even trying.

"She's very beautiful," Arthur finally said, realizing he had been standing in silent contemplation too long. "I fear she could come between us. We've already had trouble enough of the female variety."

Lancelot's face hardened, the firelight limning the hard set of his square jaw.

"Never a worry," Galahad said. "She'll choose me. It'll make it easy for the rest of you lads."

"I'm not sure walking tree trunks are her type," Percival quipped. "She seemed quite taken with me this evening."

"Too bad you took a vow of chastity then," Galahad retorted.

"Only until marriage, ye big oaf."

Arthur held up a hand and the two fell silent. "I'm not worried about you two. Lancelot?" He spoke his friend's name quietly, almost a warning hush.

Lancelot met his eyes, and a cold frost crackled in his gaze, one Arthur didn't understand. "I want nothing to do with her," Lancelot sneered. "She brings trouble."

"I'm not sure any of you have a choice," Merlin spoke, seeming to come back to life. The druid often fell still, his expression trance-like. Arthur had grown used to it, together with the wisdom that such a state would bring.

"What have you seen?"

"I have seen her drinking from the Blessed Grail," Merlin said. "Isn't that right, Percival?"

Arthur's head swiveled to look at Percival.

An apologetic look was written across the lad's face.

"What's this?" Arthur asked. Percival's connection to the Blessed Grail had not yet borne fruit, but his magical affinity to the vessel was one of the reasons Arthur had knighted him. That, and his indomitable good cheer and purity of heart.

"I thought I felt something," Percival admitted. "When I was walking with her. It was fleeting, but I dinnae think I was imagining it. She's connected to the Grail somehow. To the quest."

Merlin nodded. "She is the knight I had foreseen, though now her face has become clear. She is bound to you four, and you to her. The Fates did not make a mistake in sending her to you, Your Majesty."

Arthur crossed his arms, grappling with the excitement blooming within him. He knew he should send her away, that she would be trouble, but part of him was infinitely pleased that she had to stay. Arthur shoved that part down deep, locking the feeling within himself. He was king. He did not have the luxury of giving in to mindless infatuation, even if she were of noble blood.

"Seems we have little choice then," Arthur said. "Are we in agreement?"

"She's nice," Percival said. "I think we should keep her."

"She isn't a stray puppy," shot Lancelot darkly.

"Your vote?" Arthur asked Lancelot.

Lancelot gave a curt shake of his head, his unruly mop of dark curls swaying.

Arthur swallowed his surprise. Lancelot saying no to a woman. This business with Morgana had indeed shaken him deeply.

"I say yes," Galahad rumbled. "She earned her place."

"Very well," Arthur said. "But I will have a promise from each of you."

The knights looked to him.

"You are my brothers. I will not have a woman break the bonds between us. If she chooses one of us, or none of us, the others shall respect her choice, and bow out gracefully, and with honor."

"Maybe she'll want all of us," Percival said with sly grin.

Arthur massaged his temples. That headache had arrived in full force. "She will not tear us asunder. Do you so swear?"

His knights swore, and Arthur prayed that the vows from his sword-brothers would be enough to withstand the coming storm that was Fionna Allán.

Chapter Eleven

Fionna

ormally after battle, I slept like the dead. But last night, sleep's sweet embrace had eluded me completely.

With a groan, I sat up amongst a sweaty tangle of linen and woolen bedclothes. I longed for the single woven blanket from my bed at home, as well as my wolf pelt for unbearably cold nights. Aideen had made me the blanket gracing my cot. I picked the colors of red and orange and purple, and then Aideen wove the hemp yarns into a masterpiece of intricate intersecting lines. That was what Aideen did—beautify the world around her. That was her gift, to bring beauty and life, while my gift was to bring destruction and death.

It hadn't mattered how different Aideen and I were though, we had been inseparable since my little sister was born. We were inseparable still, or at least we had been before Donal O'Lynn had snatched Aideen off the battlefield at Ballymena, while our clanns fought with an expanding Norse settlement.

When we were girls, Aideen would sneak over from her own bed to mine more nights than I could count. And all to whisper stories and giggle beneath the rhythmic sound of our father's snores that crested and fell like waves on the rocky shores of Lough Neagh. Even when we grew too big to both fit in my narrow little bed, I would turn sideways, fitting my body around my sister's, stroking her rich auburn tresses as we murmured about lads from our village or fretted about our father's stiffening hip.

The last night we had bedfellowed, we had argued—Aideen insisting that she skirt the battlefield to heal our clann's fianna who returned injured and dying. I had argued about the danger, feeling like flint striking across the hard rock of Aideen's resolve. If there was one thing Aideen and I had in common, it was our stubbornness. And this was one time I took no joy in being right.

Sunlight streamed through a crack in the heavy wool curtains of my room, setting dust motes alive and dancing like flecks of gold. I stood, stretching my sore body, before leaning over to touch my toes. Wrinkling my nose, I lifted the lid to the chamber pot and relieved myself, and then enjoyed a deep drink from a pitcher of water a servant left the night prior on an ornately-carved sideboard. Those tasks complete, I looked around the lavish room helplessly, wondering what on earth to do next. Why, steal the sword of course. But how?

I looked about once more, taking closer stock of my surroundings. The plush woven carpet was softer beneath my toes than even the downiest pelt. Gold leaf and rich linen and wool fabrics decorated the room, from the large four-post bed, to the upholstered backs of chairs, to a vibrant tapestry covering one wall, depicting knights on unicorns battling dragons. Well, unless things were *very different* in Briton, more so than I realized, the mythical fight was mere fancy. Still, the amount of casual wealth in this fortress—in this room—was staggering. Bewitched, I fingered a silver candlestick inlaid with mother of pearl and calculated how much I could get by bartering the pair to the nearest Dál nAraidi clann. Maybe I could take a few things for my trouble when I departed.

A churning feeling returned to my stomach. The grinding anxiety nearly stole my breath.

The thought of stealing from these knights, from the king, unsettled me far too much. I wasn't sure why, but a part of me cared what Arthur Pendragon thought of me. His nearness felt right somehow. As if we were fated to be bound to one another. At first, I thought my draw was to how his smile invited my troublesome thoughts. Then, over supper, I noticed how the freckles sprayed across his nose were only the darker few. Faerie kisses touched every part of him that I could see, even the very tips of his ears. I was undone and drank two goblets full of wine, simply to forget the man's freckles, and smile, and the way he inclined his head just so when intently listening to another. Wanting to steal his good opinion of me would prove more unsafe than O'Lynn's demand.

So perhaps just the sword.

A knock sounded on the door and I flew to it, grateful for a distraction from my uneasy thoughts. I yanked on the door's iron ring to find a pretty brunette in a cornflower blue dress on the other side, teetering under the weight of several large bundles.

"Hello," the girl said, her voice sweet and tinkling. "I've brought you some things."

My breath caught. One of the bundles was my saddlebags. I pulled the heavy weight from the girl's shoulder, and then hugged the familiar leather bag to my chest. Hopefully Zephyr wasn't growing too fat and happy in the stables under Caerleon's rich care. She would never forgive me once we returned to Ireland.

The girl straightened, sighing with relief.

"Come in," I said, stepping aside.

The girl placed the other bundle on the little bench at the foot of my bed and turned to me, her eyes downcast. "His Majesty thought you might need more clothes. He wasn't sure . . . whether you would prefer dresses or breeches." The girl hurried through the words as if slightly scandalized. "So, he sent both."

I bit back a smile. "Give the king my thanks. What do they call ye, lass?"

The girl looked up, and I marveled at how her bright blue eyes matched her dress and envied the dimple in her chin. She was perhaps eighteen, just two years younger than me. "Margred, Your Ladyship."

"Simply call me Fionna, no need for formalities,

please. May I ask for yer help?"

Margred nodded enthusiastically. "I've been assigned to attend you. Whatever you need, Lady . . . er, Fionna."

"A bath," I answered, hoping the blush I felt heating my neck didn't wend its way upward to blaze my cheeks. I had consciously avoided peering toward the looking glass on the far vanity table. For I was sure I looked a fright after a day fighting under my helm. "Some breakfast, and then I want ye to tell me everything ye know about the king's knights."

Margred grinned as if we had just shared a secret. "That I can do," she said.

After eating and bathing, I felt more like myself than I had since leaving Ulster. I was as clean as a newborn babe, my long hair now washed, combed and loosely braided. All the clothes from my saddlebag were ripe from the sea crossing, so I dressed in clothes that Arthur had sent—an emerald green linen tunic trimmed in silvered threads, and tight brown breeches beneath. After I laced up my worn leather boots and buckled on my sword belt, I had to admit, I didn't form an altogether displeasing picture.

Once finished, I desired to visit the stables and check on Zephyr before seeing to any other errands and duties this day. Margred walked with me part of the way through the maze of corridors, and then pointed down the stairs and out into the bright morning sunshine before returning to her own duties.

The lass had shared interesting tidbits about the knights, all of which kept with my own assessment. Arthur, proud and fair, with the weight of the world upon his shoulders. Percival—the jester of the group, his boasting and jokes hiding a sweetness and innocence that Margred hoped he would never lose. Galahad, a powerful warrior whose heart was as big as his stature.

Apparently, he had been nursing an injured fawn back to health in the stables for a week before the stable boys grew any the wiser. If the village ladies hadn't swooned for him before, that incident had seemed to cement him as one of their favorites.

And then there was Lancelot, a man who loved women and was equally beloved by them. The gossip about his engagement to a dark fae princess, together with the relationship's spectacular implosion, had been particularly juicy. Perhaps I could use this newly gained insight, somehow.

I was pleased to find Zephyr tucked in a cozy stall, munching contentedly on a full manger of hay. The mare looked up drowsily as I entered her stall, huffing gently against my face in greeting. I looked her up and down, nodding in approval when I noticed how Zephyr's hooves had been picked and oiled and how her coat had been brushed down to a sheen, not even a fleck of mud remaining from our voyage. Spoiled, indeed. My solid-treed saddle and bridle hung neatly from hooks on the wall, the leather padding and saddle cleaned and oiled as well. At least they treated horses right in Caerleon. And tack. My respect for the place increased.

Pondering what to do next, I laid my forehead against Zephyr's velvet neck. Margred had borne no message from Arthur other than the clothes; it would seem I had the day to myself. But how to use it? I needed to strategize, to plan my theft of Excalibur. Where to start?

The sound of clashing swords reached my ears through the quiet for the stable. Curiosity piqued, I gave Zephyr's forehead a last scratch before closing the stall door behind me.

I found Galahad and Lancelot in the stable yard's bright light, sparring in furious combat, their boots eating up the paddock's loose dirt, their swords flashing in the sun. I stilled in the stable's shadow, my cheeks growing hot at the sight. Both men fought shirtless, their rippling muscles glinting with the sweat of their exertions. Galahad was huge, his biceps bunching under tawny-gold skin, the peaks and furrows of his muscled back a foreign territory I desperately wanted to explore.

Lancelot was smaller in stature than Galahad, though still tall and incredibly strong. He had nary an ounce of body fat on him. His rippling stomach flexed and tensed with each stroke of his sword. Veins roped down his powerful arms, both of which were tattooed from his upper chest and shoulders down in indigo swirls and knots—symbols of my people, the Gaels. And the Túatha dé Danann. Warrior marks. Lancelot's dark hair hung in wet curls about his head, his expression deadly serious. He fought as though the Red Hounds of Cúalu were on his heel, his sword strikes as fast and deadly as a venomous snake.

My appreciation of his male form gave way to the appreciation of his skill—deep, intricate. He was better than me. My excitement flared. Years had passed since I had fought someone better. Or found someone to teach me more. There were lessons to learn from this man.

A ringing silence echoed in the wake of their battle—their weapons now tipped toward the earth. When had their fight ended? Had I truly given into reverie for so long? Lancelot glared at me from several paces away, his chest heaving.

Galahad, on the other hand, had a disarming grin stretched across his face.

I cleared my throat, disliking the feeling of being tongue-tied. But I shook it off and strode toward them. "Lancelot. Would ye spar with me?" I asked. Might as well get straight to it.

He shook his head, beads of his sweat flicking across my cheek. "Time to begin drills with my soldiers at the Round, *Lady*," he grunted, before turning on his heel and stalking across the stable yard.

My teeth ground together, fury lancing through me at the slight.

"Don't take his dismissal personally," Galahad remarked, sheathing his sword. He strode toward the stable and then dunked his whole head into the nearest water trough. He came up with a flick of golden-blond hair, sending rivulets down the planes of his chest, each droplet of water sparkling like a diamond.

"Isn't it personal?" I managed, my voice hoarse. Then I swallowed back the forming knot, unable to tear my eyes from the sight before me.

Galahad didn't answer, pulling his hair back into a messy knot, securing his long, wild strands with a piece of leather cord. "I'll spar with you," he said, setting one hand on his narrow waist. "If you're up for a rematch."

I nodded, attempting to banish the memory of his weight upon me during our bout yesterday. "Goddess help me," I prayed under my breath. A sparring round was not at all the type of rematch I wanted.

Chapter Twelve

Fionna

The morning passed in a pleasant blur of sword strikes and parries, all the while surrounded by the steady moon of Galahad's grin, the sun on his bronzed skin, and the sparkle of his eyes. It surprised me how quickly I settled into an easy rapport with the man, joking and fighting, giving each other tips and taking them. Galahad clearly took great pride in his fighting prowess, yet he was eager for me to teach him the fighting style favored by my fiann. I had thought of my war band brothers and sisters with a pang, and then shoved the feeling down and away from my notice. I would see them before long.

When at last my muscles were quivering, my mind a soft haze, I yielded, holding up a hand, the other on my hip. "I think I've had enough for one day." I puffed in a few deep breaths, struggling to regain my wind after a particularly aerobatic sparring match.

"Thank the heavens." Galahad's muscled shoulders drooped. "Between you and Lancelot, I thought I might drop dead of exhaustion."

I pursed my lips into a fine line at the mention of Lancelot. The exiled prince clearly distrusted me, and I needed to gain trust from all the knights to accomplish my dark deed. "Should I confront Lancelot?" I asked. "Find out the cause of his great dislike for me?"

Galahad shook his head, sheathing his sword. "Lancelot doesn't like being pushed. I would wait. He'll warm to you, eventually. The man has never met a beautiful woman he didn't like."

The tips of my ears heated at the compliment. "Very well." I moved quickly past it. "I shall do as ye recommend."

"I take my leave," Galahad inclined his blond head toward me before bowing slightly at the waist. "I am off in search of a bath." And then he spun on his heel and swaggered into the stable's dark, leaving a heady scent of cedarwood and sweat and something else I couldn't name in his wake, addling my senses.

At a clean trough, I took a long drink and then splashed the cool water on my face, trying to chill the heat of desire rising through my body. *The sword. Focus on the sword, not on Galahad bathing.* I closed my eyes and huffed, trying in vain to rid the delicious mental image from my mind. *The sword.*

A distraction was needed. Something. Anything.

As far as I knew, I had the afternoon to roam or train or indulge as I pleased. Idleness was as foreign as to me as this land and my muscles, though fatigued, itched to move. But I remained where I stood and closed my eyes, hoping to hear the land's whispers. A breeze skipped over the grass and wildflowers in the paddock. I lifted my face to the warming sun. In a stall nearby, a horse nickered. Familiar sensations and sounds in an unfamiliar place. Perhaps exploring the grounds of Caerleon would prove diverting. I need to know the ins and outs of this fortress city for a quick escape anyway, including any back doors that led into the surrounding forests or to the River Usk.

A clanging rap faintly beat behind the other village sounds and I opened my eyes. A warrior should also make friends with a reliable smithy, I reasoned. Feeling a little lighter, I turned away from the stalls and surveyed the kingdom before me. First, I would wander the kitchen gardens adjacent to the stables. Perhaps next I would walk around the old Roman barracks the soldiers used, and then I would visit the blacks

After an hour of exploring and an hour of watching several thousand soldiers spar in the Round under Lancelot's guidance, I found myself ducking out a side door cut into the wooden keep's wall, tucked behind the kitchen A shadowed path led down from the hill, winding through the windswept grass toward the shimmering blue ribbon of the River Usk.

I stopped a moment and closed my eyes—I could not resist doing so all afternoon wherever I went—savoring the cool shade on my skin, the tang of wood smoke on the air, the chatter of crows gathered on tree limbs along the river or soaring high above. This country's verdant beauty soothed my soul in an unexpected way. The forests here were different from the craggy heaths of Antrim, weathered and beaten down as though by a fellow warring clann. Different than the forests of Southern Ulster and Londonderry. This place was peaceful. But somehow vulnerable too. As though the land needed protecting. I bent down and plucked a vibrant pink wildflower that grew alongside the earthen path, twirling the stem in my fingers. I had never seen a hue quite like it.

"Campion," a voice said, and I whipped my gaze up.

The druid, Merlin, stood farther down the path, his gray robes fastened with an intricately-engraved leather belt. I took his measure subconsciously, as was my habit. He was solidly built beneath those shapeless robes, probably just as fit and muscled as Arthur's other warriors. His face was handsome and rugged in a way I would normally not think as beautiful—as if Otherworldly blood ran in his veins—though much of his face was covered in a trimmed brown beard. It was hard to guess his age. Thirty? But other moments he seemed far older, a preternatural knowing in his hazel eyes. The aura of magic about him set me on edge. The clanns believed that druids who were acquainted with divination could see to the truth of a person. Arthur mentioned how his druid practiced magic. Would Merlin see the real reason behind my presence in Caerleon?

But all he did was walk closer, pointing at the flower. "Campion. The seeds, when ground, are useful for treating snakebites. Or cleansing the body from toxins."

"And the bloom?" I asked, studying the flower cradled in my palm.

"Why, it's very lovely."

"So not useful at all." I let the flower fall.

Merlin shook his head, and I found my eye drawn to the strange marks tattooed on the sides of his shorn scalp. So odd. "Beauty can be very useful. How else would the bees know how to find the flowers?" He knelt and scooped up the bloom I had dropped, and then tucked the flower into a little leather pouch on his belt.

I considered his words. I hadn't found my beauty helpful in my world. At times, my fair colorings had felt a hindrance. But perhaps in this new one, my unusual looks could have its uses. I thought of Galahad's comment. Would I dare try to use my beauty to melt Lancelot's icy demeanor?

"Where are you wandering off to next?" Merlin asked. His tone was friendly, but the gold ringing his irises flashed.

"Oh, just exploring," I said. "Trying to get the lay of the land."

"Well, the only place down this path is my cave. I would be happy to give you a tour."

My desire for immediate space from the druid

and his all-seeing eyes warred with my practical side, which insisted that I also needed to know my enemy. Plus, I didn't want to be rude and insult such a powerful man on my first official day.

"Very well."

I followed Merlin down the winding dirt and rock path, almost to the fern-lined river bank below. The forest enveloped my senses and I breathed deeply the surrounding greens and sky. Before we reached the River Usk, we turned, ducking into a very peculiar space. The cave mouth was low and wide, but upon entering, I was able to stand up straight and—

"Skies above," I whispered in awe.

Craning my neck, I gaped at the glittering ceiling, covered in tiny blue and white crystals. Merlin murmured a word under his breath and a torch flared to life in a wrought iron sconce fastened to the wall closest to where he stood. My feet forgot how to move as Merlin grasped the torch and began to move deeper into the cave.

"Come on," he said, with an amused expression on his face.

I stumbled after him. *That had been magic. Real live magic.* The first I had ever seen.

The main cavern was furnished like a disorderly study, covered in a jumble of items with a purpose I couldn't even guess. Merlin took the slightly-crushed campion bloom from his pouch and rested the bruised stem upon his carved wooden desk. "I admit, I had ulterior motives in bringing you here."

My head jerked up, my senses suddenly firing in alert.

Merlin chuckled, settling into a chair in front of a strange rocky fireplace, currently empty of flames. "All I meant is that you're a bit of a mystery to me. I would like to ask you a few questions. Would you care to sit?"

He gestured to the other chair, and I stiffly lowered myself onto the seat, albeit hesitantly. *Fool Fionna*, I scolded myself. I should never have agreed to come here or sit to answer his penetrating questions. But if I fled now, my departure would look too suspicious.

"You appeared so suddenly and have taken Caerleon by storm. Where again do you hail from?"

I relaxed slightly, reciting again the details of my heritage, my clann.

Merlin frowned. "Your father, Brin Allán you say? A chieftain. And your mother?"

I suppressed my own frown. Why did he want to know about my mother? "She was from my clann as well and died while giving birth to my wee sister, Aideen."

"Do either of your parents have any . . . magical heritage?"

I recoiled. "Magical? No, we're as plain as they come."

"I doubt that very much," Merlin murmured. "Any faerie blood?"

I shook my head. Faeries? What was this man on about?

"Do you take after your mother?"

I hesitated before replying, recalling my father doting on Aideen, stroking her auburn curls, telling her how much she looked like our mother. "No," I admitted. *Why?* I wanted to ask, but I swallowed the word, afraid of what he might tell me, of what he might suggest. I belonged to Brin and Catríona Allán, and no one else. They were my parents.

Merlin seemed to take in my discomfort, and blessedly changed the subject. "Whatever your heritage, I am glad you are here. This is a treacherous time for Arthur's rule. Your prowess and strength are a welcome addition to the court. Five is a sacred number, and Arthur needed a strong fifth for the days to come. I am confident he found this in you."

Guilt needled at me, its dark tendrils snaking around my stomach and clenching tight. I wouldn't be here long enough to help Arthur and his knights. Instead, I would be betraying them, leaving them even more vulnerable than when I had first arrived. But my loyalty didn't lie here in Caerleon, no matter what oath I had taken. My duty was to protect my family, my clann. First. Always.

"I am grateful to serve among such brave warriors," I managed when realizing he was waiting for a reply. "But I admit, I don't understand what dangers face Caerleon? Seems rather idyllic here."

Merlin sighed deeply. "This is Arthur's story to tell. I would ask him, if I were you."

"Perhaps I will," I sprang to my feet, grateful for an excuse to leave his prying eyes. "Do ye know where I can find him?"

"Likely the library," Merlin said, a weariness washing over him. "Always the library."

Chapter Thirteen

Arthur

Arthur once loved the library. This room was a place of respite, where he could find whatever knowledge he sought, and much that he didn't know he needed. But that was *before*.

Now, he was growing to loathe this tranquil space. Arthur had spent every spare hour here since Merlin discovered the truth of Morgause and Elaine's curse. The curse was about more than Lancelot's betrayal of his betrothed. His half-sisters wanted the line of Uther Pendragon removed from Caerleon's succession. Lancelot had only played into their plans.

If he hadn't known better, he would have suspected that Morgana's relationship with Lancelot was all a carefully-crafted plot. But he knew the truth. Morgana had loved Lancelot since she'd first met him as a young woman, when Arthur's mother, Igraine, had taken Arthur and his half-sisters to the

Isle of Man for a solstice ceremony. Lancelot hadn't returned Morgana's infatuation until well after she had budded into womanhood. Lancelot had claimed his longing was love, but Arthur didn't think his friend knew what falling in love was truly like. He didn't bond easily with others as it was, and certainly not with any of his sexual partners. The ability to remain objective was a perfect quality in his military's commander. Fighting for another's heart, however, wasn't the same as clashing swords on the battle field. Or maybe little differed between love and war and it was Arthur who knew little about falling for another.

They were both hopeless.

He sighed and ran a hand through his short strands. Arthur had been combing through a stack of crumbling books as high as his waist for days, and he now focused on the two leather-bound note-books containing his father's neat notes. The pages were just beginning to reveal themselves to him after weeks of study and cross-reference. The Grail was crafted by the old gods of Albion for her protection against foreign kings and their poisonous gods. When the sacred vessel served a ruler, it also served his or her land. But the Blessed Grail only served a man or woman sovereign *blessed* by the Túatha dé Danann. In the wrong hands, the Grail could become a poison. The secrets of the Otherworld's Grail—both a blessing and a curse. It was like these books spoke a foreign tongue to their Welsh and Breton minds, and his father, after years of study, had only just begun speak it. What hope did Arthur have in a few weeks? Percival knew even less of his own heritage, thanks to his fool mother. Arthur slammed one of this father's notebooks shut with a huff, seeming to banish his father's watching spirit. He may resent his father's domineering ways, but he didn't want Uther Pendragon to see him fail either.

"What did that book do to ye?" a lilting feminine voice asked from the shadows of a tall bookshelf. Fionna stood there in a tunic of green, her pale-blonde hair freshly braided and corded with black leather. She looked softer this morning—hesitant. As if a new version of herself had emerged from the fierce warrior he had clashed wills with yesterday.

Arthur rubbed his scratchy eyes. "The book refused to yield its secrets to me," he admitted.

She approached, lingering across from him, her long slender fingers tracing the table's wood grain. Her hands were mesmerizing.

"Do most things yield to ye willingly, King Arthur?" she asked.

"A king does get used to having his way," Arthur managed. It's like her presence sucked all air from the room, leaving only Fionna. He knew not whether she meant her words to sound so alluring, but his growing cock was quite insistent that he found them so. Without the dirt and sweat of a day's exertions, Fionna's beauty was even more startling, her scent of fresh herbs and heather smelling like freedom, like moors and cliffs and wild places. Even clad in a man's tunic and boots, he wanted to seize her narrow waist, to tangle his fingers in her hair and take her right there on the library table. He feared if she ever put on a dress he might implode where he stood.

But she was speaking. He tried to focus on her words, to banish his illicit daydream. She was asking him about the books.

Arthur cleared his throat. "They're books on the Blessed Grail legend. My father studied them in his youth. Discovering the Fisher King's castle became an obsession for him as he grew older."

"Ye sound disapproving." Fionna turned a book around until the title faced her. "Yet ye follow in his footsteps?"

"Not willingly," Arthur growled.

"Ye are compelled?" She raised one pale eyebrow.

"By necessity, My Lady. It's complicated."

Fionna pulled a chair out from the neighboring table, spinning it around and dropping into the seat. It was impertinent for her to sit without him giving her leave, but Arthur found he rather liked her defiance.

Her knee brushed into his as she adjusted her position while looking at him expectantly. "I think it's time I hear this story, Yer Majesty. I am now a knight of Caerleon, am I not?"

Arthur nodded reluctantly, trying to banish the tingle that a single touch of her knee sent up his leg while also ignoring his disappointment at her knee's absence. It was a *knee*, Cerridwen save him. What was he, a celibate monk from a secluded cloister, swooning at the touch of a woman's *knee*?

He shifted his attention to the more important task at hand. What should he share with Fionna? He had knighted her, but still, he didn't know her. Until she proved herself loyal, he didn't want to share the depth of Caerleon's vulnerability with her. The truth of the faerie sisters' curse.

He chose his words carefully, like a horse picking its way down a shifting mountainside. "The Blessed Grail has the ability to break any enchantment, even fae magic, and heal all afflictions set upon a sovereign-blessed man and his land. I recently encountered some . . . difficulty with several sídhe fae. Having their Grail in my possession would provide Caerleon with protection against any retaliation they might further attempt."

"Does this have anything to do with Lancelot's disastrous engagement to Morgana, yer half-sister?" Fionna asked, a hint of a smile playing on her lips. "I hear she apprenticed under Merlin's instruction for a spell."

She had been in Caerleon less than twenty-four hours! How did she—

"Servants talk."

Her smile broke free and he became a man possessed, staring beyond rudeness and far beyond his good senses. Her radiance rivaled the first ray of sunshine that appeared over the horizon, bathing the landscape in golden light. The brilliance transformed her face, from one of cold, unapproachable elegance to something more. Something hard earned—and all the more precious for it.

Shifting in his chair, he broke the enthralling silence, his voice hoarse. "I'm not sure why you even needed to hear this story from me, then."

"I needed to know why the Grail is so important. Everywhere I turn, it's all I hear of."

"Merlin foresaw a fifth knight that would help us find this Grail. That's why we held the tourney."

She recoiled slightly, playing unconsciously with the end of one of her braids. "And ye think this fifth knight is me?"

"I wouldn't have knighted you if I didn't." Arthur smiled shyly.

"But I know nothing about this Grail. I'm sorry, but I don't see how I could be of help. Perhaps this honor was meant for someone else." Her silver eyes met his, and there was an apology there that he didn't fully understand.

"Do not worry so," he reassured her. "Even if I made a mistake, Excalibur didn't." He patted the sword hilt at his waist.

Fionna's focus shifted to his sword like a falcon catching sight of prey. "Ye wear Excalibur even here?" she asked softly. "Is it so dangerous for ye in yer own keep, surrounded by barracks and soldiers?"

Arthur shrugged. "No, princess. Habit, I suppose. It's more comfortable to have Excalibur with me than not."

"Please, call me Fionna."

"If it pleases you, Fionna."

"Yes, Yer Majesty. It pleases me." She flicked her gaze to his, held him there a beat, then returned focus to Excalibur. "Do ye never take your sword off?"

"Only to sleep," Arthur said, his cheeks heating, then added, "Naturally." Did her cheeks redden as well? Or was he imagining it?

"And the flash of violet light . . . that was magic? That was Excalibur . . . choosing *me*?"

He stood, pulling Excalibur from its scabbard, handing his sword to her. "See these runes carved into the blade? It's faerie made. My sword possesses a magic even I don't understand. But Excalibur responded to you, that was clear to see and how I knew, Fionnabhair Allán, that you were our needed knight."

Fionna held the blade reverently before setting the sword gently on her knees, and then she ran her fingers over the runes, the sheen of the blade. "A remarkable weapon." Her touch lingered on the sword for a moment before she handed Excalibur back to him, almost regretfully.

He sheathed Excalibur again, relaxing slightly as the familiar weight settled again at his side.

Silence fell upon them, and Arthur found himself biting his lower lip, anxious, wishing he could kiss her. Never feeling so awkward in his life, he struggled for another topic. Perhaps their previous one was safer than he originally thought. "We will leave to find the Grail as soon as I figure out where we're going," he said with a little laugh, turning back to the books and away from her. The desire to chase her lips with his was growing by the second. Did they taste of the wild strawberries they enjoyed mid-day in the Great Hall?

"Perhaps I could help ye look." She pulled one of the books closer.

He softly said, "I wouldn't accomplish much with you here, Fionna."

"Why?" She cocked her head.

Arthur realized his misstep and fumbled to cover

it. "I . . . I work best alone, is all."

"And what am I to do in the meantime, Yer Majesty?" Fionna traced her finger along the spine of the book next to his hand. "Do I have duties as a knight? Tasks I must complete?"

"What do you mean?"

"What do I do all day?" Fionna asked, gesturing wide. "I'm not used to such free time."

"Oh." Arthur furrowed his brows. "The other knights never seem to complain. Your time is your own, to train, or study, or find leisure that suits you. Lancelot trains the soldiers, but he seems to have that well in hand. I will assign tasks, if I have them. I've received word of raids near the Kingdom of Gwent's northern border. Once my scouts return, I may dispatch several soldiers under the direction of my knights to secure our borders."

"So, in the meantime I . . . do whatever I fancy?"

Arthur nodded, slowly, his brows still furrowed. Why did she seem so put out? Lancelot, Galahad and Percival enjoyed running their own days. Though, perhaps, if he had given Lancelot more to keep busy, they wouldn't all be in their current predicament.

Fionna snatched a book off the table, and tucked the tome under her arm, standing. "Then I think I will learn about the Blessed Grail legend. If I am meant to help ye search, then I better know something about this sacred vessel."

With that pronouncement, Fionna spun and strode out of the library, leaving Arthur with one less book and the laces of his breeches strained tight.

Chapter Fourteen

Lancelot

ancelot needed a hobby. Once, enjoying the company of women had been his unofficial hobby. But it seemed dalliances were yet another thing Morgana had ruined. There was always the company of men, he supposed. Though, engaging in relations with either gender didn't feel satisfying for once. He couldn't pretend away how his careless choices harmed the people—and the land—he cared about. A people and land he was willing to die for. Maybe that was why his mood felt as black as tar. When was the last time he had been celibate for a whole month? At least Percival didn't know what he was missing out on.

This morning, Lancelot visited the stable yard to clear his head from yesterday's fog, to exhaust his body until he had no energy left to remind him of how alluring he found their newest knight. The plan had worked for a time, but then *she* had appeared, like a specter from a dream. He was too spooked to remain in her company. He didn't trust himself around her.

Still, from the shadows, Lancelot had watched as Fionna sparred with Galahad, jealousy twisting in his gut. Fionna was the siren *and* the rocks, and Lancelot wanted nothing more than to bash himself against them, to be bludgeoned and torn apart by loving her. Needing to leave but unable to remain away, he drank in the sight of Fionna from afar. Every flash of her sword, every peal of her laughter ringing out bright and clear, the look of her cheeks flush with exhilaration from the fight. He drank long and deep before he finally made himself turn away, walking stiffly back toward his chambers.

He really did need a hobby. Double drills for the soldiers? Archery? Hunting, perhaps? A hunt might be good for him. Maybe he should talk to Percival. What did celibate knights do all day?

Lancelot had settled on a nap, and so was quite disoriented when a knock sounded on his door. He stumbled to open it, his eyes blurry with sleep. On the other side stood a wide-eyed servant.

"His Majesty asks that you attend him in the throne room. We have an ambassador from Tintagel."

Tintagel. The word struck him like an arrow, jolting him awake. "A moment," Lancelot said.

He flew about his chamber, grabbing his boots and hopping into them quickly, pulling a gray-blue tunic over his head. He retrieved his sword belt from where he'd abandoned his effects on the floor and buckled the leather and weapon around his waist while hurrying after the servant. Lancelot ran his hands through his hair, trying to tame his wild curls. An ambassador from Tintagel, where Morgana and her sisters lived. This couldn't be good. What fresh horrors had Morgana, Elaine, and Morgause decided to visit upon Caerleon now?

Arthur was sitting on his throne, the carved, high-backed chair gilded in gold. His king thought the throne too ostentatious, but for moments like this, it suited. Percival stood on Arthur's right, leaving a spot for Lancelot between them. And on Arthur's left stood Galahad and Fionna. The image of the three other knights startled him, and the reality of his predicament truly began to sink in. She was a part of their lives now—day in, day out. They were five. Gods help him.

"Nice of you to join us," Arthur murmured as Lancelot took up the position by his right hand.

"Do we know why they've come?" Lancelot asked.

"Regardless of their reasons, I ask that you *please* remain quiet."

"Even if you're in danger?"

"From an ambassador?" Arthur narrowed his eyes to slits. "Do not cause a scene. I need to mend relations not give Tintagel an excuse to declare war."

A muscle twitched in Lancelot's jaw as his king

held his gaze. Their ambassador was still fae and, thus, still dangerous. *Still*, he ground out a simple, "Yes, Your Majesty."

Satisfied, Arthur nodded to the servants by the door, who opened the two large wooden doors.

The ambassador was strangely beautiful, typical of most sídhe males. Unnaturally tall and thin, though well-muscled, and pale as a stalk of winter grass, bleached by the cold. His nose, cheeks, and jaw cut at captivating angles, and his lips curved upward in a disdainful twist. Fae. Lancelot found his hand gravitating toward his sword hilt. Though the ambassador was the sort of male Lancelot once enjoyed when he roamed the sídhe courts for pleasure, he never forgot fae were predators and humans mere prey.

Arthur seemed to little mind the ambassador's strangeness. Or his rudeness. Or his king merely did a better job of hiding his sentiments than Lancelot. "Welcome to Caerleon," Arthur said warmly. "I hope your journey has treated you well."

"Well enough," the faerie male sniffed. His tunic glimmered a pale green with embroidery in a pattern of twisting leaves running up the sleeves. "My name is Alworn. My mistresses, the ladies Morgause, Elaine, and Morgana desire to express their congratulations to you for your joining of a fifth knight."

Arthur's brow wrinkled slightly at that. "Our new knight was only selected yesterday. But your journey must have taken a week at least . . ."

Alworn inclined his head to acknowledge the incongruity, a small smile twisting his arrogant mouth.

Lancelot wanted to smack the insolence off his perfectly sculpted face. Bloody faerie magic.

"As you no doubt know, the mistresses of Tintagel are powerful priestesses. They had foreseen the knighthood of Fionnabhair Allán, and they celebrate her arrival." Alworn's eyes swiveled to Lancelot, and the man's shit-eating grin broadened. Lancelot's blood heated. Of course, Morgana knew Fionna would be joining them, and knew Lancelot could not help but love her. The cruelty of Morgana's curse took his breath away. Here was the woman Lancelot hadn't known he wanted—no simpering maiden swooning at his feet, but a woman fierce and bold as she was beautiful. An equal. And Morgana had made sure he could never have her—that he would live the rest of his days with an empty bed and aching balls. Gods, he wanted to break something.

The ambassador continued. "My mistresses relay their pleasure in how you have taken a fifth knight of such unusual skill and power, and a woman no less. For surely it could not have been easy for Lady Fionnabhair to overcome the prejudices of Briton to rise so far. They wish to give her a gift for her bravery and courage."

All eyes turned to Fionna. She held herself stiffly, her lean face betraying no hint of what she might think of the male's offer. Lancelot wanted to lean over to tell Arthur to reject the gift, but Arthur was already nodding. "Lady Fionna?" He gestured her forward.

Lancelot cursed inwardly. Faerie gifts came with strings attached. Strings tied to unforeseen dangers and tricks. He didn't know what the sisters had against Fionna, but this "gift" surely brought trouble.

Fionna glided down the stairs to stand before the ambassador, her eyes narrowed in such a way that made Lancelot wonder if she had ever met a fae in the flesh. If not, he hoped she well remembered all the faerie stories she had surely heard over the years, and would guard herself against tricks or unwittingly given favors.

Fionna's tunic and sword were odd for a lady in Arthur's throne room. Yet, she appeared every inch regal—an Irish warrior princess—looking Alworn straight into his unnatural aquamarine eyes, framed by white lashes. Seeing the two of them face each other gave Lancelot pause—it was like peering into the reflection of a looking glass. Fionna's pale coloring and white-blonde hair mirrored Alworn's. Though, Lancelot knew people of the North were fairer in coloring, even with hair so blond the strands shone white as Fionna's. He had traveled once to Northern Ireland and the Kingdom of Denmark. And he knew the Kingdoms of Strathclyde and Alba in Scotia as though his own hunting grounds. Still, the pair of them together unsettled him.

The ambassador presented a small wooden box carved with snaking vines and glistening dewdrops, and Fionna took it, opening the lid. Lancelot craned his neck to see while fighting his urge to rush down the steps and bat the box out of her hand.

"A necklace," Fionna said, holding up the gift. The silver chain held a pendant shaped like a budding lily, iridescent and sparkling and pure white.

"Lovely," she said, bowing before the male.

Good, she didn't thank him.

Alworn inclined his head. Again. "It would please my mistresses greatly to see you wear their gift, I'm sure. May I?"

"Of course," she said after a moment's pause, handing him the necklace. She pulled her long cord of braids over one shoulder and turned her back to the man. "I fear this isn't proper attire for such a grand necklace," she added with a little laugh.

Warning bells rung in Lancelot's mind. "Don't—" he grit between clenched teeth, but Arthur grabbed his wrist in an iron grip, silencing him.

Lancelot ground his teeth together harder as Alworn clasped the necklace around Fionna's neck, letting the chain fall. "Lovely," he murmured, echoing her earlier sentiments.

"We must celebrate your visit here," Arthur said to the ambassador. "We will have a feast tonight in your honor. Perhaps we can convince Lady Fionna to wear something to better suit her new gift?"

Fionna glared daggers at Arthur as she stalked back up the stairs to resume her position at Galahad's side.

Arthur chuckled nervously. "Or perhaps not."

Alworn dipped his head. "I look forward to the feast, Little Dragon King." The ambassador turned and retreated from the throne room.

"Thank you for attending," Arthur said once the thick doors closed behind him. "And Fionna, thank you for entertaining the ambassador so graciously."

She gave a curt nod while inspecting the necklace hanging around her swan's neck.

"Sir Lancelot, a word?" Arthur asked, and the others took his cue to disappear.

Arthur stood as the others filed out, stretching his back. "That chair is as hard as a rock," he complained.

"You shouldn't have let Alworn place *that* necklace on her," Lancelot said, gritting his teeth again. "We know not what the pendant does."

"Perhaps, but if we had refused the gift, it would have further alienated Morgana and her sisters from us. And we can ill afford more enmity between the Tintagel and Caerleon."

"Still—" Lancelot protested.

"I chose a risk of harm over a certain one. Sometimes that's the only choice before a king."

Lancelot studied his fingers, the muscles in his jaw clenching tighter. He decided not to mention how Arthur had chosen a risk to Fionna over a risk to his rule, which didn't seem very kingly at all. But he supposed Fionna was part of his rule now, so perhaps Arthur saw them all as one and the same.

"Lancelot," Arthur said. "Might be best if you skip the feast tonight. With your and Morgana's history . . . we should minimize your interaction with Tintagel for the time being."

"Very well," Lancelot said woodenly. How things had changed. A knight of Caerleon, banished from a feast in his king's own Great Hall. "But promise you will be careful, Arthur Pendragon. Do not thank the male, or you will be beholden to him or his mistresses. Remember, when you sup with sídhe faeries, you must be on your guard."

Chapter Fifteen

Galahad

The Great Hall looked resplendent, all dressed up for the feast. *And so do I, if I don't say so myself,* Galahad mused to himself. Candlelight flickered across the hall as though dancing will-ó-the wisps. Fern and wildflower garlands draped across rafters and festooned banquet tables. And fresh rushes released a soft, earthy scent with each step.

His thumbs hooked into his sword belt, Galahad whistled a bawdy tune as he strolled past clan lords who were clustered together for a hearty debate. Galahad wore his finest tunic—a rich woven linen fabric of maroon and gold, cinched with a leather belt stamped with interconnected lines and knots—a gift from his father when Galahad had left home for Caerleon. He had even bathed and trimmed his beard, wanting to look his best this evening, his hair brushed to a sheen and falling around his shoulders.

The moment he stepped past the visiting lords

and their families, his eyes were searching for her. They found Percival instead, who popped into his line of sight, his expression eager. Percival grabbed Galahad's tunic and gave him a little shake.

"What is it man?" Galahad said with amusement, clapping his sword-brother on his shoulder.

"Wait 'till ye see her!" Percival said with un-adulterated delight. "She's a beauty. An enchantress. Nae—a goddess!"

The youngest knight's tongue seemed to trip over itself while searching for the right word. The poor lad was akin to an awkward lamb trying to walk on shaking legs for the first time. And this, just by noticing a woman at a feast. Still, Galahad had no doubt of whom Percival spoke. And when he caught sight of her, his own legs grew shaky. She was all the things Percival had said—and none of them. Because no word could encompass the vision that was their fifth knight.

Fionna stood against the far wall amongst a gag-gle of nobles from neighboring chiefdoms, a pewter goblet held daintily in her hand. Her white-blonde hair hung free, cascading in ripples to her waist but for a few pieces pulled back from her temples and braided around the crown of her head. She wore a dress of the deepest blue embroidered in silver, and the shimmering yards flowed over her form like a moonlit river. His eyes snaked up the same path, fol-lowing her curving hips past her trim waist, leading to firm breasts that begged to be kissed. Her dress bared the milky skin above her plunging bodice line—as though a Roman goddess carved of marble—

revealing the faerie necklace nestled atop her cleavage.

"Yer hurting me," Percival choked, and Galahad turned to him with a start.

"Sorry." Galahad released his crushing grip on Percival's shoulder.

The young man rubbed his neck with a grimace. "Not verra sporting to kill yer competition, arsehole."

"Competition?" Galahad raised an eyebrow. He slung his arm around Percival, leading him toward the head table, where a goblet of wine waited with Galahad's name on it. "With that little vow of celibacy, I'm not sure you're even allowed to play the game."

"There are plenty of ways to play without . . . taking the queen, ye ken," Percival said, nearly rolling his eyes.

Galahad guffawed. "Been skulking around, listening to the maid's gossip, have we?" he asked.

Percival was well on his way to becoming a powerful fighter, but in the ways of women, the lad was greener than a newly budding leaf. Stars shone bright in the young man's eyes, but Percival wasn't real competition. Not when it came to a woman like Fionna. He'd known a few women like her before, though none so remarkable. She was capable and crafty and above all—in control. She needed a lover to ignite her passion until she blazed white hot, not as a warrior or noble, but as woman set on fire by the kind of searing, breathless pleasure that could only be given by a man. Galahad would be more than happy to fill that role.

"Hardly need to eavesdrop on the maids," Percival was saying when Galahad pulled out of his head. "Lancelot shares every intimate detail of his exploits. Or at least, he used to."

That was true. Lancelot had some most interesting conquests. And he was never shy about kissing and telling. Until Morgana that was. "Where is Lancelot?" Galahad craned his neck to take in the crowd, searching for a familiar mop of curly black hair. His sword-brother was conspicuously absent.

"He won't be joining us," Arthur said, approaching. The king shone like the high-noon sun in a tunic of gold and black thread, matching the auric tones of the oak-leaf crown resting on his brow.

Galahad frowned, but swallowed the question as Fionna joined them. "I kept waiting for someone to rescue me over there," she said, blowing out a slow, measured breath.

"Are you now the type of lady who needs rescuing?" Galahad winked.

"I would much rather face a Saxon horde than a grasping clann lord who's maneuvering for power."

"We share your sentiments," Arthur remarked.

Percival flashed Fionna a wicked grin. "Did Lord Tyrin tell ye about his goat breeding program?"

Fionna gaped. "How did ye—"

The knights laughed. "He can talk about his goats for hours," Galahad said. "Trust me, if he hadn't yet spouted poetry about the flavor profiles of Cheviot versus Snowdonian goats milk, you are lucky indeed."

"Isn't a goat a goat?"

"Nooo." Arthur shook his head in mock horror. "Never let him hear you say *that*."

Fionna heaved a withering sigh. "I do believe I need more wine."

"See? And ye lads were worried. Our Fionna is already familiar with our ways around here." Percival threaded his arm through hers, a waggish smile on his proud face. "Regardless of the question, the answer is usually 'more wine.'"

The feast now reveled in full swing. The musicians played a toe-tapping reel, the courses were plentiful, and the company was excellent. Fionna had just finished regaling their group with a tale of one of her fiann mates tangling with an angry mother badger, which had sent them all into roars of laughter. *The woman was funny, too?* Galahad groaned inwardly. It was hardly fair.

The merry atmosphere between them dimmed slightly, however, when their guest of honor arrived. Alworn had fashioned his long silver hair in a braid, and he had changed into an even more elaborate tunic of white linen beaded in tiny pearls. Galahad stifled a snort. Never had he seen a more impractical garment in all his twenty-four years.

Tucked under his arm, the fae male carried a bottle that piqued Galahad's interest, though. The ambassador approached the head table where Arthur and the knights sat, inclining his head.

"Little Dragon King," Alworn began, preferring to use Arthur's nickname among the Túatha dé Danann. The male's voice was like snakeskin, smooth yet slithery. "Another gift, to add to tonight's festivities. Sweet woodruff wine, one of Tintagel's finest May vintages." He offered the bottle to Arthur, who took the gift from his outstretched hands.

Arthur dipped his head in answer. "Shall we have a toast?"

A servant hurried over with a tray of fresh goblets and wild strawberries. Alworn came around the table and settled into the empty seat on Fionna's right as the servant poured the wine, plunking in a wild strawberry or two per May wine tradition.

Galahad accepted a goblet and sniffed the libation with interest, savoring the ambrosial scents of vanilla and honey from the sweet woodruff. He hadn't much of a nose for wine, preferring ale. But this smelled tasty and brought him back to village days with the Manor Lord who squired him.

Arthur stood and raised his cup. "A toast, to our honored guest, Alworn of Tintagel. To a long and prosperous friendship between our two lands."

"Hear, hear," the revelers cried, raising their own cups in answer.

The wine's taste was even richer than the aroma—the sweet flavor was lush and full on Galahad's tongue. Utterly intoxicating.

Even Arthur regarded his goblet with an expression of pleasant surprise. "I've enjoyed May wine countless times, but I have never tasted one quite like your vintage."

"I brought a second bottle, Your Majesty." Alworn leaned in conspiratorially, a wide smile breaking across his pale features. "When you're ready."

On Arthur's other side, Fionna set her goblet down, her pink tongue flicking across her lower lip to capture a stray drop. Heat coursed through Galahad and pooled into a singular ache to know how good that tongue would feel. Would taste. Sharing more stories suddenly seemed a waste of an evening. Why weren't they dancing? He wanted to pull Fionna's lithe body against his, to feel the fit of her hipbones in his firm grip.

Galahad downed the rest of his May wine in one swallow, pushing back from the table. He strode behind Arthur and held out his hand. "Fionna, would you do me the honor of this dance?"

Fionna looked from his outstretched hand to his face, a flicker of indecision in her eyes. "I'm not sure I know the steps . . ."

"I've been told I'm an excellent teacher," he pressed, not willing to take no for an answer. He needed her in his arms. Yesterday. "And if this is to be your home now, learning a dance or two might come in handy."

She slinked out of her seat in a graceful arch, laying her hand in his. As soon as their palms touched, a buzz of energy—of awareness—coursed through Galahad and his chest tightened. He led her around the table onto the dance floor, feeling more alive than he had in years. Galahad took her into his arms, tucking her against him more tightly than was strictly necessary.

Her body fit perfectly against his, the warmth of her hands in his, the firm press of her breasts against his chest, her low neckline giving him an excellent view. And gods, the way she shifted against the bulging length of his throbbing cock. He couldn't breathe. He hissed in a breath when she shifted again. Without her armor on, she was softer, disarmed. A woman—a strong and fearless one, yes—but still tender too. Yielding. And impish. She knew what she was doing to him.

"I believe this is the part where we begin dancing," Fionna said, amusement sparkling in her eyes. He had been studying her, noticing every freckle, the silver of her eyelashes.

"I thought ye were teaching me," Galahad said, struggling not to growl the words. His longing for her was pulsing within him like a feral beast, roaring to be set free.

"I believe that's the opposite of what I was promised," Fionna pointed out, arching a single pale eyebrow.

"Well, I'm a man who delivers what he promised." Galahad pulled her tighter against him, running his thumb up the arrow of her spine. "Let's dance."

The musicians struck up a slower tune, the melody all the invitation Galahad needed. He pulled her into the steps, moving around the floor, weaving between the other nobles who spun around them. Heat flooded his wildly pounding pulse as they danced. Each time he spun her away, he pulled her back closer and, in such a way, she pressed against his length until he wished there was nothing between them but gasps and moans. The feel of her softness against his hard lines was maddening, her scent of heather and steel a headier concoction than he had ever known. The bodies around them seemed to fade away, and it was only him and her, and one possible end.

Galahad lowered his head to her ear, growling into it, made breathless by his need for her. "You have enchanted me, My Lady, leaving me utterly defenseless against your charms." He had planned to wait, to bide his time, to woo her as a man should. But his plans were but ash on the wind in the face of the power she had over him. "Come to my chamber with me," he murmured. "And allow me do the same to you."

Chapter Sixteen

Fionna

Galahad surrounded me. The pressure of his fingers splayed against my back, the scratch of his beard against my cheek, the heat of his words in my ear. My senses galloped about like an unfettered wild horse. Dance. I needed to focus on dancing. My hand clutched the soft linen of my skirt and I moved to the drumbeat.

Clann wars and power plays by greedy kinsman perpetually decorated me in leather and shields. Not since we visited the High King of Ireland four years past had I worn an elegant dress such as this, or known the melodious footwork inspired by instruments instead of clanging metal on metal. Or received an offer that I hadn't responded to with a bawdy retort or knife blade to the man's throat. I can't remember when I had last received an offer I wanted to accept. And I wanted to accept Galahad's offer. Badly.

My lungs seemed to press against the ties of my

dress. Was the large hearth stoked too hot?

My feet had a mind of their own, happily following Galahad across the dance floor.

"From your silence, I believe you're considering my invitation," Galahad said with a little laugh. A pleasant buzz tingled down to my slippers at the husky sound.

I really shouldn't. But oh, how I really should. I was wading through the argument in my heated, sluggish mind when the music stopped, breaking the spell. The crowd clapped politely while dance partners bowed to one another. I pulled back from Galahad, relieved as cool air flooded the space between us.

"I need to sit, Sir." I tore my hand from his grip and my gaze from the intense expression on his flushed face.

He was like a man possessed at the sight of me, and the aroused expression he wore both thrilled and frightened me in turn. I took a much-needed deep breath, trying to slow my heart's staccato beat. *Getting involved with Galahad romantically would be a terrible idea*, I told myself. *No matter how toe-curling our dalliance might be.* My body protested, however, refusing to relinquish its memory of his strength and vitality as he pressed his hard-muscled chest to mine. Goddess help me, I would need a cold bath tonight. But first, a chair.

I rounded the head table toward my blessed seat in a rush. My thoughts were so tangled that I didn't notice a body blocking my escape until I ran right into its solidity. "Percival!"

"Fionna . . ." Instead of flashing a smile and cracking a joke, as I was coming to learn was his way, he snaked a strong arm around my waist and threaded his other hand through my hair. Percival pulled me flush against him, tugging my hair so my head tilted back, my lips at the perfect angle for kissing.

The quick bite of pain in my scalp shocked me, but nothing surprised me so much as the expert way Percival seemed to fit me against his body. A bolt of desire coursed through me. Any other man might have received a knee to the groin for his impertinence, but I balked, trying to reconcile the smoldering heat in this man's brown eyes with the playful Percival I knew.

"Percival!" I pushed against his chest, pulling in a ragged breath. His scent of bergamot and sage washed over me, fresh and clear. "Have ye lost yer wits?"

"Ye have bewitched me, lass. There's only one way I will be free from yer spell."

Dread fluttered in my belly at his strange words. My heart thundered as though a mere yearling in battle, feet frozen to the blood-soaked ground. But I was a battle-hardened warrior who knew how to listen to the warnings in her gut.

I pushed harder against his chest. "What about yer vow? The Grail?"

"My vow means nothing. There is nae dish I would rather drink from than ye."

He wasn't talking sense. I shook my head, my heart sinking into my churning stomach. Something was definitely wrong. "Percival, no. I'm returning to my seat." I shoved my elbow against him, breaking his hold on me.

Thankfully, he released me, but not without a pained expression on his face. I hurried to my seat, crumpled onto the ebony wood, and then hid my shaking hands under my thighs. What was going on? Galahad had been forward, yes, but I knew he was attracted to me. I had seen his interest when we sparred. But Percival?

"Are you well, My Lady?" Alworn leaned over to me, concern written on his ageless face.

"No need for worry." I struggled to paste on a smile. "A friend is acting a wee bit strange, nothing more."

"Perhaps he can't hold his wine." Alworn touched a hand to his chest. "I hear tell it's a problem some mortals have."

I chanced a look to the dance floor, where Galahad and Percival now danced with new partners. The knights' flushed faces pressed close to the women's own, a preternatural gleam in their eyes.

A faintly predatory smile teased Alworn's lips. He hadn't touched the wine in his own goblet or the food on his plate.

"Remind me, what kind of wine did ye gift?" I asked.

"Sweet Woodruff. A special May blend."

I nodded slowly, my thoughts racing. Alworn was an emissary from Morgana and her sisters. Wasn't this the family Lancelot had offended by breaking his engagement to Morgana? What if this wasn't a diplomatic visit at all, but a veiled attack? The blood drained from me, the rich food roiling in my stomach. Had Arthur and his knights been poisoned? But no, Galahad and Percival didn't seem ill. They only acted strangely. And I had drank the wine, and I felt fine.

I needed to talk to Arthur and warn him that something might be amiss. But how, with the ambassador sitting next to us? I turned to Arthur, who watched the dancing, his chin resting on a fist. "Yer Majesty, would ye do me the honor of a dance?"

Arthur was on his feet in a blink, his hand out to me.

I started at his sudden movement, but stood cautiously, placing my hand in his long fingers. His hand felt warm—feverishly hot.

As we approached the dance floor, the other revelers began to clear for their king to claim the floor.

"Carry on!" Arthur called out, and then gestured to the musicians to take up a tune once again. As a lovely ballad began, Arthur wrapped his arm around my waist like a vise.

My breath hitched in surprise.

He leaned in, his voice low and purring in my ear. "Less prying eyes this way." His hard cock pressed into my stomach.

My whispered warning died on my lips. By the goddess, Arthur was infected too!

We began to dance, my mind racing for a solution.

"You are more beautiful than a starlit night," Arthur murmured, burying his face into the crook of my neck. "Your hair like the fall of moonlight on a snowy field."

Skies above, I couldn't concentrate with his whispered poetry. Still, I tried to remember what I had learned about faeries. All I recalled were children's stories and fireside myths. I had no idea how to break the spell of tainted faerie wine. And if I didn't, would my knights dance and dance until their feet fell off? Was that Morgana's plan?

And then two conflicting realizations struck me like bolts of lightning. First, I had thought of them as "my" knights. When had they become *mine*? Second, Arthur was addled beyond belief. Now would be a perfect time to steal Excalibur and get the hell out of Caerleon. Arthur and his knights wouldn't be able to pursue me for some time. Zephyr and I could be on the next boat for Ireland before Arthur even stopped dancing. If he stopped dancing. Guilt needled at me. I couldn't really leave him like this, could I? Leave all of them like this?

"Would your skin leave stardust on my lips?" he whispered hoarsely into my neck.

Arthur stroked my ear and pressed a kiss to the delicate flesh right beneath my lobe. I couldn't stop the shiver of pleasure that ran through me, all thoughts fleeing from my mind. Arthur smelled like the forest—oak and cypress and . . . home. My heart nearly stopped. Home? But I didn't have long to think of what *that* could mean when he trailed a line of kisses down my throat and over my collarbone. My head fell back, my breath trembling. I no longer thought of tainted wine or faerie swords or anything but Arthur. This close, he was magnificent.

My fingers took on a mind of their own and roved over the hard lines of his muscles under his soft tunic, caressing each dip and valley, while my eyes took in the freckles across his nose, the gleam in the golden crown across his brow. This man was a king. This land, this fortress, these subjects belonged to him—he could have anything he desired. But he wanted me.

And I wanted him.

His mouth captured mine, and my eyelids fluttered closed as my world tilted on its axis. I melted against this strong, thoughtful man, the room around us fading away. There was only Arthur, and the velvet strokes of his tongue against mine, and the heat pooling between my legs. His lips were firm and soft, and he tasted of May wine. Of magic.

My eyes popped open. This wasn't Arthur. This was the wine. Arthur and his court were under attack. My heart grew sick. I would rob him and betray him, but the manner in which I would do so was of my choosing. Not like this. I would never leave him like this.

It took every ounce of my self-control, but I pulled back from Arthur's heady kiss.

His green eyes were hooded with longing, his breathing rapid.

"I'm sorry, Yer Majesty," I said. "But we must stop."

Arthur's brows creased before he dipped down for another taste of my swollen lips.

"I said *no*, Yer Majesty." I shoved off him and fled through the crowd toward the large hewn doors, feeling the crawling gaze of Alworn on my back.

I stumbled against the stone wall outside of the Great Hall, my hand on my chest as if the pressure from my palm was the only thing keeping my heart from beating out of my body. An errant tear broke free and rolled down my flushed cheek. Two days in Caerleon and I was a wreck. Galahad, Percival, Arthur . . . my emotions were ragged, my body desperate with need. Who was I—this gasping maiden in a hallway, so thoroughly disarmed by the knights of Caerleon? I needed Fionnabhair Allán back. I needed my fiann; I needed my armor; I needed someone to slap sense into me and tell me to do what needed to be done.

"Lancelot." I said his name like a prayer. Blessed goddess, I needed Lancelot.

Chapter Seventeen

Lancelot

Pounding on Lancelot's door startled him out of his bitter reverie. He unwound himself from his chair, where he had been staring morosely into the fire.

More pounding, followed by a muffled shout. His name.

He huffed, stalking to the door and yanking it open. "I thought I wasn't welcome—" The words died on his tongue. Fionna. And Fionna's breasts. His gaze traveled down her midnight blue dress that dipped low Roman style. A dress, he cursed silently, that hugged every curve of her firm, supple body. He thought he had a fighting chance of resisting her when she was dirty and sweaty and strapped into her armor. But like this? . . . Sweet merciful gods. Tamping down his desire, he snapped, "What do *you* want?"

Perhaps he did too good of a job, because Fionna recoiled slightly, her expression darkening. "I'm sorry to interrupt yer valuable time, but I thought ye would wish to know that yer king and fellow knights have fallen under a strange spell." She whirled to go, tossing over her shoulder, "I must have been wrong about ye."

He reached out and grabbed her wrist. "Wait."

She looked down at where his hand held her captive. Clenching his jaw, he released her more than a little reluctantly. It was the first time he had touched Fionna, and felt the heat of her. The realness.

"Tell me," he somehow managed.

"The ambassador offered a toast. May wine he brought from Tintagel. I think the bottle may have been laced with something."

"They drank faerie wine?" Lancelot asked, incredulous. He stabbed his fingers through his black curls with a furious groan. He never should have let Arthur banish him from that feast! His hand fell to his waist in angry defeat. Arthur was altogether too trusting sometimes.

Guilt wrinkled her smooth brow. "I do believe so, yes."

"Rule number one when dealing with faeries," Lancelot seethed, "don't eat any food or drink they offer. Idiots!"

When Lancelot was a young lad of twelve, a lord visited the Isle of Man. Drunk on faerie mead, he had grown so enchanted by Vivien, Lady of the Lake, that he cut off his own feet in order to become a merman and wed her. So drunk with magic was this visiting lord that he had failed to see Vivien's two feet planted in the wild grass and ferns. Lancelot had watched in horror as the noble bled out—the man grinning with the headiness of death. His foster mother knelt in a pool of the dying man's blood and kissed the final breaths from his lungs, then used his air to blow his limp body into the rippled surface her lake like a dandelion on the wind. Traumatized, Lancelot had refused any drop of alcohol until well past his eighteenth birthday. The memory sent a shudder down his spine.

"I think they didn't want to offend him," Fionna offered weakly.

"Of course," Lancelot sneered. "When someone offers you poisoned wine, of course you drink it, so as not to *offend them*!"

Fionna set her jaw, as if steeling herself against the buffeting force of Lancelot's anger.

He took a deep breath and exhaled slowly through gritted teeth. "What are they doing? Just dancing? Making merry?"

A blush colored Fionna's cheeks, the rosy hue softening her seemingly untouchable beauty. "They've grown . . . forward."

"Forward? Spit it out woman."

"Arthur kissed me," Fionna whispered, a hushed confession. She peered over her shoulder before settling a level gaze back onto Lancelot. "And Galahad asked me to come to his chamber. And Percival . . ." she ran her hand over her eyes, as if attempting to banish the memory. "They're not themselves, Sir."

"Bloody hell," Lancelot muttered, pulling his door shut. "Let's go."

Fionna hurried after him down the hallway, the

folds of her gown clutched in her fists. "How are ye going to fix them?"

"Damned if I know," Lancelot shot back. "This is magic wine. We need druid magic."

"Merlin!" Fionna's eyes lit up. "I forgot about him."

"Probably the first time that's happened," Lancelot said wryly. He looked at her sideways, trying to ignore the pleasant bounce of her breasts as she strode beside him. "When I get my hands on Alworn, I'm going to throttle that male. Like Morgana and her cursed sisters haven't wreaked enough havoc on Caerleon!"

Fionna looked at him with interest. "What do ye mean? What else have they done?"

Lancelot realized his mistake too late. Arthur hadn't told Fionna yet about the curse. He raced for an excuse as they rounded the corner into the main hallway that led to the Great Hall. "Morgana demanded that Arthur execute me for my . . . crimes against her. She didn't take it kindly when he refused, swearing vengeance."

"Execute ye! That's preposterous. Ye weren't even married yet." Fionna's lips formed a straight line. "Aren't faeries notoriously promiscuous? Ye would think Morgana would be a little more understanding."

"Morgana is wrath and ruin, not understanding. She's unlike any other faerie I've known," Lancelot admitted.

"Oh goddess," Fionna breathed as they passed through the wide-open doors into the Great Hall.

The scene was even worse than Lancelot could have imagined. Arthur, Galahad, and Percival were standing in the middle of the spacious room, shouting at each other—a circle of wary onlookers curving around them. Treacherous Alworn was nowhere to be found.

Percival pushed Galahad with an angry oath, who pushed the younger man in return, sending him stumbling back into a hapless lord standing nearby.

"I claim her," Arthur shouted, and the sound of steel echoed in the room as he drew Excalibur. "I am king and you will, therefore, desist all claims!"

The circle of onlookers stepped back. Gasps and worried whispers fell over the gathering like rain.

"Arthur!" Lancelot pushed through the crowd, Fionna close on his heel.

Arthur, Percival, and Galahad spun toward him, each of their blank faces homing in on Fionna like hungry predators catching the scent of prey.

Lancelot skidded to a stop, throwing up an arm to stop Fionna from approaching any closer.

At the sight of the clashing stags, Fionna blanched, burying her fist in the tunic at Lancelot's waist. She took a step behind him, shielding herself with his body. "It's worse than when I left," she said and, for the first time, Lancelot thought he heard a waver of fear in her voice.

"Fionna," Arthur strode toward them first, Excalibur swinging wildly in his hand, his green eyes glowing with need. A path parted between them as feast-goers scrambled away from his careening weapon.

Lancelot and Fionna backed up slowly toward the door, her other hand grasping his wrist, even as he held his arm out over her protectively.

"Feast is over," Lancelot bellowed to the other guests. "Time to retire to your chambers. The show is over."

"Where are you going?" Galahad rumbled angrily. Galahad and Percival were following like fish on a line, towed by an invisible current. Linked inextricably to Fionna.

"Fionna," Arthur begged. "Please—"

"Put away Excalibur, Yer Majesty," Fionna commanded, still backing away slowly into the hallway. "And come with me. Ye . . . ye shall have what ye w-wish." She stumbled over the words, the strain evident in her voice. "All of ye."

That well and truly hooked them. The three men followed like eager puppies, and Fionna turned to Lancelot, her eyes shining with angry tears. "It's awful," she said. "Their free will is gone. How could someone do this to another human being?"

Lancelot squeezed her hand once before forcing himself to let her go. Her righteous anger for his sword-brothers touched something deeper within him than even her haunting beauty. He struggled to ignore it. "Faeries aren't human beings," he said. "We're pets to them. Playthings. You can't trust them."

She stared at him in horror—one beat of his thundering heart, then two—before they ducked out the door and into the cool of the night. The moon was full and low that night, illuminating the rocky path as they picked their way toward Merlin's cave.

Lancelot shivered, the skin on the back of his neck crawling with the feel of someone watching him. He took a steadying breath. The night's events were simply unsettling him. They weren't *actually* being watched.

"Where are we going?" Percival asked behind them. His voice was dreamy—false.

"Somewhere to be alone," Fionna said, her eyes fixed firmly on the ground, her hair shining like a halo around her.

They ducked into the darkness of Merlin's cave, their party silent but for the rushing of the River Usk over the mossy rocks below. The sharp tang of herbs and the cave's musty smell washed over him and, for once, Lancelot found the scents comforting.

"Merlin!" he called out, his deep voice echoing on the damp stones. A torch on their right sprang to life, and they all jumped back.

"I thought we were going to be alone," Arthur said suspiciously.

Fionna shushed him, then whispered, "Soon, My King."

From the flickering shadows, Merlin appeared, his gold-ringed eyes glowing in the dark. "All the knights of Caerleon at my door—I sense magic."

"Faerie wine," Lancelot said, disliking the pleading in his tone.

Merlin clucked his tongue but motioned them forward into the main cavern. "Come, fool lads."

Galahad cozied behind Fionna, snaking his arms around her waist and burying his face into her hair.

"At last," he whispered. A hand roamed up her taut stomach toward her breasts; the other seized her chin and tilted her head back toward him.

Jealousy roiled hot in Lancelot at the sight of Galahad's hands where he wanted his own to be.

"A little help?" Fionna yelped, trying to squirm out of Galahad's iron grip. The knight was lowering his lips to the curve of her neck. "I don't want to hurt him. But I will—"

Merlin murmured under his breath and the three enchanted men swayed on their feet as their eyes fluttered shut. Lancelot lunged for Percival, catching the wiry lad before he toppled forward, while Merlin went for Arthur, catching him under the armpits and lowering him to the floor. Galahad, who was thoroughly twined about Fionna, crashed backwards like a felled tree, pulling her down onto him. With a muffled curse, Fionna rolled away and flopped onto the floor as Galahad's huge arms went limp.

Reclining on one elbow, she panted for breath. "A little warning next time, druid."

Merlin inclined his shorn head and walked to his shelves, pulling items into his arms.

"Can you fix them?" Lancelot asked.

"I can," Merlin said. "The magic in the wine was more whimsical than deadly. Lighthearted faerie fun. I can undo it."

"Remind me to never have fun with a faerie." Fionna pushed herself to her feet and straightened her dress, pulling her long, flowing locks and braids over her shoulder.

"It's lucky you two didn't drink the faerie wine."

Merlin deposited his ingredients onto his carved desk, then looked at both he and Fionna.

"I wasn't there," Lancelot said. "Or I would have stopped the fools from drinking the wine too. But . . ." he turned to Fionna, his brows drawing together. "Why didn't you drink the wine?"

Fionna shrugged, an unreadable emotion playing across her face. "I simply didn't want any," she said. "Alworn left me far too unsettled."

Lancelot nodded slowly, studying her, trying to read the truth behind her silver eyes. And failing. There was something she wasn't saying. She may have clasped his hand that night, but he would do well to remember: their fifth knight kept her own counsel.

Interlude

Morgana

The crow watched from an oak branch as the fae male transformed into a white wolf and loped into the night-shadowed forest. She launched into the air, silently tailing him until he reached a safe distance from prying human eyes.

The crow flapped her moonlight dusted wings, swooping onto the deer trail the white wolf followed. She cawed as he approached.

The wolf's hackles rose, an answering snarl escaping his snout. The night provided ample darkness and whispered prayers and she transformed in a rush of wind and decaying leaves.

"Alworn," Morgana said simply, touching the wolf on his head.

Her ambassador vaporized into his male form, all slender lines and angles. His haughty gaze found hers before, remembering himself, he stumbled into a hasty bow—one knee to the forest floor, his head low.

"Your Highness," he intoned. "How may I serve you further this night."

"I require your confession."

He looked up then, graceful eyebrows drawn together. Under the moon's watchful eyes, his hair glinted silver and his eyes paled to their unnatural aquamarine shade. "Confession?"

"Do not play coy with me, Alworn. I observed the whole sordid affair from the rafters."

"Then surely you saw how your brother and his knights made fools of themselves with the witch."

Morgana laughed. Crows slumbering in the branches above awakened and joined their caws of laughter with hers.

A sliver of fear tightened the muscles of Alworn's beautiful face.

She stepped close and traced along his bottom lip, drawing blood with her sharp fingernail.

"Surely you witnessed how our May wine failed to enchant the witch. Why is this, dear Alworn?"

"I am as baffled as you."

Morgana bared her teeth as blood dripped from Alworn's mouth, then leaned toward his ear. "Convince me not to peck your eyes out," she whispered, her voice sultry and inviting.

"Must be her . . . m-magic protecting her. B-but the necklace," he stammered. His body shuddered under her touch and she smiled, satisfied. "She w-wears the n-necklace you enchanted, Your Highness."

"Yes," Morgana hissed, drawing out the sound until the word slithered from her tongue into his ear.

"The necklace." Releasing him, she stepped back. "It is enough, for now. I will spare your eyes this time. Do not fail me again or you will wander blind until a pack of wolves scents your weakness and shreds you to ribbons."

"You are m-merciful, Your Highness." His eyes fixed onto the dirt beneath his feet.

"Go, Alworn." Morgana touched his forehead and he vaporized into his white wolf form once more. "Be swift. Return to Tintagel and keep my sisters company."

The white wolf tucked his tail and loped into the distance, disappearing between the inky silhouettes of tall, swaying trees.

A dark breeze ruffled Morgana's hair and she lifted her face to the sister moon. "Guide my journey . . ."

The rest of her whispered prayer was lost to the night as the crow appeared once more. She joined the twinkling stars and low-hanging clouds high above Caerleon, her mind filled with thoughts of freedom, and magic, and revenge.

Chapter Eighteen

Fionna

I pressed my forehead to the slick glass of the latticed windowpanes and tried, in vain, to cool my feverish skin. An hour had passed since Merlin's magic banished the strange echantment gripping Arthur, Galahad, and Percival, since the five of us walked in silence back up the path to the wooden keep.

We parted ways by the corridor's mouth that led to my room, the knights heading to theirs. I had never seen them so morose, or so quiet.

I didn't know if the men remembered what they had done while in the faerie wine's grip, but I did. My body burned with the memories. Arthur's velvet tongue in my mouth; Percival's hand gripped tightly in my hair; Galahad's massive arms locked around me. Their remembered words were flint striking in the dark of my mind, kindling a fire within me that burned so hot it frightened me. And then there was

Lancelot—ornery as a penned stallion one moment, ready to protect me with his life the next.

Even I had my limits as a seasoned fighter. I could fight one—maybe two—men. But three strong, skilled warriors? A sick feeling twisted in my stomach once more. I both enjoyed and loathed their advances, for how the feelings forced me to question my morality and sense of honor, while also embracing how each man made me feel desirable. The nausea swirled stronger and I had to admit the real truth— my mind was drifting farther and farther away from my father and sister and the sacrifice I must make for their lives.

I pushed back from the window, heaving a sigh, before crossing the room to the sideboard. I poured water from a silver pitcher and splashed cool liquid onto my face, desperate to find myself again. My body no longer felt like my own. Nor my heart. Many a song declared the misery and ache of a stolen heart. Is this what I felt? My heart torn between two lands and two callings?

I blotted my face dry. I didn't understand this . . . this confusion. I had been with two men before— one, a lad from Aghanravel, another a warrior in a fiann I fought beside. Both had been pleasant enough experiences, though short and somewhat underwhelming. In truth, I had set thoughts of sex aside and dismissed intimacy with another as something that held little interest to me. Fighting and sparring and honing my skills as a warrior—these were the physical activities that inflamed the passion in my blood.

Until I came here.

I wondered if I knew myself at all. I thought of Lancelot's question about the faerie wine. I had hoped neither he nor Merlin would pick up on my sudden discomfort. I should have known I wouldn't be so lucky to escape their inspection. I didn't know why I had lied. I drank the faerie wine. So why wasn't I affected by the enchantment? Did the tainted May wine only affect men? Or could I have some other magical immunity?

The silver necklace dangling around my neck caught the firelight, and I lifted the pendant, examining the jeweled lily. Could the necklace be a form of protection? My skin crawled at the thought of anything from Alworn touching me. I grew overcome with the need to toss the gift far from me. I reached back to remove the necklace, but the clasp stuck. My fingers fumbled with the delicate mechanism. I grunted, spinning the chain around, trying to work the clasp from the front. The clasp's lever didn't budge. I tried to pull the chain off over my head, but the length was too short, too tight. Frustrated, I yanked on the chain and grimaced at the biting pain in my neck.

I let the necklace fall, huffing. I guessed Tintagel's gift was staying on. For now.

Between the excitement of Alworn's attack, the ache in my loins, and the guilt-tinged pang in my chest, sleep would elude me tonight. I slipped out my door into the dimly lit hallway, candle in hand. Perhaps I could find a book in the grand library to explain my immunity to the faerie wine. That would set my mind at ease.

My jittery mood settled as soon as I had a task before me. My shoulders sagged slightly in relief. Nothing like boring, dusty books to distract me from the tumbling confusion in my head and the yearning heat deep in my belly.

Or so I thought. The library was lit from within. Candlelight flickered gentle amber light onto the stone walls.

"Fionna . . ." Arthur whispered my name from behind a table. Shadows smudged the skin under his eyes.

I briefly contemplated excusing myself, but it was the look of him that convinced me to move forward. His short hair was tousled, his full lips pinched, his brow twisted with worry.

"Yer Majesty," I said, needing the formality to remain. I settled into the chair across from him, grateful for the expanse of wood and books that stretched between us like a barricade.

"Please Fionna, Arthur is fine," he said, his voice soft and shy. "Percival calls me 'pumpkin' behind my back. You may at least call me by my first name."

A smile tugged on the corner of my mouth. "Pumpkin?"

He closed his book and, in a single blink, met my gaze. "I don't understand his reasons. I'm sure it's only a matter of time before he crowns you with a mildly insulting moniker as well."

"Percival's terms of endearment?"

"Precisely." Arthur smiled weakly over one of his books, his eyes glossing red in the candlelight. "About tonight . . ." He rose from behind the table and knelt at my feet, bowing his head. I bit back a gasp, unable to process a king lowering himself before me as Arthur did so now, his shoulders slumped, dejection posturing the angle of his head. "I cannot express how utterly sorry I am for what happened, for my behavior. All of our behavior."

"Do ye . . . remember?" My cheeks flamed and I swallowed at the forming knot in my throat.

Arthur lifted his head and searched my eyes, almost pleading. "I wish I did not, but I do. Every wretched moment."

His confession stung. Wretched? He wished to forget our kiss? Or the different sort of magic that enveloped us as our lips touched and breath mixed? But even as the thought surfaced, I scolded myself. Of course he desired to forget. He had embarrassed himself in front of his entire court. Anyone would want to forget such a moment.

"I did not behave as a king should, nor a man of honor," Arthur continued, his voice shaking. "I deeply regret how you were subjected to my shameful actions. I shall never forgive myself nor will I ever forget."

I softened. "Ye were not yerself, Arthur."

"Matters not, for tonight still happened. Do not excuse how we—how I—treated you, and publicly no less. You're not an object to appease our carnal urges and deserve my utmost respect before my court." He rubbed his face, as if he could banish the memories. "My father . . ." Arthur trailed off, leaning his head back to gaze at the ceiling. I watched as his Adam's apple bobbed and his eyes blinked back growing emotion.

"My father and my mother," he began, almost a whisper. "Their union was not . . . consensual. He used magic to disguise himself as Gorlois—the Duke of Tintagel, a fae male from the Túatha dé Danann who gave up immortality for my mother, and my half-sisters' father—and then Uther bedded my mother. That same night I was conceived, my father placed Gorlois at the front lines in a battle against several Saxon clans and . . . and he died—violently. His body was returned the next morning to Tintagel, mutilated. I . . . I was eighteen when my father died after he drank from a spring the Saxons had poisoned in his war camp. The Lady of the Lake dissolved any gossip of my rightful claim to Caerleon's throne through Excalibur." Arthur's green eyes brimmed with anguish as he met my gaze. "I am born of rape and deceit, and I watched my mother live under Uther's obsessive claim over her for eighteen years, helpless. I swore that I would *never* condone that form of cruel behavior in my kingdom. To allow a woman to suffer such indignities where I had the power to stop it." His green eyes searched everywhere, landing anywhere but my face. "And then to find . . . it was I . . . who perpetrated them." His voice lowered to a near growl as he said, "Perhaps I'm more like him than I thought."

Grief flooded through me like a swollen river. How was it possible for a man in this dark world—a king no less—to have such a tender heart? In that moment, I would have done anything to soothe the guilt chafing at Arthur. Even, it seemed, tell the truth.

"Our kiss was consensual," I managed, swallowing.

Arthur's eyes met mine as the words hung between us. "You forcefully had to tell me no and shoved me away."

"A surprise, certainly. The wrong venue, absolutely. But . . ." I closed my eyes, struggling against my embarrassment. What was I doing? Admitting to the king of Briton that I had wanted to kiss him! Was I a fool? I opened my eyes again, meeting his firmly. "Yes, I had told ye no, and I do not make excuses for ye. Simply, I knew ye were under a spell ye could not control. If I continued our kiss, is that not the same as taking advantage of ye?"

His chest rose and fell, though a hint of light chased away the shadows on his beautiful face.

"And, if I had truly felt unsafe," I continued, encouraged, "I would have knocked ye on yer arse, king or no."

A sad smile touched his lips, flushed from his sorrow. "I imagine that's experience talking?" he asked, softly.

"Men have a funny way of feeling entitled to something from a woman, especially when their blood is up. I've had to remind a few over the years that my body belongs to no one but me. And yer body belonged to ye, not the faerie wine."

He bowed his head toward me, the lines on his face relaxing. He whispered, "Thank you, Fionna."

"Ye're welcome, Arthur," I whispered in return, my heart squeezing in my chest.

He slowly rose to his feet and locked eyes with me before returning to his seat, saying, "Quick thinking, finding Lancelot. You're an asset to this kingdom. We're lucky to have you."

His praise warmed me like a hearth in winter. Who was the eager puppy now? I *wanted* this king's gratitude, his esteem. His view of me shouldn't matter, but skies, I found that I craved his good opinion. What would it do to him when I took the sword? The one granting him sovereignty over his land? Or when I fled from here? What would it do to me? How had I sank so deep so fast? The longer I stayed here, the greater my blood price would become. I needed to focus. I needed to remember my father and my sister, held prisoner by Donal O'Lynn. In danger.

It was in that moment that I saw what my muddled emotions had hid from me. My vision narrowed to a point. Arthur's hand rested on his thigh, where his fingers normally curled around the pommel of Excalibur. A pommel that was conspicuously absent.

I hissed in a breath, trying to keep the excitement from my face. He didn't have Excalibur with him. Now was my chance.

Then pain lanced through me. Blood drained from my face as I accepted my fate. I would deal with my treacherous heart later. First, I had to save my father and sister from certain death.

"Are you well?" Arthur asked. "You seem as if you've seen a ghost."

I scrambled for an excuse, standing. "My mind refused to tire after all of today's excitement, but exhaustion has finally found me. With yer leave, I will retire to bed."

"Of course," Arthur said, rising to his feet and bowing. "I should probably head to bed as well."

"No!" I nearly shouted, before realizing how unhinged I sounded. "I disrupted yer study. Please, stay and finish whatever ye were working on. Perhaps tonight will be the night ye will have yer breakthrough and find yer Grail."

"Your lips to the gods' ears," Arthur said, lowering himself back into his chair.

I relaxed—slightly.

"Good night Arthur," I whispered, my eyes tracing the planes of his handsome boyish face, memorizing every inch.

For what I really meant was *goodbye*.

Chapter Nineteen

Fionna

My footsteps thundered in my ears as I hurried toward the East Wing. My heart galloped in my chest like a wild stallion. Was I really doing this? I was really stealing Excalibur.

The fortress slumbered at this hour, and no one blocked my passage. Not that they would have any reason to, I reminded myself. I was a knight, after all. I could go anywhere I pleased. I straightened my shoulders and slowed my steps. I needn't skulk about like a common thief. *Though you are a thief*, my conscience whispered at me. *Curse you, Donal O'Lynn for putting me in this impossible situation!*

Perhaps I could leave a note. I dismissed that idea as soon as the thought surfaced. A note would be a clue to help them find me more quickly. Best that they not know why I've left or where I journey. A messenger then. When the deed was all said and done, I would send a messenger to explain everything, especially where to find O'Lynn. A grim smile crossed my face. That would be a worthy vengeance. As soon as I had my family free, my fiann would join with Arthur and his warriors in slaying O'Lynn and reclaiming Excalibur. Relief swelled in me. The very thought was enough to quiet the guilt gnawing at my gut.

The corridor leading to the knights' rooms was dark. It seemed a lifetime ago when I had pounded on Lancelot's door, demanding his aid. This night had felt like five nights, these last few days—a lifetime. I passed Galahad's door next and an ache of desire coiled deep within me. In other circumstances, I would have accepted Galahad's invitation gladly. And then I passed Percival's door, and whispered an apology. An image in my mind of his unflappable smile falling when he heard of my betrayal was almost too much to bear. I looked away, toward the staircase at the end of the hallway. Arthur's chamber tower. I could do this.

"For ye, Aideen. Papa. For ye, I'll do anything," I whispered to the shadows as I crept up the stairs.

Arthur's door was unlocked and I slipped inside silently. I let my eyes adjust to the dim space first, taking in my surroundings. His chambers were slightly larger than mine, but not by much. Nor were they gaudy and ostentatious as some kings favored. Rather, his personal space was neat and orderly, with simple, carved-oak furniture, and tidy stacks of books. A sad smile crossed my face at how very Arthur it all was. And then I went to work.

Knowing my time was short, I turned every inch

of his chamber upside down as quickly and as delicately as I could. The four-post bed, the oak-hewn chest, the heavy desk, the bookshelves. Excalibur was large with an Otherworldly shine, incapable of hiding. Yet, the faerie sword was nowhere to be found. I rose to my feet after riffling under the bed for the second time. No, definitely not there. I brushed off my gown and huffed.

Slowly, I spun around again, taking in every nook and cranny. The coveted sword wasn't here. Excalibur wasn't with Arthur, but it also wasn't here.

My mind raced as I slipped down the stairs and back into the corridor. Chewing on my lip, my feet dragged as I twisted and untwisted possibilities. Perhaps Arthur had left the sword in Merlin's cave? I paused and closed my eyes, trying to replay the scene in my mind. Had Arthur removed Excalibur when Merlin administered the antidote to the faerie wine? If the sword was indeed with Merlin, I had no chance of stealing the blade tonight. But . . . if he had left Excalibur somewhere else—

"Fionna?"

A baritone voice startled me. My hand flew to my chest as I jumped as though a startled deer.

"Galahad . . ."

I pressed my body to the far wall as I willed myself to calm. I had been so lost in thought, I hadn't realized that I had stopped right in front of his doorway. Which he was now filling. Shirtless. His long blond hair tousled around his shoulders.

I swallowed as I took in his form, limned in torchlight—the flat planes of his pectorals, the rippling ex-

panse of his abdomen. Behind me, I placed my palms
flat against the cool stone wall. Without anchoring
myself to something real, I feared I might float away.
Had a man ever looked so devastating in firelight?

"What are you doing in the East Wing?" he
leaned one muscled arm on the doorjamb.

I practically groaned at the way the movement
displayed his muscles before me, my skin coming
alive in his presence. "Couldn't sleep," I managed.
"Simply enjoying a midnight walk."

"And your walk brought you to my door?"

His low chuckle rumbled through me, hardening
my nipples against the fabric of my dress. I licked my
dry lips.

Galahad shifted in the doorway, and I pressed
myself harder to the far wall. With this space between us, I could retain some coherence of thought.
If he came over here . . . I might grow weak, to my
shame as a tested warrior.

Goddess, he moved toward me—was before me
in a flash, his calloused hands taking one of mine. He
loomed in my vision, a golden sight that I wanted
to drink in until I drowned. Without a sword in my
hand, without my armor on, I felt small compared to
him. Distinctly female.

"Please forgive me for my ungallant behavior tonight," Galahad said. His dark blue eyes were earnest, sorrowful. "I would never think to impose myself on a woman who was not interested. My mother
and sisters would have my hide, if they knew." A sad
smile flitted across his lips. "If I offended you, I apol-
ogize profusely."

"I wasn't offended," I managed to say. My voice sounded hoarse to my ears. "I understood there were . . . extenuating circumstances."

He heaved a sigh of relief. "You are most gracious for understanding." The light in his eyes shifted, sending a trill of excitement up my spine. "Though, I would be false if I said I had not thought of my invitation before." His thumb drew lazy circles on the back of my hand. "Though I am naught but villager's son compared to other company you could keep, know that you are welcome in my chambers any time it pleases you." He winked at me before leaning forward and placing a soft kiss on my cheek, bracing one hand against the wall by my head. His lips were like a brand upon my skin, marking me his with one simple gesture. He lingered there, his lips hovering by my ear, the heat of his bare skin and his breath warming me like a Beltane fire. Allowing the choice to be mine.

I didn't want the choice to be mine. I wanted his passion to overcome my senses, my better judgment, so I could tell myself in the morning that I had been swept up in the madness of his offer. But that would be a lie. My emotions warred within me—wanting this man yet knowing my betrayal would hurt him even deeper should we become tangled up in each other's lives this way.

Galahad pulled back, sensing my hesitation, a sweet smile dimpling his cheek. Did he fear I judged him for his birth status? My heart spasmed painfully with the increased space between us, seizing my will. I had been teetering on the edge of a knife's blade, and I threw myself off it.

"What about tonight?" I heard myself whisper.

His smile turned sultry, and my pulse thrummed through my veins in response. He traced the line of my face, my ear, down to my chin, which he gently held between his fingers. "You're sure?"

I gave a little nod, as sure that this was a terrible idea as I was that I wanted him more than I had wanted anything in a very long time.

In one lithe motion, he scooped me up in his arms. His smell of cedarwood and leather teased my senses.

"Tonight," he murmured as he pushed back through his door, closing it with a bare foot, "you are a queen, and I your humble servant."

A spasm of need jolted through me with his words, and my breath grew shallow.

Wanton.

In one playful motion, he tossed me down upon the coverlet. I scrambled back as he pounced on top of me, finding myself giggling like a maid. My fevered grin was matched by one on Galahad's handsome face. And when he kissed me, his lips tasted as sweet as honey. All thoughts of O'Lynn and Excalibur and tomorrow fled from my mind, leaving only Galahad.

Chapter Twenty

Galahad

Fionna was in *his* chambers. Beneath him on *his* bed. In a dress sewn from folds of the night sky by Freya herself. Stars above, what delicious madness was this?

Two princes and a king slept on either side of his walls. He flirted and teased, but he didn't expect her to choose him. Especially not choose him over Arthur. As the son of a blacksmith—in a home of ten—as the one who was squired at a young age to help provide food for his sisters and brothers, he could not fathom why a princess would choose him.

Galahad nibbled on her lower lip before pulling away to confirm that he was not lost in a dream. He stilled at the sight before him.

A wicked gleam glimmered in her silver eyes—one that disarmed his hold on her waist and puddled every thought at her feet. And then she rolled out from underneath him as though they sparred in the paddock.

Galahad boomed with laughter, ready to pounce again.

But Fionna's lips, the ones he had just tasted, curved into a flirtatious smile as she rose onto her knees—and he stared, beguiled by the toned muscles of her arms, her long, graceful neck, and the way her gown dipped low between her breasts. Lifting an elegant arm, she pulled a few pins from atop her head. A waterfall of braids joined the moonlit tresses spilling to her waist.

His breath caught. Just to feel the fall of her hair about his face, her breasts pressed to his bare skin—it would be heaven and hell rolled into one. And she wasn't done tormenting him yet.

Tilting her head, Fionna trailed the tips of her fingers down his broad chest in a feathered touch, down his stomach ribbed in muscle, lower still. Galahad's muscles jumped and flexed. She was killing him. When her fingers reached the drawstrings of his breeches, she dipped forward and kissed the broad expanse of his pectorals.

"Gods," he whispered as his head fell back against his shoulders.

Her tongue explored his skin, roaming southward to his abdomen. His chest heaved as he watched her, mesmerized by every little movement, every languid sensation. Silver eyes locked onto his hungry gaze and she grinned, right before her pink tongue flicked below his navel, where a thin patch of hair traveled below his breeches.

A white-hot flame blazed through his groin and

Galahad growled her name. He was unraveling by the second. Fionna laughed at the sound, as if taunting another warrior in the round. If a fight was what she wanted, a fight was what he'd give her. And this time, there would be no tie.

Tangling his fingers into her hair, Galahad lifted her cruel mouth to his. Their lips crashed in a bruising kiss, drinking each other in. Desperate for more. Longing for release. His hands slid up her waist until his thumbs brushed along her pebbled nipples. She moaned into their kiss and sagged against the hard planes of his body.

But only for a moment.

As if remembering herself, Fionna pushed away and narrowed her eyes. She thought she could take him. Do with him as she wanted. But he had other plans. Tonight was about *her* pleasure. Control, he knew, was a climax all its own. The corner of her mouth lifted in a challenge—come and get her—if he could.

Fionna tried to scramble off the bed, but he curled an arm around her waist and then flipped her onto her back in an easy motion. She thrashed beneath him, laughing, feigning a struggle. She wanted a chase. He wanted to win.

Nudging her legs open with his knee, his hand slipped under the folds of her skirt and caressed her calf, behind her knee, her thigh. She drew in a ragged breath of anticipation. The curve of her hip fit perfectly into the palm of his hand. Her eyes fluttered closed and her lips parted.

Galahad lowered his weight onto her and ground

his throbbing cock between her thighs. Fionna arched, moaning, her breasts offered to his lips. He rolled his hips into hers again, sucking her breast into his mouth through her bodice. Her nails dug into his back as she bit back a cry.

He was dying. Heat curled violently in his blood. Vicious tendrils that burned and consumed. His muscles tightened and shook with need. And, Odin save him, he wanted her to know the same torture a tongue could inflict. A fair fight. Not that she fought fair, not even once since arriving. She didn't take kindly to losing either, a thought that billowed his determination.

Biting the edge of her bodice with his teeth, he tugged the fabric away until her breast sprang free. Fionna was perfect, ample and soft, cold moonlight caressing her skin. Her curves rose dangerously near his lips and then falling away. He wanted her rendered immobile. Unable to escape his returned attack.

Gently, Galahad grasped her wrist, freeing the nails that dug into the flesh of his back. He placed one hand above her head, then the other. She was now pinned down, but he knew she submitted willingly—for a moment, at least. Finding her heated gaze, he held it, allowed a wolfish grin to form, and then he licked her nipple with the tip of his tongue—flicking, toying, drawing circles—as his hardened length pressed against her once more.

A moan escaped her mouth, rumbling through him. He moved against her again and again, desperate for every sound. She melted into the sheets and bucked her hips to increase their friction. He dragged his lips to her mouth to silence her heavy breaths and hums of pleasure. And stars, his pulse was drunk, intoxicated by the feel of her body, the taste of her lips, the way she moved beneath him. Especially when her hips danced to his in a rhythm that grew frantic.

"Tell me what you want, My Lady," he whispered in her ear, breathless. "Command me and I will obey."

"Taste me," she sighed in answer.

He nipped the skin beneath her earlobe and whispered back, "Only if you remain silent."

"If I—"

"Silent," he repeated. "Do you accept my challenge?"

Fionna lifted herself up onto her elbows to glare at him. "Am I not in command?"

"Command comes with a price. Self-control." A devious smile curved on his lips.

"I have plenty of discipline," she parried. "Or have ye forgotten how I matched ye during the tourney?"

Galahad winked, rubbing the rough edge of his thumb against her exposed nipple. "Then what are you afraid of?"

Her eyes narrowed farther, and she tried—unsuccessfully—to suppress the shudder his motion was sending through her.

"Fear you will lose to me?" He pressed his cock to her sex next, grinding—lazily, erotically—his gaze never leaving hers.

Fionna's eyes widened in a flash of sensual anger and something else—*want*. The liquid heat in her gaze almost unraveled him. Almost.

"Fine," she said. The reply was meant to be sharp, he knew. But the single word came out in a quivering breath. "I'll be silent."

"Good," Galahad breathed into her ear. Then he kissed her jaw, her neck, her breasts, down to her stomach. "I want to drink my fill and not be interrupted." He smiled into her gown, bunched at her waist, when her hands fisted his coverlet, white-knuckled with frustration.

But her legs willingly opened for him as he pushed the skirt of her dress up, running his hands up the smooth expanse of her thigh. Her scent enveloped him and his arms nearly weakened at how beautiful she was while spread out before him. . . and how beautifully wet with arousal. To test the waters, he kissed the inside of her thigh and waited. Fionna sucked in a quiet gasp.

"Silent," he purred from between her legs.

His hot breath on her skin sent a tremor across her body—both in frustration and desire. He knew she was ready to raze him to the ground and it took everything in him to not laugh. Instead, he kissed the inside of her other thigh. Happy when she didn't make a sound, he flicked her swollen nub with the tip of his tongue. Her entire body tensed as she gripped the coverlet tighter, sinking her other hand in the long strands of his hair.

It was the sight Galahad desired, and he buried himself in her. Her thighs shook with the effort to not cry out in deep-sated moans as he lapped and drank, as his lips slid between her seam. The taste of salt, honey, and sex danced in his mouth as she writhed against his tongue.

Now he was truly dying. Never had a woman tasted so divine nor felt so right in his battle-worn hands. It drove him deeper, made him more desperate to earn his name on her lips. Especially when her hips began grinding against him. When her fingers clawed his shoulders, fisted in his hair. Her back arched, her breasts swelled, nipples taut as she climaxed under his torment. Every part of her trembled and he was heady with the power she granted him over her.

A wild heartbeat later, Fionna's fingers released. Her thighs no longer straining under his pleasure. Still, he wasn't quite done with her yet and licked her one last time right as her body seemed to fully relax. Her reddened lips, swollen from his kisses, parted as a faint moan escaped before closing into a furious line.

She had lost.

And she knew it.

A surprise attack to repay hers on the tourney green.

Amused, he sat back on his knees, his cock hard and his balls tightening with need. But not tonight. He would make her wait for victory against him. Perhaps even beg. A bout he looked forward to fighting in, if he was lucky enough to receive a second match. He prayed he was.

"I think I won that round," he said, a triumphant grin on his face. "Perhaps you need another lesson in self-control."

Fionna sat up, emotions warring on her beautiful face. Her eyes blazed and he stole a quick kiss, wanting her to taste herself on his lips. She struggled to appear unmoved, though he knew she was affected when her eyelids began to droop in a drowsy blink. He pulled back from her and she straightened, head thrown back, shoulders squared. To a warrior as fierce as Fionna, defeat was unacceptable. Galahad flashed his most cherubic grin in reply, almost challenging her to a second duel.

"I shouldn't linger here," Fionna forced out to cover for her slip in reaction. "I will sleep well now, thank ye." In a proud huff, she extricated herself from his bed and marched toward the door, a little wobbly on her feet. Pride rushed through him. He had weakened the mighty Fionnabhair Allán, knocked her off balance.

Before pulling on the iron ring of his chamber door, she peered over her shoulder at him, her face imperious, the plunging seams of her bodice pulled closed in her fist. "Actually, I have won Sir Galahad. For it seems I'm the only one who will depart satisfied this night."

And, with that, she left his chambers in a rush of skirts and wild, white-blonde hair.

Galahad released a thunderous laugh, one that rumbled clear to his toes. He hoped she heard his humor too.

Chapter Twenty-One

Percival

Percival pulled a pillow over his head to muffle the banging on his door. The stuff of nightmares. The day wasn't even light yet! Perhaps if he didn't answer, the offender would just skulk away.

The knock sounded again—louder this time.

"Go away!" he shouted, instantly regretting his movement. He felt like he had been trampled by a pair of cart-horses. His head pounded; his mouth tasted as if a small rodent had crawled behind his tongue and died; and his balls ached with unmet need.

Bloody faeries.

Percival let out a groan when his door opened.

"Good, you're up," Arthur said, pushing farther inside the room.

"Am I being punished?" Percival asked as Arthur crossed the room and threw open the heavy drapes. Dim, watery moonlight pooled through the windows, laying shadowed diamonds on the large rug beneath his bed.

"It's not even dawn." Percival had hardly slept an hour last night, tossing and tangling in his covers, thinking about Fionna. He was torn between embarrassment and longing, remembering the feel of her body against his as the faerie wine stole his better judgment. His behavior had been wrong, yet . . . touching her had felt so very right. Her scent of heather and moss, the catch in her breath as he seized her. Gods, he wanted this Grail business to be over, so he could be a real contender in the race for her heart. So, he could give up this ridiculous vow of chastity.

"I was in the library all night," Arthur said, plopping down on Percival's bed with a bounce.

Percival pushed himself up gingerly, trying not to jostle his pounding head. Arthur looked wild-eyed, stubble shadowing the cut of his jaw. A far cry from his normally immaculate self. "Is everything all right?"

Arthur waved a hand. "Besides the Túatha dé Danann meddling in my court and making us all fall like idiots over our newest knight? Things are fine."

"About that . . ." Percival said, trailing off. He didn't know what to say. None of them should have drank that wine. He remembered the ominous shrill ring of metal as Arthur pulled Excalibur from its sheath. Percival shivered. They were lucky Fionna and Lancelot had arrived when they did.

"I talked to Fionna, she understands. We're all forgiven for our impertinence."

"Good." Percival heaved a sigh of relief. "It's her

own fault for being so beautiful. She had to know something like this would happen. If she were ugly, this would be so much less complicated."

"You cannot blame a woman for your own behavior, Percival, regardless of her fairness of form and face."

"Och, I know, forgive me. My brain is still addled. I speak more of my own ability to resist my attraction to her."

Arthur pursed his lips, holding back a smile. "Perhaps we should demand that she wear her stag helm each day, to make things easier on you."

"That's the first good idea I've heard in days," Percival said. "Ye're king. Make it happen. Though . . ." he paused. "Her figure is quite distracting. Anything you can do about that?"

"Shapeless sackcloth shift? Will that do?"

"Perfect," Percival said, grinning. "Make sure the sackcloth hangs down to her toes though. I'm not sure I can resist a flash of ankle. A man can only endure so much."

Arthur shook his head, a laugh escaping from him. He seized the pillow from Percival's hands and smacked him with it. "You're an idiot."

"Yes, well, I'm yer idiot. So, what does that make ye?"

"King of idiots, I suppose." Arthur tossed back the pillow to Percival, who tucked it behind his head while leaning back against the headboard, his hands interlocked behind his neck. "Now, I assume this isn't a social call. If it is, we need to talk about yer timing."

The mad gleam in Arthur's eye flared back to

life. "Like I was saying . . . I found something." He pulled out a folded piece of parchment from his tunic's pocket and held it out.

Percival took the aged, wrinkled parchment, unfolding it. He blinked his eyes to clear them, to make out the cramped scrawl. "A letter?" Percival asked.

"To your father," Arthur replied. "And not just a letter. The missive references a secret."

Percival blinked at that, scooting up. "The note is from a Lord Bronn."

"Do you remember him?" Arthur asked eagerly. "Is the name familiar?"

Percival nodded slowly, searching his memories. "Aye. He was an old friend of my father's. If I recall, he helped my father when he was ill."

"Yes, that's what the letter says. He tells your father that he could not leave a wounded man to die on his manor lands."

Percival nodded, barely. Gods, his head. Drawing in a long, deep breath, he exhaled slowly, then said, "Nae, not an illness. He was injured. Lance to the thigh or some such thing. When he was hunting. I think Bronn lived nearby. He found my father bleeding and took him in." Percival scanned the letter. Lord Bronn did mention a secret. He read the note aloud. "*Lay your fears to rest that I will spill your secrets, or usurp the knowledge for my own uses. The things you said while you were wracked with fever are yours to keep. I understand the heavy burden resting upon you as Keeper of the Grail. I would be a man without honor were I not to respect your noble task.*"

Arthur's face was alight with excitement. "Don't

you see? Your father said something when he was beside himself with fever. Details about the Grail. This man, Lord Bronn, promised to keep your father's secrets. He could know the location of the Grail!"

"Where did ye find this?" Percival asked, his mind racing. Arthur was right. This could be a clue. A real clue. It seemed like a lifetime ago, when he had lived with his parents in his father's grand manor at Caer Benic. Before his father died. Before his mother had gone half-mad, stealing him away to the darkest woods of Strathclyde in Alba, where they lived like hermits, away from the prying eyes she thought were searching for them. Before the Otherworld shrouded Caer Benic from mortal eyes to protect the Grail in the absence of a Fisher King. Before the sun had broken through the dark clouds of his life in the form of Arthur Pendragon. His way out of the gloom.

"The note was tucked inside a book in the library," Arthur answered, unaware of Percival's thoughts. "A dusty tome with your father's name scrawled on the front page. I think the book was from his personal library."

Percival stilled. "My father's books are in the library here?"

Arthur's brow softened. "When your father died, and you and your mother disappeared, I believe my father visited your father's known holdings in Northumbria. He must have brought a few of your father's personal books back with him. It's the type of thing Uther would do. He always took what he wanted, regardless of whom the property belonged to."

Percival frowned. He knew Arthur spoke not of books, but of his mother. Married to another man, until Uther Pendragon cast his eyes on her, and coveted her for himself, using fae charm to disguise him as the Duke of Tintagel. He supposed Arthur had ghosts enough of his own to haunt his past.

"You can have them, if you so desire," Arthur continued. "The books. I didn't know they were here. But they're yours by right."

Percival shrugged. "They can stay in the library with their bookish brethren. The Grail quest is more than enough legacy for me."

"Do you know where Lord Bronn lives?" Arthur asked hopefully.

"It's been a long time. But I think he lived in Chester, North of Wales in the Kingdom of Mercia. I think . . . I think we visited him once." Percival closed his eyes, trying to focus. "I have a memory of his manor. There was a statue shaped like a gryphon, and a huge oak tree that I played in. A brook I fell into. An old Roman fort is nearby. Aye, I believe I could find my way back there."

"That's not far. Perhaps a three days' ride, if we stick to the Roman roads."

Percival raised an eyebrow. "Do I sense an outing in our future?"

"After the messiness of last night, a journey will do us all good. Plus, there's been raiding near Ewloe, not far from Chester."

"What, the Kingdom of Gwynedd dinnae fight raiders now? I always did think the Northern Lords were all bark and no bite, a bunch of self-important arseholes. King of the Britons, ha! Does their king still claim this ridiculous notion despite the Lady of the Lake's pronouncement that ye are the rightful Pendragon?"

Arthur played with a worn corner of the leather-bound book in his lap. "There was a call for aid to all the Kingdoms of Wales, be they king or peasant. The raiders have left a trail of wreckages down the River Dee. Perhaps we can speak with the townsfolk of Ewloe to ask if they know of Lord Bronn as well as see if we can take care of whoever has been terrorizing them. We can kill two birds with one stone."

"Count me in. Let us Southern lads show those pompous Northern Lords who the real Head Dragon of Wales is." Percival threw his covers off, springing to his feet. The thought of a trip out of the keep—a real chance to find the Grail—had invigorated him, banishing his headache.

Arthur groaned, shielding his eyes with a hand as he stood. "Give a man a little warning next time."

Percival looked down at his naked form. "I could say the same for ye. Ye're the one who barged into my chamber unannounced."

"I'll consider myself reprimanded." Arthur strode toward the hallway.

"Arthur," Percival said, and this king paused at the door. "When do we leave?"

"No time like the present. I'll tell the servants and have Lancelot ready the soldiers to stand guard. This morning."

"Excellent," Percival said, hands on his hips.

"And Percival?"

"Hmm?"

"Wear pants."

Chapter Twenty-Two

Fionna

Back in my armor, I felt more like myself than I had in days. My knives were strapped into their vambraces on my forearms, my sword on my hip. Now if only I had armor to surround my heart. And this damn faerie necklace off. The thing was clasped tight, refusing to yield. I had even tried to cut the chain free with one of my knives, to no success. I supposed the necklace was staying, for the time being.

Zephyr plucked an apple from my hand. This was our tradition before I cinched her saddle tight and loaded her up with my bedroll and saddle bags. She pawed the hay in her stall until I offered her another freshly plucked apple from the neighboring orchard. She could smell her favorite treat in the pouch hanging from my sword belt and I smiled.

Only an hour earlier, Percival had shown up at my door, bright eyed and bouncing, announcing how we were leaving on a mission. I had nodded cheerfully, hiding my discomfort the best I could. But when I had closed the door, I sagged against the rough wood with a shaky breath. I wasn't sure what I feared most. To be alone with all four knights? To find an opportunity to steal Excalibur? Or afraid that the others would see how something had happened between me and Galahad? My skin flushed as I thought of last night.

Zephyr curved her head back toward me, lipping my hair with her soft mouth. I leaned my forehead into her velvet neck, breathing in her comforting scent of hay and leather. My pulse became a wild, unfettered creature as the scent of leather reminded me of another. To distract myself, I braided a piece of Zephyr's mane, an occupation to banish the tempest of sensations flooding over me of where Galahad's fingers had marked me like woad. I didn't think I would ever be the same.

I had told myself I was going into Galahad's room last night only to keep him from suspecting the real reason behind my presence in their hallway. But that wasn't true. I entered his private chamber because I had wanted to, because I had desperately longed to forget myself for a while, yearned to feel the earth beneath me and the heavens before me when man moved both while loving a woman. And goddess, I received more than what I had bargained for, and then some.

Galahad's touch—his expert tongue—had me burning and quivering in an explosion that swept me away, obliterating my universe into nothing but a

sweet ache and pleasant haze. And beyond his devil-
ish smile, his playful banter, had been an earnestness
and care that shook me more than my climax had.
Galahad cared for me. Truly. And when I took Excalibur and ran, it would ruin him. My deceit would
ruin them all. I feared O'Lynn's task would ruin *me*.

"You're looking well this morning, Fionna," a
man's voice purred from beyond the stall. I turned
and hid my surprise when my eyes locked onto the
source.

Lancelot.

"Ye as well," I said, forcing a smile on my face. It
was true, the man did look beyond handsome, with
his ebony hair tousled from sleep, his leathers partially unbuckled to reveal the broad plane of his chest.
A peek of indigo ink brushed along his upper chest,
near his shoulder, in vined swirls and lines. I forced
my eyes back to his and said, "Fair morning for a
journey."

"Indeed. A fine spring day."

It seemed that some of Lancelot's ice had thawed,
and I felt I should not let this moment pass, even if we
had little more to discuss than the weather. "Thank
ye for yer assistance last night. I am in yer debt."

Lancelot waved a hand. "Think little of it. If
someone was indebted to me each time I saved these
animals from a tight spot, I would be staggering under the weight."

"Isn't it a touch early to be stroking your ego,
Lancelot?" Galahad chose that moment to swagger
up, clapping the other knight on his shoulder.

Lancelot pursed his lips, but his blue eyes were

mirthful. "It's never too early to stroke anything, that's what I say."

Galahad boomed a laugh. "I would have to agree. What about you, Fionna?"

I busied myself with tightening my saddlebags, but I could hear the grin in his words. "I'll leave the stroking to ye men." I pushed out of the stall and pulled Zephyr's substantial body between myself and the two men. The heat in Galahad's expression as I passed by made my body clench with need. Skies, this would be a long few days.

"Glad to see you're back to your old self, crabapple," I heard Galahad say behind me.

"You and me both, chipmunk," Lancelot replied.

I pressed my lips together to keep from smiling.

The day grew warm and bright, and Arthur and his knights were in even brighter spirits. Galahad seemed able to talk to me without filling very sentence with sexual innuendo and, after a few miles, I relaxed into Zephyr's rocking gait, laughing and jesting with the other knights. Even Arthur seemed to have forgotten the mess of the faerie wine, his cheeks flushed with life, his green eyes as rich as the forests surrounding us. I felt comfortable with these men, as comfortable as I was with my fiann, though I had only known these knights for a few days, and I had fought in my fiann for years.

The realization snuffed out my good mood. My eyes flicked to Excalibur hanging at Arthur's side, the rubies in the pommel winking in the sunlight. The sword suited Arthur—a beautiful blade for a beautiful man. To see such Otherworldly beauty hanging on Donal O'Lynn's hip would pain me to no end. The man deserved nothing so fine. The man deserved a knife in the gut.

Arthur slowed Llamrei, his black mare, to match Zephyr, and smiled at me. He didn't wear his golden oak-leaf crown today. Without it, he looked lighter. Freer. I said as much, and he smiled ruefully. "It pinches."

A startled laugh escaped my lips. "Ye're not what I expected, King Arthur of Caerleon."

"What did you expect?"

"I am really not sure." It was the truth. "For a man who's supposed to conquer all of Briton, ye seem remarkably content just riding through the countryside."

He snorted. "Conquer? No. The only reason I even accept Excalibur's charge to wear the coveted title Pendragon is to hopefully prevent even more war. Briton has bled enough since the Romans. And I like to think I am a decent enough king. I would do what I could to rule Briton justly."

"Ye're a wonderful king." My voice grew soft. "All of Briton will be lucky to have ye, once united."

"Thank you Fionna. I'm sure life is quite different here than the home of your father and clansman you've left behind. I hope you've found your time pleasant."

"Most pleasant." I swallowed, trying not to think of Galahad's honey-blond head between my legs. "In truth, I enjoy not being a princess—with the eyes of everyone constantly upon me."

"I doubt they're looking just because you're a princess," Arthur said, rubbing the stubble on his jaw.

I looked at him in mock confusion. "Why King Arthur, whatever could ye mean?"

He blushed and, for a shy heartbeat, appeared a young man and not a battle-worn king. A small smile flitted across his lips with the amusement on my face. "I promised Percival I would make you wear your helm all the time, so as not to distract us."

"And a sackcloth shift!" Percival called out from behind us. The young man was eavesdropping. I swiveled in my saddle to stick my tongue out at him, and he grinned, giving a little bow in his saddle while Galahad laughed beside him.

"Very well," I said. "Though my helm pinches, I'll wear it, so long as ye all wear yers too."

"Why Fionna . . ." Lancelot and his mount took the spot on my left, flanking me and Arthur. "Does this mean you find us distracting too?"

A smile twitched on my lips. "I think there's a reason why Arthur's feasts are attended by two women to every one man."

"Hmm," Lancelot seemed to ponder. "I hadn't noticed."

"That's because when ye bed one, she becomes invisible to ye!" Percival called.

"Percival." Lancelot turned back toward the other man. "I'm in need of a sparring session tonight. I think you are too."

Percival groaned so loud a flock of birds alighted from a nearby copse of trees. "There's no healer for miles!"

"I'll spar with ye, Lancelot," I offered. The man's skill with a blade impressed me, and I wanted to try myself against him.

The playfulness slipped from Lancelot's face, leaving an emotion I couldn't quite read.

"Unless ye're scared."

Lancelot inclined his head, accepting my challenge. "Saved by a woman, Percival," he called back to the other knight.

"Saved by a *knight*," Percival replied. "And a gallant one at that. Fionna can carry me off into the sunset any time."

We made camp in a meadow nestled between a grove of beech trees and a winding stream. The evening was warm, and I laid my bedroll down beside a scattering of wildflowers. The knights made quick work collecting firewood, watering the horses, and arranging bedrolls. Arthur did his chores as cheerfully as any of the knights, reminding me yet again he was no ordinary king. No ordinary man.

After a meal of cured sausage, rye bread, and goat's cheese, Lancelot stood, stretched, and gestured to me. We tramped through the wildflowers together, our swords in hand, and squared off against each other while the setting sun gilded our landscape.

And then, as easily as if he were tying his boots, he came at me.

Lancelot's movements were as smooth as water over the stones of a river—each one flowing into the next. His footing was firm, his stance unshakable. He kept twisting his attacks, working his way around me until the sun glared in my eyes.

"Quit it," I panted, feinting at him and finding only air.

He chuckled. "A smart warrior uses the terrain around them." He attacked, his flashing sword coming at me with one, two, three blows in quick succession.

I bared my teeth, my frustration growing. He was winning. My sword arm felt like a ton of bricks, and sweat poured down my forehead, stinging my eyes. But I was too proud to yield, to admit defeat. I caught sight of a discarded tree branch on the ground and stifled a smile. I danced around him and redoubled my attack, driving him back toward the branch. Closer—closer—our blades met and locked, and we grappled against each other, the veins in his arms straining. I pushed with all my might, and his feet tangled in the branch. My eyes narrowed with victory, only to widen in surprise as he hooked his hand in my sword belt, pulling me down after him.

We hit the ground in a tumble, the meadow's tall grass a screen of golden-green around us. My heart hammered in my chest as his weight settled half atop me; as I realized, this close, his blue eyes were flecked with silver, that he smelled of mint and fresh soap.

Lancelot was looking at me, examining my face, my eyes, my mouth. He brushed a long, white-blonde tendril off my neck, his fingers grazing the soft skin there. For a moment, I thought he was going to kiss me.

But then he pushed himself up, offering me his hand once he stood. "Good fight."

I took his hand, pulling myself to my feet and trying, terribly, to ignore the feel of his calluses against my palm. "Someone once told me that a smart warrior uses the terrain around them."

He snorted, before turning back toward the camp.

I headed to the stream, needing a moment to compose myself, to pull the pieces of myself back together. I splashed cold water on my face, my neck, my chest. I walked back to camp on wobbly legs, knowing that it wasn't the night's exertion that was shaking me. It was this place. This land of caramel sun and sweeping verdant meadows. It was these men. Charming and arresting and playful and kind.

I walked past where the others chatted around the fire, to my bedroll. Tears were prickling my eyes. As I reached my bedroll, I stopped in my tracks. There where my head would lay down to rest, sat a bouquet of bluebells and violets. I didn't know which of the men had left them for me. It didn't matter. I fell to my knees, lifting them up in my shaking fingers. The dam burst within me, and I shattered.

Chapter Twenty-Three

Lancelot

The melodious chirps of robins and goldfinches pulled Lancelot from the cold, rocky ground beneath his bedroll. Upon opening his eyes, his gaze flitted across the campfire's ring of stones and onto Fionna's angelic sleeping form. The white tendrils and corded braids of her hair seemed to glow in the dim light of dawn, her skin smooth and milky as marble. One hand clutched a dagger, tucked neatly under her bedroll, beneath her cheek. The image was so very Fionna. How could a single sight fill him with so much joy and equal parts despair? He heaved a sigh and pushed up, running a hand through his bed-mussed hair.

"Not you too, brother."

Lancelot shifted to look at Arthur. The man pulled his scarlet cloak tighter around his shoulders, then clasped hands around his drawn-up knees. Arthur was studying her too, his eyes drinking her in.

"I wish I could say otherwise," Lancelot admitted.

"Tell me we're not lost," Arthur said, his voice quiet and tender.

"You're not." A stone dropped in Lancelot's gut. Still, he quirked an eyebrow playfully. "The king usually gets the girl."

"Even if that's true, how could I enjoy my life knowing my pursuit deprived my dearest friends of their happiness?"

"I do not know. But these sentiments are why you will remain our dearest friend. No matter what happens."

Arthur squinted up at the lavender and gold brushed sky, a wistful smile crossing his face.

Feeling restless, Lancelot rose to his feet and dusted off his breeches. "Now, let's talk of more pleasant things. Faerie curses and vengeful half-sisters and ex-betrotheds."

Arthur laughed. "As you wish."

The Roman road to Chester was a well-worn route through fertile green farmland and peaceful woods. As their band rode by, deer scattered in their path and herds of sheep watched with placid black eyes. Lancelot reveled in the sun's warm caress on his skin while the cool spring air kissed his cheeks.

He almost felt like himself again.

Here, he could almost forget.

They passed through the shade of beech and maple trees. The filtered light dappled shadows across the mossy, leaf-littered forest floor and craggy stones. This was a place where the fae might govern, but the passing greenery felt friendly, almost welcoming. Lancelot flitted a veiled glance Fionna's way. Not for the first time, he wondered about her. There was something "otherly" about her that reminded him too often of Vivien, his foster mother. Fionna said she didn't possess any sídhe blood, yet she rode through the trees like a faerie queen. Perhaps he only noticed her noble heritage and bearing and nothing more.

The sunlight brightened as the trees thinned. His horse danced for a moment, most likely from the shadows elongating up ahead in the clearing. He shushed his stallion gently and nudged him along. His stallion's ears flattened and his muscles from head to tail quivered, but he obeyed Lancelot. They were just passing out of the forest and into a meadow when Lancelot noticed that Arthur had fallen behind, his horse now pulled to a stop.

Lancelot slowed his horse and turned toward his king. "Arthur?"

Arthur was staring between his horse's ears as if he'd seen a ghost. "I . . . I'm not sure. I just have a strange, unpleasant feeling." He met Lancelot's intense stare and lifted a faint, shaky smile. "I'm fine. Let's go."

Lancelot placed a comforting hand on his skittish horse and considered Arthur's odd premonition.

Some believed that moving from the woods and into the meadow was like leaving the Otherworld. Maybe they had crossed through a forest the fae governed.

He and Arthur rejoined the others, who were waiting a few hundred yards ahead, where they had stopped.

"Everything all right?" Galahad asked.

Arthur nodded, his face still pale.

It wasn't until they crested the next hill that it became clear that everything was most definitely *not* all right. His king—and Lancelot's stallion, for that matter—sensed true.

"My gods," Lancelot said as he surveyed the landscape before him. A river snaked through a checkerboard of farmland below. But everything the river touched seemed to have—*withered*. Dry and cracked crops shaded into the brighter green health of adjacent fields around them. As if the river carried poison, killing everything the tainted water touched. But only in this area. Was the disease spreading?

"What could do this?" Fionna breathed out, her mouth pinched in sorrow.

"Reminds me of old faerie tales about the Formorians," Lancelot said, unable to hide the disgust in his voice while mentioning the ancient enemy of the Túatha dé Danann.

"The Fomhóraigh?" Fionna asked, eyes growing wide.

Arthur didn't answer, kicking his horse into a canter.

The knights followed not too far behind, riding after him toward the blighted fields. As they neared, the destruction became more evident. Dead fish lay on the riverbank, their carcasses bloated and white. The bodies of birds and even a deer who had the misfortune of approaching for a drink littered the affected land.

"The water's been poisoned," Percival said, his eyes wide with horror. "Who would do such a thing?"

But Lancelot knew exactly who. And if Percival thought for a moment, he would too. Morgana. Elaine. Morgause. And their bloody curse. A curse on the building elements of Caerleon. A curse of destruction.

Lancelot swallowed the bile rising in his throat. This destruction was a result of his recklessness. His choice. He memorized it, taking in each withered blade of grass, each dead, glassy eye rotting on the bank. This was the cost of betraying a fae. This was the cost of a faerie curse. This is what would happen—and worse—if he gave in to his weakness and slept with Fionna. This. This. *This.* He beat himself with the word, with the images, an intentional self-flagellation. He wanted the wounds, the memories, to dig deep. So deep that he wouldn't forget the next time his cock stirred in Fionna's presence.

Arthur had dismounted and was kneeling at the edge of the blighted line, his fingers brushing the stalks of spring wheat that still lived.

A crow cawed loudly in the trees behind them and Lancelot jumped. He swiveled in his saddle and regarded the bird, its black-feathered head cocked to one side, seeming to watch him through one glassy eye. Icy fingers of fear crawled up his spine as he remembered Morgana fleeing from his chamber, leaping out the window and into the night air, borne aloft on dark crow wings. He shook himself. Crows were commonplace. The bird was just here for the carrion below, a decaying feast along the riverbank.

"What did this?" Fionna asked, summoning his attention back toward the group. Her voice was hard and angry. "We will kill them for it."

Arthur stood slowly. "I don't know," he said, turning back toward them. Lancelot hid his surprise when the king sent a knowing look toward him, Percival, and Galahad. He didn't want to share the truth of the curse with Fionna. Why? The other knights seemed to understand Arthur's silent admonition and stayed quiet.

Arthur pulled himself back into the saddle and nudged his horse forward with his heels. "But rest assured, we'll find out."

They rode in silence the rest of the day, each knight in quiet contemplation. Sorrow warred with anger and guilt within Lancelot. And somewhere, deep down, a kernel of hope. Merlin had seen a way out. With Fionna's help, they could find the Blessed Grail. And, if they found the Grail, they could fix this. They had all grown distracted by her beauty, by the light she infused in their little brotherhood. The river was the clear reminder they had all needed. This wasn't a game. It wasn't fantasy. This was life and death, and their enemies were playing for keeps.

The village of Ewloe which, according to Percival, bordered Lord Bronn's manor house, appeared first as a smudge of smoke on the horizon two days later. Three days in the saddle with the earth for a bed and stars for a blanket. But as they approached, the smoke proved black and oily, not the cheerful puffing of wood-burning hearths.

"Something's wrong here," Galahad rumbled.

Arthur pulled Excalibur from its sheath and the others followed suit.

They rode into the village at a slow walk, their horses shying from the strange smells. As soon as they saw the first body, Lancelot's spirits sank. This village had been attacked.

"Skies," he hissed under his breath.

No building was spared and, it seemed, no villager either. The thatched homes had burned to ash and rubble, many with their inhabitants still inside.

Fionna swung down from the saddle, her arm thrown over her nose to ward off the smell. "A day ago, perhaps?" she said. "The fires would be out by now, if the attacked had happened before then. And these bodies aren't too ripe yet."

"They seem pretty ripe to me," Percival said, his face white as snow.

Fionna knelt in a patch of charred grass, pulling an axe from the back of a woman's body, and then examined the wood-carved handle and blade marks. "Flaming hells," she swore, standing.

"What is it?" Arthur asked, dismounting and

striding over.

She held out the axe to him. "See this detailing on the handle? It's Dál nAraidi. And this symbol? The blackthorn tree? I know this clann. It's the Uí Tuírtri."

"Who are they?" Arthur asked.

Fionna bit her lip, seeming to hesitate. "They're a rival clann in Lough Insholin who wants to rule in Antrim, including the lands of Allán. I know the leader, Donal O'Lynn. He's a bastard. But . . . I don't know why his fianna are raiding here. I didn't even know they'd been to Briton."

Lancelot narrowed his eyes. Fionna's explanation rang false. Did she know more than she was letting on? Yet, Arthur knew more than he was telling Fionna. Perhaps there was a good reason for her to keep her own secrets.

Arthur threw the axe into the ground, where the blade stuck, quivering. "They picked a fight with the wrong king. The Kingdom of Gwynedd cannot rid themselves of these pests, but I will. If they're only a day's ride, we'll take them." His words rolled and boomed like thunder.

"Arthur," Percival said. "If the raiders came here . . . they might have visited Bronn's manor. Spoils to be had, in a house like that, ye ken."

Arthur's skin sickened to a greenish pallor. "Do you think . . ." He looked at the body by his feet, pale and unmoving.

Percival grimaced. "I think we better find out."

Chapter Twenty-Four

Arthur

Lord Bronn's house was a large, sturdy lime-washed cob and black timber manor with thatched roof, surrounded by stone walls, even as they approached, Arthur's senses rang in alarm. Adrenaline coursed through his body. The grounds were too quiet.

Fionna's hand rested on a dagger at her side; Percival rode with a sword in his hand.

A bird burst into flight from a nearby bush, swooping low across the dirt trail before them. Arthur jumped in his saddle, spooking his horse, Llamrei.

Galahad's horse danced in reply. "We're a cheerful bunch, aren't we?" the big warrior muttered.

They rounded the last curve and the manor's front came into view. Arthur let out a muffled curse. The wide oak door hung off its hinges, splintered and cracked.

The knights dismounted and pulled their swords from their scabbards. They crept into the manor.

Signs of raiders were everywhere. Mud trekked onto the plush woven carpets, dishes smashed to the floor, the lime-washed walls singed with smoke.

Up the stairs they went, one at a time, with Arthur leading the way. Then he saw it. A booted foot, poking out from around the corner.

His heart sank.

The man was broad and well-muscled, with thick dark hair and a neatly-trimmed beard. His brown eyes stared wide and vacant, frozen in death. A dark bloom of dried blood colored his white shirt.

"Lord Bronn is dead," Arthur said, his voice dull. The first lead he had received in years, and the man was dead.

Percival knelt by Lord Bronn's face and gently closed his eyes.

"Damn it!" Arthur cursed, swooping a hand across a nearby bookshelf. Papers and books scattered amongst the raid's detritus.

Fionna recoiled slightly at his outburst but, in that moment, he didn't care. He leaned his forehead against the bookshelf, closing his eyes. They had seemed so close. First Fionna, next finding the letter from Lord Bronn—a clue to the Grail mystery that had haunted his family for decades. Veiled hope had blossomed inside him, too powerful a feeling for him to remain guarded. And now that hope was dead, cut down as easily as poor Lord Bronn.

"We'll find another way to reach the Grail," Percival said softly.

Arthur heaved a sigh. "The first lead we have had in years. We can't wait years to find another. Caerleon can't." His frustration and disappointment kindled into rage within him like sparks striking dry tinder. These Dál nAraidi, this clan, had sailed into Wales and England and killed and maimed and took. He was supposed to protect these people as their High King. To defend this land, regardless of whether the Kingdoms recognized him as their Head Dragon. But he had failed. The people of Ewloe had died, and who knew where these Dál nAraidi snakes were slithering to next.

Arthur spun to the others, who stood mutely around the room. "We ride," he said. "We find the men who did this and we make them pay. I will not have these Irish bastards returning to their shores and gloating that Wales is ripe for the picking. Mount up." He wanted to rage and thunder and plunge Excalibur deep into the gut of whatever raider did this. Those men had taken something precious from him and they would pay for it. With their lives.

"No," Fionna said, her voice sharp as steel.

"What?" Arthur growled.

"Not until ye tell me why this Grail is so important. There's something unspoken between ye, and it's thick as sap. As much as I want to kill Uí Tuírtri, I'm not plunging into battle without knowing why."

"Isn't it enough that these Irish slaughtered my people?" Arthur asked.

"It would be, if that's the only reason we're here. But it's not. If I am to fight at yer side, Arthur Pendragon, if I am yer knight, I deserve to know the truth."

The other knights exchanged wide-eyed, pregnant gazes.

"She's right, Yer Majesty," Percival said. Arthur opened his mouth to tell Percival to shut it, but the fool man kept talking, his words coming faster. "Either we trust her or we dinnae. The Fates brought her to us so she could help with this quest. Let her help us."

Arthur ground his teeth in frustration. He didn't know exactly why he had been keeping the secret of Morgana's curse from Fionna. No, that wasn't true. The reason was his pride. He didn't want to admit to this beautiful stranger that he was fallible. That his kingdom was cursed and, by extension, so was he. But Percival was right. He had knighted Fionna. Excalibur had shown her to be the one. He couldn't keep her on the outside anymore.

"Fine, Percival." Arthur's shoulders sagged. "You tell her. But on the way. I'm not letting these dogs get one more minute on us."

"Should we bury him?" Galahad asked as they trampled down the stairs and out into the fresh air.

Arthur took in a shuddering breath, letting the cool air fill his lungs—banishing the oppressive stench of death. "Yes. On the way back. We can't risk losing the raiders."

The knights mounted, and Arthur kicked Llamrei into a gallop. Sometimes he felt that his horse was his oldest and truest friend. She sensed his mood better than most. And, right now, he wanted to be borne away by Llamrei's powerful strides, to let the whip of the wind wipe away his worries and fears and failures.

If only resolving matters were that easy.

Behind him, he knew Percival was shouting at Fionna, explaining to her the messy sordid tale of Arthur's failure as a diplomat. His half-sister's wrath and her sisters' cruel magic. Lancelot's fool mistake, falling in love with a faerie, and then his even worse mistake of falling out of love with one. He kicked Llamrei's heaving flanks with his boots, urging her forward, the landscape bleeding into a blur of green grass and golden fields and blue sky.

And then she was beside him, her white-blonde braid trailing behind her like a pennant, her dappled grey mare matching Llamrei stride for stride.

"How could ye not tell me?" she shouted at him. The wind's pull almost stole her words from his ears. "Did ye not think I needed to know?"

"You know now," he said, not able to confess to her the real reason, to admit that sometimes he wasn't an infallible king, but just a man.

"Percival had to convince ye," she said accusingly. "Ye should have told me yerself. Ye should have chosen to trust me."

"And do you not keep your own counsel, knight?" He needed to sting her back, push her away, keep her from getting too close.

She recoiled as if struck. Nor did she shout back a clever retort.

"Tell me of this clan. What do I need to know?"

"They bleed as red as any men. Seems that's all ye care to know," she said, before reigning in her mare and falling behind him.

Arthur slowed Llamrei as well, though he stayed before the other knights. The raiders' trail wasn't hard to follow, with a dozen men on horseback heavy laden with treasures but, in his haste, he didn't want to miss a turn or change in the trail. His mind was a whirlwind of three thoughts—Lord Bronn and the Grail, the crimson need to cut down these Irish for what they had done, and Fionna. Always Fionna. Had he driven her away by keeping the secret of the faerie curses from her? Would she forgive him? And what would he do, if she didn't? The very thought of being without her felt crippling. Felt like a cloud passing before the sun. She had become a firm fixture of his court. He didn't know why she had fought in his tourney, but he knew this: she belonged here. With them. He would convince her of that.

The whicker of horses was his first warning that they were coming upon the raiders' camp. The smell of campfire smoke was the second. A small, cautious part of him knew that he should reign in Llamrei and survey the camp with a measured, dispassionate eye. But that part of him was an ant compared to the lion of his anger. A need roared within him to rip apart these men for what they had done to that village, for killing Lord Bronn and murdering Arthur's chance at finding the Grail.

And so, he urged Llamrei forward and ignored the muffled curses from his knights behind him. He pulled Excalibur from its sheath and rode toward the Uí Tuírtri clan, a savage smile on his face.

Chapter Twenty-Five

Fionna

I had a ritual I always followed before battle. I would wash my face and hands, and carefully paint on lines with blue woad in the runic patterm that marked my clann—Beith, the silver birch. With blue stained onto my fingertips, I would then pray to The Morrígan, sister goddesses of war and fate, that my sword would swing true, that my shield would hold fast, marking each weapon with Beith runes as well. Afterward, I would sit in silence, if even for a few moments, feeling what it was to be inside my body, fully aware of the breath in my lungs and the blood in my veins. These were gifts that were fleeting, and I never felt that lesson so keenly as before battle. Small and fragile and mortal. After battle, I thrummed with power like the sister goddesses themselves, invincible and terrible.

But not today.

Today there wasn't woad or prayers or quiet contemplation. There wasn't even a plan. Today there was a wild gallop into a force of men three times our size. If this is how these knights fought, I had a thing or two to teach them.

And, today, there was a whirlwind of anger and emotion, hurt and betrayal, gut-twisting guilt. Arthur had lied to me from the moment I had arrived here. But I had done the same. Who was one liar to judge another? I needed time to think. To scream and shout into the uncaring breeze and pound a sparring strawman with my sword until my shoulder ached from the force of it.

I would have no chance to do any of it. Caerleon was cursed. And if Merlin and Percival were to be believed, I was a key to undoing that curse and finding the Grail—the one item that could stop the creeping elf-shot sickness that was overtaking this lush land. And I was leaving. Stealing Arthur's most prized possession, his sovereign-blessed connection to this land, and running with my tail between my legs back to Ireland.

Was I really willing to do that?

Could I truly abandon these men and leave Arthur's entire kingdom to its fate? Was that worthy punishment for a lie? Only the goddesses knew. I had told myself I would pay any price to ransom my father and sister back. But now I grasped for another way. How had things become so twisted so quickly?

All these thoughts spun in my head, a blizzard of emotions where the quiet calm before battle should be. I tried to focus on the force before me, to absorb the details that might save my life.

The Uí Tuírtri were camped in a sparse wooded bluff overlooking the River Dee. Their left side was flanked by a trickling stream that poured over the bluff in a waterfall down to the river's banks, while the right was guarded by a pile of large boulders that were arranged as if they had been tossed there a thousand years ago by a Fomhórach, an Underworld giant. This area was a smart and defensible position and, in the end, Arthur's mad dash was a fairly effective strategy.

We were amongst them—swords swinging and hooves trampling—before the sixteen raiders were hardly up from around the fires, scrambling for their weapons. I recognized one warrior, a tall burly bear of a man with long hair tightly braided down his back. I registered all this in the instant before Excalibur speared him through. The blade's scintillating length blazed in the afternoon sun like a sacred relic.

Then the clannsmen seemed all the same with sneering faces and flashing teeth and eyes shining manically with the frenzy of sudden battle.

I sliced one man across the back as he went for his weapons. I whirled in my saddle and stabbed another through his throat before he slashed at Zephyr's belly. I vaulted off my charger and then whacked her flank with the flat of my blade to send her running. She'd linger nearby for me when the battle was done. The quarters were too small to fight on horseback, and I wouldn't risk her.

Arthur and the other knights had dismounted too. They now fought like the Danish berserkers I had seen in Aghanravel's neighboring Norse settlements. Their swords swung so fast that I could hardly see them. Drops of red arced through the air as Dál nAraidi clannsmen fell, their leather armor soaked through, their lifeblood spilling into disbelieving fingers.

And as quickly as that, we had cut down half the clannsmen, leaving eight. These men were the best of their clann, grizzled warriors with years of fighting seasons under their belt. Professional killers who lived for the sword and died for glory. They faced the knights with a ferocity that I think startled even Arthur out of his battle haze.

A big man came at me with a Danish axe and a blood-curdling shout in Irish, "Bua nó bás!" I recognized his words as the Uí Tuírtri clann motto, meaning "victory or death."

I screamed back at him as I brought my sword up to meet the fury of his blow, wishing I had my sturdy wooden shield. His shout was every warrior's motto, in a way. I would win today, or I would die.

I lashed out with a vicious kick to the man's gut. He stumbled back, providing me a moment to take stock. Lancelot was across the camp by the boulders, fighting two men. The dark knight's sword struck fast and deadly, slashing the men on arms and thighs, bleeding them from a dozen different places. Arthur fought two men as well; Galahad was grappling with one over the fire. And Percival had the last man— they slipped and splashed on the slick, mossy stones of the river.

No, not the last man. That was seven.

I rolled out of the way as my opponent swung

at me again. His huge Danish axe's blade sliced into the ground until buried. My eyes fixed on the man creeping around behind Percival, raising his axe to throw.

"Percival!" I screamed, and then pulled one of my throwing daggers from its sheath along my forearm. The small blade loosed in an instant, borne aloft by muscle and whispered prayers. I watched as the dagger plunged into the man's chest. A relieved smile crossed my face when the raider stumbled backward. But there was no time for relieved smiles in battle. I realized a split second too late that I had lost sight of my opponent—that I couldn't account for the position of his battle axe's blade. Instinct possessed me and I jerked sharp to the right, knowing I needed to move somewhere, anywhere.

It was that instinct that saved me. Had I waited a mere second more, the axe blade would have severed my spine rather than glance off my shoulder's muscle. Still, pain exploded through my side as the blade rent leather and flesh. A tangled scream escaped from my mouth, so high and animal I hardly recognized it.

I rolled to see the clannsman's eyes gleaming with the light of his killing blow, his certainty that he had me beat. But all I could think was how I couldn't let them all down. My father and sister, Arthur and the knights. If I lived, I would have to choose, but if I died, I failed them all.

I was on the ground, the Uí Tuírtri warrior looming above me. So, I did the only thing I could think of. I pulled out the wicked little dagger from my boot, and lunged forward, burying the blade into the meat of his groin. He bellowed with rage and pain as I yanked down in a jagged slice, seeking the lifeblood of his artery. Warm blood gushed over my hands and his axe thunked to the ground beside him. I shoved him away from me and he toppled backward, writhing in pain and shock.

I looked about for my knights, wild with fear. Had I missed an attack? Had something befallen any of the four while I was too distracted to help? One by one, my eyes drank in the sight of them. Percival, his chest heaving as he wiped his sword on the grass and moss, his opponent now face down in the river below him. Lancelot, pulling his sword out of a man's chest. Arthur, running a shaking hand over his short hair. Galahad. Where was Galahad? The world seemed to tilt and I blinked through the fog as Galahad ran toward me. Wisps of honey-gold hair that escaped from their tie floated about his head like a halo. Relief welled in me.

They were all safe.

They were all alive.

"Fionna," Galahad's hand was beneath my head, cradling my neck. The other roamed over my body, checking for wounds. "There's so much blood—" he breathed. His voice sounded distant and thin.

"Not mine," I croaked. Everything felt faint and far away.

His hand was roaming over my back now, and came away wet with red. "And this?" he asked.

"Oh. That's . . . mine," I managed. My tongue was thick in my mouth, heavy with fatigue.

The other knights were by my side now. My vision blurred and swirled until all I saw was their colors. The colors I knew by heart. The blue ice of Lancelot's eyes, the grass-green of Arthur's. The copper of Percival's hair, the tawny warmth of Galahad's skin.

"Fionna, stay with us," Arthur said.

I wanted to do as he asked. I wanted to honor them, please them, protect them. I wanted to love them. But I couldn't. I felt consciousness slipping from me. Their colors draining into darkness. Then darkness carried me away.

Chapter Twenty-Six

Galahad

Fionna was bleeding. Fionna was injured. These were the words sounding in a loop in Galahad's head. This could not be.

He cradled her body to his chest as they moved away from the Uí Tuírtri camp, a few hundred yards up the river. They didn't want to move her far, but none of them were eager to stay amongst the dead.

"Here," Galahad called as they reached a sun dappled clearing next to a flat expanse of slow-moving river. "Lay out a bedroll."

It was Arthur himself who pulled his bedroll off his black mare, unfurling the hide layers at Galahad's feet. The other knights' faces were pinched with worry and fear, but none more so than Arthur.

Good, Galahad thought savagely. It was Arthur's furious dash into the enemy camp that placed Fionna into this mess. Let him feel the guilt keenly.

Fionna moaned as Galahad lay her down as gently as he could on the bedroll. She looked ghostly, her skin pale and flecked with blood. As if all the color had drained from her. Except crimson.

"Someone fetch water, someone start a fire so we can boil it, and someone retrieve my medical kit from my saddlebag," Galahad ordered, not looking up from his administrations to see who was jumping to which task. He was no healer, but his mother hadn't had eight children or a farm full of animals without some meager medical skill, and Galahad had always watched by her side, soaking up her instruction. As a page boy, he learned even more animal husbandry tricks.

There were times his limited medical and sewing skills and easy way with people of lower classes singled him out among the nobles of Arthur's court. From birth, they had the privilege of coin to hire tailors, apothecaries, and men of medicine. But right now, Galahad was grateful for his low-born knowledge.

Percival dropped to his knees at Fionna's side and delivered Galahad's meager kit of medical supplies. "Will she fare well?"

"Don't know yet," Galahad replied, keeping his voice impassive. She would be all right. She had to be. Fionna was the fiercest woman he had ever known. It would take more than a nick with an axe to end her.

Galahad unbuckled her leather armor, gently pulling the plates and guards from around her arms. "Help me turn her?" he asked Percival.

Together, they gently rolled Fionna onto her stomach, revealing the bloom of red blood on her white shirt.

Percival bit his lip, his eyes wild. "Looks bad," he said in a hushed whisper.

"Percival," Galahad said. He needed the lad out of here, distracted. "Fionna's horse is missing. The mare should be around here. She'll be beside herself, if she wakes and we haven't found her. Could you—"

Percival sprang to his feet, eager for a task. "I'll find her."

"Fionna will be in your debt," Galahad said, but the young man was already bounding toward his own charger.

Galahad ripped Fionna's shirt in two, revealing the slender arrow of her spine, the smooth stretch of pale skin as well as the muscles of her back.

Arthur had the fire going now and Lancelot had set a pot of water on a stand above it.

Galahad used his knife to cut strips from Fionna's shirt, silently apologizing for mangling her tunic so. They'd buy her a hundred new tunics when this was over. He folded a scrap neatly and pressed the linen to the wound, not wanting to examine the injury until he had washed his hands.

Lancelot knelt at Galahad's side and reached out with inquisitive fingers toward Fionna's wound, then let his hand fall. "Your assessment?"

"The wound is deep, but the location was lucky. The blade cut into muscle, but muscle will heal. The biggest risk will be infection. If I clean the laceration well and stitch the skin up, she should be fine."

"The slice isn't deep enough to pack with moss first?"

"No, I don't believe so. But if she continues to bleed after stitching, we will pack her wound."

Lancelot nodded, relaxing perceptibly.

It was almost painful, the way Galahad's heart twisted in his chest when he looked at her, the longing he felt, this unquestionable need for her. The exquisite taste he'd known the other night had only kindled his need all the brighter.

"She looks like an angel when she's like this, doesn't she?" Galahad asked.

"An angel of death," Lancelot whispered.

Arthur appeared with the pot of water, and Lancelot's odd response was forgotten. The three men went to work—washing and sterilizing the strips of cloth, cleansing Fionna's back, and finally, with clean, lye-scrubbed hands, Galahad bent over Fionna's back with a needle and gut and began to sew.

As he pierced Fionna's skin with the needle, she exploded awake with an anguished scream, struggling beneath Galahad. He pushed one forearm to her back to hold her still. "A little help!"

Arthur sat on her legs and Lancelot grabbed her shoulders as she cried out with a moan of pain.

"Fionnabhair . . ." Lancelot crouched low while still holding her, peering into Fionna's eyes, just inches from her. "Be still, warrior. Galahad is stitching your wound."

Her muscles relaxed and unclenched as Lancelot's words seemed to sink in. She let out a hiss of pain as Galahad pulled the needle and string through her skin, but held still.

"It will be all right," Lancelot murmured to her, stroking his fingers down her face before tucking a small braid behind her ear. "You will be fine."

Arthur shifted his weight off her to sit in the hard dirt, his face buried in his hands.

Galahad continued to sew, while Lancelot whispered soothing words to Fionna, and while Arthur buried himself deep into the despair of his own thoughts.

Galahad was wrapping Fionna's wound when Percival reappeared in the clearing, leading Fionna's dappled mare by the reins. Percival swung down and led the horses toward the river to drink. "How is she?"

"Good," Galahad murmured, tying off the bandage. Finished, he pulled a blanket over her sleeping form and then strode over to the river beside Percival to wash his hands. "She'll be fine."

"When I saw all the blood on her . . ." Percival trailed off with a shaky smile. For once, the lad seemed lost for words. He tied the two horses to a nearby tree, before both he and Percival walked to join Arthur and Lancelot around the fire.

Percival, as usual, talked as if unaware of the tension brewing between the men. "The Kingdom of

Gwynedd has plenty of warriors and enough ego to slay thousands of invaders. If they requested aid to defend the River Dee from raiders, why were the villages left unprotected?"

Arthur peered up from his perch beside the fire but remained silent.

"Perhaps these were not the raiders spoken of in the missive." Galahad volunteered. "Could be the Northern Lords and their warriors were already caring for the problem, not expecting a second set of raiders."

Lancelot tossed a twig into the flame. "Or the note was false."

"A fake request for help?" Percival asked, head angled in confusion. "Not verra sporting of Gwynedd."

"Not from Gwynedd," Lancelot drawled in irritation. "Obviously."

Arthur cleared his throat and nervously chanced a look their way. "You believe Tintagel is behind the Irish raiders?"

"They did ask for my head in a box and they knew of Fionna only one day after her knighting."

Their king closed his eyes tight as his face reddened.

Galahad's ire rose at the sight. "Arthur—"

"You don't need to say anything." Arthur held up a hand. "I know. I put us all at risk today. I was angry and I let reason give way to emotion. And, for that, I am truly sorry."

But Galahad didn't want to let his king off so easily. Fionna almost died. This reality wasn't something a simple apology could wipe away. "You can't risk her like that."

A strange look came over Arthur's face. "I value each of your lives over even my own. But I am king and you are my knights. Fionna included. Sometimes I will have to risk her."

"But she isn't *just* a knight," Galahad rumbled, his fingers curling into a fist.

"What are you saying?" Arthur asked.

"He's saying he's in love with her." Lancelot threw up his hands. "The whole lot of you are."

"That's the pot calling the kettle black, don't you think?" Galahad retorted. "I've never seen you push a woman away the way you've done to Fionna. That can only mean one thing. You're afraid to let her get close."

Lancelot was as mysterious as his fae foster mother when it came to some things, but not women. When it came to women, the man was as simple as a strawman. He wanted them, he bedded them, he left them. And since Lancelot hadn't bedded Fionna yet, he must still be in stage one.

"Or, maybe I learned my lesson with Morgana." Lancelot threw a small stick into the fire and then glared at Galahad.

"Is that why you were whispering to her while Galahad stitched her up?" Arthur pointed out.

Lancelot rolled his eyes. "I was calming her down. I would have done that for any of you."

"I dinnae recall Lancelot ever murmuring sweet nothings in my ear," Percival said. "What about ye, Galahad? Arthur?"

"Nope," Galahad said, unable to hide his victory from his icy sword-brother. His grin grew wider when a muscle pulsed in the other man's jaw.

Lancelot stood, his expression dark.

"No," Arthur commanded. "Sit. You're not walking away from this conversation. Any form of attraction to Fionna concerns all of us."

Lancelot dropped back down, crossing his arms before him, and then stared into the crackling fire.

"Well, I'm definitely in love with the lass," Percival said, chipper as usual. "I'm not ashamed to admit my feelings. I'll gladly wipe the floor with all of ye in the contest for her heart."

Arthur sighed. "She's captured my heart as well, despite my better judgment."

Galahad took a breath, his thoughts warring within him. Normally, he would keep the truth of what had happened with he and Fionna to himself—he wasn't a man like Lancelot, who liked to kiss and tell. But if the other men thought they had a fair claim to Fionna, it was only right to tell them that they had missed their chance.

"I'm afraid to break the news to you lads, but Fionna has already made her choice. She came to my room the night before we left Caerleon," Galahad said.

The other knights fell silent, shocked expressions on their faces.

Galahad struggled to keep another grin off his face. He would be lying to himself if he didn't admit that some part of him was pleased to stun them into silence.

"Did you—" Arthur tripped over his words, his mouth open and closing like a fish gasping for water.

Galahad shook his head. "No, but I made sure the lass enjoyed herself, if you catch my drift."

Percival apparently did not. "What do ye mean?" He leaned forward, his eyes wide.

Lancelot cuffed Percival over the head, but the gesture was gentle. "We'll tell you later."

Arthur furrowed his brows, seeming to pull his kingly mantle around himself. "She kissed me too. We don't know . . . what her attentions mean. What she wants. We vowed we wouldn't let her come between us. We let her choose. Maybe she'll choose Galahad and maybe she won't." Arthur's eyes met Galahad's, and there was a challenge there so powerful that Galahad recoiled slightly.

Arthur wanted Fionna, that much was clear. And who was he, the son of a Danish blacksmith, to stand between a king and what he wanted? Galahad knew that he should back down and step aside. But didn't he deserve to be happy too? If Fionna preferred Galahad, why should Arthur have her, just because he was born with noble blood and crowned King of all Briton?

"We let her choose," Galahad said.

The other men nodded.

"Trouble," Lancelot mumbled under his breath. "The lot of them."

The four knights turned and looked at Fionna's quiet sleeping form, her white-blonde hair peeking out from beneath the blanket. Galahad didn't envy her the choice. Or the fallout.

Chapter Twenty-Seven

Fionna

Hot pain rippled through my shoulder as my eyelids fluttered open. I gulped in a startled breath before the pain stole the air from my lungs. Darkness filled my space. As did a strange, unnatural silence. Not even the low crackle of embers drifted to my pricked ears. Where was I?

Unsure, I remained still, not wanting to alert anyone nearby to my return to consciousness. I glimpsed a sliver of light in the corner of my eye and turned toward it, achingly slow, gritting my teeth until I locked onto the source. A narrow band of moonlight crept through large, heavy drapes and across the wooden floor, illuminating timber-constructed walls. Mentally, I took stock of my surroundings. I was in a spacious room atop a luxurious feathered bed. My armor was on the floor beside me, and a man slept in a separate bed across from me.

My heart thundered at the many possibilities. Our

ambush defeated O'Lynn's men. Why wasn't I under the stars on a bedroll beside my fellow knights? Was I still with my knights?

The word "my" twisted my insides. I had no right to claim those I would destroy. And, yet, I found the treacherous organ in my chest equally as treacherous as the woman I would become.

Memories flashed in my mind as the last thought spurred my rapid pulse—of Galahad sewing my wound shut, of Lancelot cupping my face and whispering words of encouragement, of Arthur burying his face in his knees, as if ashamed. The only face I couldn't remember was Percival's. Did he live? He must. I would know.

And then I felt the knowing ache, the sharp pang bleating behind my ribs. Not for Percival, but for them all. These men had wedged their way into an unknown chamber of my heart and this occupation, this residency was almost more than I could bear. Pushing up with my good arm, I clenched my jaw and rolled to a seated position. My breath came quick and heavy after such a simple task. But the pain was welcome compared to the breaking of my heart. How was I to do this? I forced myself to turn from my haunting thoughts to the body in the bed across from me.

Pale silvered fingers of light caressed the planes of the man's face, and I relaxed. Even dusted in moonlight, Arthur appeared boyish, all freckles and muscle, hair cut short but long enough to be disheveled by sleep. Such a contrast to the large presence he commanded when awake. My gaze trailed the length of him, uncovered and still fully armored. Except Excalibur, which no longer hung from his hip, but rested upright against the bed near his head.

"Goddess no," I whispered under my breath. I wasn't ready, not while injured. But when would I find a better opportunity? If my instincts proved true, we were back in Lord Bronn's fortress, which meant the Irish Sea was only a few hours up the River Dee from the port in Chester. I could hire a sailing vessel and be on my way long before the men awoke from their battle and travel fatigue.

Inching from the bed, I crept over my armor and tip-toed toward Arthur. My hands shook as hard as an untested warrior facing her first blood-stained field. This was all wrong; I should have prepared, gone through my ritual before I faced battle—even a fight with myself. My injured shoulder screamed similar sentiments with each step. Too late. I could brush the faerie sword with my fingertips this very moment. Just one more step and . . . cold metal branded my palm with guilt. Arthur would lose his gifted sovereignty as king. His land and people would suffer until a new king was appointed by the Otherworld.

And, yet, my father's land and people suffered *now*, and for similar reasons. Brin Allán's sovereignty was in question, for what king is taken from battle? Better to fall on his own sword than become paraded, tortured, and demeaned by his enemy.

Excalibur glinted in a pocket of moonlight as I used every breadth of control to lift the steel and jeweled scabbard. A shudder dragged long, jagged nails down my spine and I fell to my knees as gracefully as possible, my face contorted in a grimace. Pain seared down my arm and I nearly dropped the sword. Excalibur was too heavy for me to carry. Or perhaps the weight was in my mind—the weight of power over kings and men and land.

"Fionna?"

I whipped my gaze toward Arthur and stilled.

His face was mere inches from mine. Sleep softened the lines around his mouth and eyes, and he appeared so young without the weight of duty on him. So vulnerable. So incredibly beautiful, as if each feature were hand carved by the gods.

"Mmm, you smell of heaven and earth," he murmured, his eyes fluttering closed. Then, to my horror, he adjusted closer to the bed's edge and reached out. With eyes still closed, his fingers touched my cheek and slid to my mouth—as if he had touched me a thousand times. As if he always found me, even when separated by darkness. "With your permission, a kiss?" His voice held the same moonlight illuminating the hard lines of his armored body.

My thoughts tumbled like racing leaves in a black wind as a whirlpool of dread formed in my already soured gut. I wasn't sure how to respond, how to fight the shiver of desire coursing through me. His hand cradled my cheek and pulled me closer. His breath pulsed on my lips.

My mouth parted in anticipation, eyes closing, body leaning forward, wanting to feel the soft warmth of his lips on mine.

Tipped off balance, I dropped the sword. Metal clanked on the wooden floor and I bit back a curse.

Arthur's eyes flew open and he instinctually grasped for the sword no longer by his side. Not finding Excalibur, he jolted upright, his attention snapping wildly onto me.

My heart galloped through my veins as I knelt before him, hands now empty. At least I didn't wear my armor, an oversight that was now a blessing. Forcing myself to breathe, I pulled my gaze up to his and prayed that the guilt wasn't plain in my eyes.

A worried expression flitted across his face while he picked up and then rested his blade against the timber wall. "Did you tear your stitches?"

"I don't think so."

He scrubbed calloused hands over his handsome face before they fell to his lap. "Are you in . . . pain?"

"A little."

Even in the shadows I could see a blush color his stubbled cheeks. Did he think I approached his bed for pleasures? The sharp pang returned to my chest as I held my king's humbled gaze. I would steal away his inheritance and he looked at me as if I were his very salvation.

"Where are we?" I somehow managed to ask.

"Lord Bronn's estate." Arthur swallowed and blinked back shyness. "We buried him this afternoon."

"Ye stayed by my side . . . "

"Yes," he breathed. "I caused your injury with my foolish anger." He looked like he wanted to say more but didn't. Instead, he took my hand in his and bowed his head. "I am so sorry, Fionna. Please forgive me."

The vise in my chest ratcheted even tighter. "I am a warrior and I swore upon my life to follow ye into battle, King Arthur Pendragon."

A sad smile played across his lips as he stared at my hand in his.

"In Ireland, men do not fuss over women so," I continued when he didn't offer a reply. "We are their equals, not a delicate object to protect from harm's way. Not unless that is what the lass desires."

Arthur bashfully met my gaze once more. "I fuss for other reasons." Then his gaze dipped to my lips before he looked away, whispering, "I dreamed of you consenting to a kiss just now and I awake to find you real and near as if . . . as if you—"

"Almost kissed ye?"

"This guilt I carry over your pain is mine to bear." The voice of a king returned and I almost flinched. "You may be my sworn warrior, but I am responsible for you, for all of my knights." His shoulders slumped and his fingers gripped mine tighter, then he lowered his voice to an intimate whisper. "If I could, I would take your pain as my own, Princess Fionnabhair Allán. I would have you know only pleasure and happiness."

Tears burned the back of my eyes. Though the gesture seared hot across my shoulder, I rested my head against his leg. Never, in all my years, had I yielded myself before a man in such a way. But, as I knelt before my king, before a piece of my heart, I only wanted him to know pleasure and happiness too.

I blinked as the tears threatened to roll down my

cheeks. My shoulders began to shake. Gently, Arthur lifted my face until our gazes touched.

"You *are* in pain," he said simply.

I was, but not in the way he believed. I couldn't confess my dilemma or how the very thought shattered me. Nor how my sister and father held captive by O'Lynn already tormented me until I wanted to double over in agony. I didn't want to think of it. I didn't want to think of anything.

Raising my hand, I cupped his face and whispered, "Help me to know only pleasure and happiness."

He sucked in a quiet breath.

"I give ye permission, Arthur."

Our breaths mingled as we held each other's faces. Vulnerability pooled in Arthur's gaze and I understood. He didn't give himself easily to another, not intimately at least. The realization lanced me anew.

Taking great care to not aggravate my wound, he tenderly scooped beneath my knees and lifted me to his chest before laying me upon the covers. I rolled to a seat before he could protest or join me on the bed. Then, unable to resist the temptation, I reached for his side and unbuckled a strap. And another. Arthur stood before me, his gaze unwavering, as I removed his armor piece by piece. Until only a loose tunic and breeches remained. My shoulder throbbed, but still I continued until I tugged up on his tunic. Arthur pulled the soft linen over his head, tossing the garment to the floor.

Goddess above, he was beautiful. A king forged from grace and battle. And as I had often secretly hoped, faint freckles covered his chest and muscled abdomen like a spill of stars. I wanted to kiss each one, to touch every mark and scar—to know every part of this incredible man.

Arthur leaned down until his hands settled on either side of my hips and then he brushed his lips across mine. He pulled back just enough to catch my gaze and gauge my reaction.

I smiled to encourage him. Where Galahad was all fire and fight, Arthur was sweet wine and the simmering warmth of home.

Home.

It wasn't the first time Arthur birthed this feeling in me. But I didn't have long to question why or ponder the strange emotions the word conjured.

His lips had returned to mine as he tipped my head back, reverently lowering me to the pillows below. My injury jolted with sparks of fire as my shoulder pressed into the bed. Breath fluttered free from my tightened chest, and I held back a grimace. But every ounce of pain dissolved when Arthur slowly crawled over the length my body, his skin practically glowing in the dusty moonlight. I watched, bewitched by the play of muscle and sinew across his chest, arms, and shoulders as he trailed soft kisses up my legs, around my navel, then between and under my breasts, before he buried his face into my neck.

"I feel as if my body knows yours already," he whispered across my skin. "As if I were made for you and you were made for me. Do you feel it?"

Pain tightened my chest once again as I whispered the word. One word that fully sealed my betrayal. "Yes."

I did feel this connection, and strongly. The pleasure was unlike any I had known before, slow and languid and devastating. He seemed content to explore the expanse of my skin with lips and soft caresses, ever careful of my wound. And yet my body reacted as though he were making love to me.

Perhaps he was, emotionally. And perhaps I wished him to.

We couldn't get enough of one another, memorizing each other's bodies in reverence, tasting passion's sweetness with one kiss after another. His affections were one of the most fulfilling experiences of my life. Every touch felt as though we joined completely, even though he remained respectful of my injury. We continued our exploration until the moon shifted from the window and the room shadowed into blissful darkness, a stillness broken only by our ragged breathing.

Until Arthur fell asleep, lips flushed and skin salted with sweat.

I stared at the ceiling, listening to the rise and fall of his peaceful slumber. This time I let the tears fall as my heart withered into brittle leaves and crumbled beneath the weight of my guilt. My choice was made, however.

My toes touched the cold floor and I crept back to the other bed where I gathered my armor, sword, and daggers. In the quiet hallway, I dressed, the tears still slipping down my flushed cheeks. When finished, I strode into the room, giving Arthur every opportunity to wake and stop me. But he remained sprawled across the bed, lost to pleasant dreams.

"Ye're a beautiful man, Arthur Pendragon," I whispered to his shadowed form. "It is I who asks for yer forgiveness."

My breath shuddered. Then, I pushed past the pain in my shoulder and in my chest and grabbed Excalibur.

I expected a knight to call out, "Traitor!" as I barreled out of the building and across the field. Yet, the only sound I heard when I reached the stables was a crow on a nearby branch, cawing. Strange for a crow to be active before dawn. I shook off the omen and threw Zephyr's saddle over her back.

The last sound I heard before Zephyr and I thundered onto the road that would carry us to the river port was that same crow. But this time the bird sounded as if it laughed.

Interlude

Morgana

The crow swooped low and trailed behind the witch's shadowed side unseen. Hooves turned up clods of dirt and grass. Her beast heaved and the charger's coat glistened with sweat. Occasionally, the crow could hear the witch hiccup with pathetic sobs. The task had broken her fierce spirit and weakened her focus. Good. The smell of her sickened grief was delightfully bitter and fed the crow more power to remain aloft.

Soaring on the wings of Arthur's destruction, the crow cawed with laughter. And if the witch heard? The better. Let the crowed triumph settle in the witch's bones. Let the mocking sound turn her blood to ice as she raced against the night and dawn and her failed destiny.

Arthur would spurn the witch now and, thus, his salvation. The crow laughed again, her caws growing louder when swollen silver eyes peered over an injured shoulder.

The witch pulled on her reins, and the horse slowed to a canter. The beast huffed large, hot puffs of vapor from her nostrils before shaking her head and flattening her ears.

The acrid smell of smoke still hung in the air. Crude wooden structures lay splintered in charred heaps. Bodies of villagers littered the dirt streets and soaked the ground with their innocent blood. And their boats—the ones the witch needed—rested half-sunk, still tied to posts in the River Dee.

The witch kicked her beast in the flanks, turning her away from the ruined village. Ghostly white strands of hair streamed after her in a macabre dance as she galloped along the river bank toward the Irish Sea.

O'Lynn's men were idiots. How did they plan to sail away? Or was this a suicide mission from the onslaught?

The crow no longer laughed. Plans that were firmly within her claws now loosened and slipped. When Arthur and his knights gave chase, they might catch their little white whore. No, she couldn't allow Excalibur to touch the Little Dragon King's fingers ever again.

With a furious beat of her wings, the crow soared past the witch and her heaving beast toward the next big port town.

Chapter Twenty-Eight

Arthur

Arthur awoke to a honeyed kiss of morning light streaming through the drapes. He stretched slow and deep, his body alive and humming with the pleasure of last night's exertions. Fionna. Even her name tasted sweet on his lips. He closed his eyes, letting the memories wash over him.

It had been like a dreamscape—Fionna an enchantress, spinning his world into a string of miracles and wonders. The heat of her lips on his, the silken feel of her skin beneath his hands, the exquisite press of her lithe body against his. Arthur shivered at the memories, unable to keep the smile from breaking across his face. Every touch, every movement was careful, with her injured shoulder. But Arthur hadn't minded taking things slow or waiting for their coupling. The kisses and caresses they had shared last night had been gentle and deliberate and perfect.

Arthur heaved a soft sigh. He couldn't remain floating in a pleasant haze of daydreams all day. They needed to return to Caerleon and start the hunt for the Grail all over again. They had turned every inch of Lord Bronn's house upside down last night while Fionna slept, and found nothing that even mentioned the Grail, let alone contained a clue to the vessel's whereabouts. Arthur sighed, pushing himself up and out of bed. The bed where Fionna had lain was empty. He frowned. Perhaps she had already left for breakfast. Had he lingered abed so late?

Arthur pulled on his tunic and pants, sitting on the edge of the bed to lace up his boots. Once finished, he reached for Excalibur's familiar weight. And froze.

The sword wasn't there.

Arthur spun in a circle, his panicked gaze searching the room. He remembered setting his sword by his bedside last night. And . . . he wracked his mind, trying to recall details through the fog of sleep. Yes, Fionna had knocked Excalibur over. And he had set his blade against the wall. He stared at the empty spot where the sword should be. It was gone. His eyes swung to Fionna's bed. Fionna was gone. His heart seized in his chest. Panic charged through his veins. Perhaps she had taken Excalibur downstairs with her?

Arthur flew down the stairs and swung around a stone doorway leading into the dining room.

Lancelot, Galahad, and Percival sat at a long wooden table with trenchers of food and goblets of ale before them.

"Morning sleepyhead," Percival said cheerfully.

"Fionna . . ." Arthur breathed, his mind racing almost too quickly for words. "Where is Fionna?"

"*You* were the one who insisted that *you* stay with her." Galahad wrinkled his brows in a scowl. "And now *you've* lost her?"

"Excalibur is gone," Arthur rushed out, ignoring Galahad's impertinence. He couldn't believe it. This couldn't be happening. "And so is Fionna."

Lancelot was on his feet in an instant. "You sure?"

"It's a big bloody sword, I'm pretty damn sure," Arthur snapped. "None of you have seen her?"

The knights shook their heads.

"Could there be more Irishmen about?" Percival asked. "Could they have taken her? And the sword?"

Arthur bit the inside of his cheek. "I don't know how they could have moved past without me waking. I suppose stealing her out from underneath me is possible." As horrible as that would be—an injured Fionna being captured by a hostile clan—the thought was far preferable to the other one that seized him.

Of course, it was Lancelot who voiced his real concern. "Or she took your sword."

"Fionna wouldn't have stolen Excalibur," Galahad protested, pushing up from the table. "She swore an oath to serve Arthur. She's loyal."

"Stop thinking with your cocks for one minute," Lancelot said. "We've known her for less than a week. She showed up out of nowhere and disguised who she was to win the tourney. She seduced Galahad—"

"I seduced her, man," Galahad rumbled. "Get

your facts straight."

"I thought you said she showed up at your room?" Lancelot pointed out.

"Well, she was . . . in the hallway. She didn't exactly knock on the door."

"You know who else's room is down in that hallway?" Lancelot lifted one dark brow. "Arthur's. Perhaps she went to seduce *him*, and you got in the way."

Lancelot looked from Arthur to Galahad, his blue eyes sharp as daggers. It took all of Arthur's self-control not to look away from his knight's accusatory gaze. If what Lancelot was suggesting was true . . . Arthur's mouth went dry. Last night's stolen kisses and heated caresses jumped into stark relief, exposed under the piercing light of Lancelot's suggestion. Had Fionna only kissed him last night to lull him into a false sense of security, so she could take his sword? His mind rebelled at the notion. The thought was too terrible.

"What night was it that you and Fionna . . ." Arthur trailed off.

"The night of the faerie wine," Galahad said.

Arthur wracked his brain again, recalling. "I wasn't in my room that night. I was at the library."

Galahad crossed arms over his chest, and Lancelot frowned, dragging angry fingers through his hair.

"Disna matter," Percival cut in. The young man had been staring forlornly at his plate, and now stood. "She's our fifth knight. Excalibur chose her. And she's the key to finding the Grail. I feel this as surely as I breathe. Perhaps she was taken, or perhaps she took the sword herself. If she did, I'm sure she has a good reason."

Lancelot sighed. "The world doesn't work that way, lad."

Percival jutted his chin out stubbornly. "Just because ye betrayed Morgana disna mean Fionna will betray us." The other knights flinched at that, but Percival pushed on. "Wherever she is, Excalibur is with her. We need to find them both. Every minute we waste here is another minute between us."

"Percival speaks sense," Arthur relented. At this moment, it didn't really matter who had taken his sword. They just needed to get Excalibur back. "Be ready to ride in five minutes."

The knights flew from the room, gathering belongings, and then dashed toward the stable to saddle their mounts.

Arthur was glad that his body knew by heart the familiar motions of saddling and bridling Llamrei. For his mind was useless to him, trapped in a spinning loop of fear and sorrow and self-loathing. Excalibur was his most precious possession, the gift that marked him as sovereign over Caerleon, the Kingdom of Gwent's overking, and the High King of all Briton. First, Morgause had cursed his blade, and now, he'd lost it, all in a span of a month. Were the gods testing him?

Perhaps he didn't deserve to rule Briton, if the promise of one night with a beautiful woman was all it took for him to abandon his charge to rule this land. Fionna. Bewitching and fierce . . . and duplicitous? He didn't want to believe this version of Fionna possible, but Lancelot was right. They knew little about their fifth knight, despite how deep the connection he felt with her. Perhaps she was a spider, carefully spinning a web of illusion and lies—a trap for a king. His face burned with shame at the thought that what he and Fionna had shared may have only been a clever ruse. Is this what his half-sister felt, he mused, when Lancelot had betrayed her? Embarrassed her before the entire kingdom? Arthur felt a newfound surge of kinship.

Llamrei stamped her hoof and Arthur started, realizing he was pulling the girth too tight. "Sorry girl," Arthur murmured, slipping the buckle into the correct notch in the leather. He led Llamrei into the open and swung onto her back.

Arthur's shame burned into anger and he let roiling feelings spark into a blaze within him. He welcomed the searing heat, a purifying fire burning away the softness of his emotions. The weakness of his desires. Until only rage remained.

A grim smile split his face. They would track and capture whoever had Excalibur. Perhaps Fionna was guilty, perhaps not. Whoever the thief, when he found them, he would make them pay.

Chapter Twenty-Nine

Lancelot

A small part of Lancelot refused to believe that Fionna would betray them. Lancelot saw the dim hope in Arthur's eyes. The rigid set of his shoulders spoke of Arthur's desperate prayer that Fionna had been taken somehow—that she wasn't the treacherous snake she now apeared to be.

But, sometimes, the simplest explanation was the right one.

The wind streamed through Lancelot's hair, his horse's rocking gait smooth beneath him. They were eating up the ground in their pursuit of her, or whomever had the sword.

"Arthur!" Galahad's booming shout sounded behind them, almost stolen by the wind and the distance. But their king heard and turned his mount, galloping past Lancelot, to where Galahad had stopped and pointed to a patch of mud on the road. "Tracks. A single horse."

Galahad and Lancelot exchanged a grim look. One horse meant just Fionna. She hadn't been taken. She had stolen the sword and run. All on her own. Sometimes Lancelot hated being right.

Arthur straightened in his saddle. "This is a well-traveled road, we don't know—"

Galahad cut in gently. "Possibly. I think it's safe to assume the tracks belong to Fionna's mount."

Percival was shaking his head, as if he didn't want to believe it either. A surge of compassion for the lad overcame him. True, perhaps Lancelot was more jaded than most, but there came a point in every man's life when he realized that life and love wasn't all courtly romance and fair maidens. Men were moths and women the devouring flame—they kept a man warm at a distance, but if he were foolish enough to get too close, they would burn him up in an instant.

Arthur was nodding woodenly, processing Galahad's unwelcome words, before saying, "Good. If we only face her, then Excalibur will be easier to recover. We ride." He kicked his horse's flanks. Llamrei spun about and then launched back into a gallop.

Lancelot sighed, urging his charger forward to match Arthur's pace.

It didn't make sense. Morgana's curse had said the Gwenevere would tear them apart. Would ruin Caerleon. And Fionna was certainly doing that, by taking Arthur's sovereign blade. But . . . Lancelot hadn't slept with her. He had exercised superhuman restraint against the most fascinating woman he had ever met. So . . . why was the curse coming true? Could Morgana have lied to him somehow about the nature of this curse? He didn't think that was possible. Fae couldn't lie. But they could omit details. He wished he had his foster mother to talk to about this situation. Vivin would know a thing or two about curses.

Should he tell Arthur? He looked at his king's back a few paces before him. No. Lancelot didn't think he had ever seen Arthur so unmoored. Now wouldn't be a good time to tell him. Besides, he didn't even know if his curse had anything to do with the current situation. He had stayed away from Fionna. He had done his part, regardless of how hard his heart and loins pulled him toward her with a ceaseless tug.

They continued to ride, past the raided village of Ewloe down the River Dee. Countryside blurred in greens and smoke. The stench of death carried on the wind and followed their trail.

Perhaps only a half hour later, they approached a crossroads and Arthur held up a hand as he reigned his horse in. Both he and Arthur slowed to a stop. Galahad and Percival were close behind and quickly came clattering to a stop as well. Their horses huffed and heaved for breath while anxiously pawing the ground. Each poor mount was caked in dust and sweat.

"I think I should have done without breakfast," Percival muttered, twisting in the saddle to relieve a crick in his side.

"That way leads to another port on the River Dee a touch southeast of where we stand," Arthur said. "The village there would be the fastest way for her to sail north to the Irish Sea since Ewloe's destruction."

"There's smoke on the horizon that way," Galahad pointed out. "It's the nearest port outside of Brunanburh. The raiders would be fools to land in a Danish sea town, though. If the Uí Tuírtri visited this shore, the village southeast of here would have been ravaged before Ewloe. There might not be any boats there either."

"Or anyone to man them," Arthur agreed. "North we go, then. To Brunanburh. The river port is less than two hour's ride that way."

"If she made straight for Brunanburh, she could already be on a boat," Lancelot offered apologetically. "She likely has at least a few hours on us."

Arthur's face blackened.

"If she tried for the River Dee, she would have lost a few hours," Galahad pointed out.

"She isnae on a boat," Percival said. He was staring into the distance, a strange expression on his face. "She's coming up that road." He pointed to the left, from the direction of the river village. Lancelot stilled, the hairs on the back of his arms raising. He'd been around magic long enough to know the telltale mental tug and intuitive heightened awareness, and magic was definitely dancing in the air.

"How do you know?" Arthur asked. "Makes little sense that we would catch up with her so soon."

Percival shook his head, his copper hair flashing in the sun. "I just know."

"So, we take her." Arthur's fists tightened on his reins. "And whoever she's with."

"Arthur, are you mad?" Galahad protested. "Do you want to get killed? If we get into an all-out chase with her then someone will break their neck. Or end up on the point of a sword. And I don't know if you remember, but Fionna isn't bad with a sword. It might be one of us."

"What do *you* propose, then?"

The words were tight, clipped. The strain of this was breaking Arthur. Lancelot could visibly see his struggle. Gods, his king really loved Fionna. How could she have spit in his face like this? Especially after the tear of village raids and the loss of Lord Bronn? After their small band had made her one of them? Welcomed her into Caerleon with open arms?

"We lay a trap," Galahad suggested, pulling Lancelot from his ranting thoughts. "Perhaps Percival was right. Maybe she had a good reason for taking the sword. If she did, I for one would like to hear her tale before we come to blows. Let us not strike first and ask questions later."

"What kind of a trap?" Arthur asked.

"I will wait here for her. You three sneak around and hide—someone beside the road where we came, the others on the River Dee side. She'll slow when she sees me blocking the path. I'll find out what I can. If she tries to run, she'll be surrounded. We capture her, hopefully without killing her," Galahad looked meaningfully at Lancelot, "and get back the sword."

Lancelot grunted. It's not like he wanted to kill the woman! He was just apparently the only one of them who hadn't completely lost his mind for her.

"She comes soon," Percival added, his voice faint.

"Hurry," Galahad ordered. "To positions."

Arthur didn't seem to mind being commanded in

that moment.

"I'll cut through the woods and circle back around to her," Lancelot said, trying to be kind by giving his grieving king the easier route. "Arthur, you take the road from Chester. Percival, wherever you would like."

Arthur nodded and Lancelot wheeled his horse, plunging into the sparse forest bordering the road. He looked behind him and didn't see Percival following. The knight must have decided to go with Arthur. Fine. It would be good for his friend to have moral support, if he had to do the worst.

Lancelot slowed his horse to a walk when he got far enough from the road to be hidden from sight. Then he turned to cut parallel to the path Fionna would emerge from. He wouldn't have to go far to be able to circle around and pen her in.

Trepidation filled him as the sound of stilted hoofbeats reached his ears. Whatever came next, it wouldn't be pretty.

Chapter Thirty

Galahad

Galahad sat at the crossroads, his heart in his hands. A small plume of dust rose in the distance as a rider limped up the road from the River Dee. How could the rider be Fionna? How could it not?

It's strange how much had shifted for him in the past few days. As effortlessly as a thread on a loom, Fionna had fit into the fabric of their lives as if she had always been there. Had there ever been a time when she wasn't supposed to be their fifth? It felt hazy and distant—her presence in their lives a given. And then this morning, everything shifted again. But now, instead of feeling comfortable and right, things felt strange and chaffing, like putting one's boots on the wrong feet. Fionna wasn't their enemy. Galahad didn't know why she had taken the sword, but he knew this much at least: she wasn't their enemy.

The white of her hair and the foam-flecked flanks of her limping horse came into view first. Had Zephyr thrown a shoe? Or gone lame? His eyes traveled back to Fionna and his pulse stuttered at the sight of her, each wounded beat of his heart panging with confusion.

Galahad took a steadying breath, clicking his tongue to turn his large charger sideways, to block most of the road. With Zephyr's injury, he knew she couldn't gallop away. This was more for show, to gain Fionna's full attention. He kept his sword in its scabbard, though he rested his hand on the big pommel. He prayed he didn't have to use his blade. Might as well cut off his own arm, as cut down Fionna. Still, through his trepidation, he marveled at how quickly he had come to love her. And love her he did.

Fionna caught sight of him and hauled on her gray mare's reins. Spooked from the pain, her horse slid to an agitated stop in a clatter of hooves just feet from Galahad. Fionna's lovely face was covered in a sheen of sweat, her white braids a wild tangle behind her. Her expression—he recognized it. Grief and heartbreak thinned her pink lips into a tight line, weariness drooped her proud shoulders. And over those shoulders, strapped to her back, the glittering pommel of a sword that winked in the morning sunlight.

Excalibur.

"Good morning, Fionna," Galahad said, grateful that his voice was clear and strong.

She let out a strangled laugh. "That's all ye have to say to me?"

"A few other things come to mind, but I thought we could skip those and be civil. Give us the sword,

Fionna." He held out his hand toward her, like one might toward a wild animal, to let the beast test the stranger's scent on the air. "Excalibur doesn't belong to you."

"I know," Fionna choked out. "I'm sorry. I'm sorry for everything. But I need this sword more than Arthur does." Her mare danced beneath her, seeming to sense her rider's anxiety.

Galahad tensed, in case she was about to bolt. Though, her mare wouldn't travel far, if she did. And Zephyr could become permanently damaged too. He decided to keep her talking.

"He needs Excalibur most of all. Without this sword, his claim to the kingship of Caerleon, the Kingdom of Gwent, and all of Briton is lost. You swore an oath to protect him, to serve as his knight. Did that mean *nothing* to you?" He didn't ask the question that was ringing loud in his mind. *Did we mean nothing to you? Did I?*

Fionna looked up at the heavens, her mouth twisting as if she was fighting back tears. "Of course, my vows meant something. But I made another oath. As a daughter. And a sister. And that means more. It has to."

Galahad frowned. What was she talking about?

"Galahad—I'm sorry for what I did to ye. Our time together, every moment meant something to me. But we can never be."

"It doesn't have to be this way," he said tenderly. How was he to show her how much their moment had meant to him too?

She plunged on, choking on her apparent anguish. "And tell Arthur . . . tell Arthur I'm sorry. That I appreciated all he did for me. All . . . that passed between us."

"Tell him yourself," Galahad suggested. "Come back with us. Return the sword. Our fellowship can be as it once was."

She shook her head, her braid whirling. "That's impossible Galahad, and ye know it. I've ruined everything. The only chance I have now is returning home with this sword."

"You're not leaving Briton with Excalibur. Do you think Arthur would not come for you? That he would not ride to the ends of the earth to take back what is his?"

"I just need Excalibur for a time. After that, he can have his sword back. I'll even help him get his blade back."

"I don't understand."

Fionna licked her lips nervously, her gaze darting around as tears rolled down her cheeks. "I'm sorry Galahad, I've tarried too long. Tell the others . . . I don't know. Something to make the betrayal softer."

Even knowing an attempt to flee might happen, despite her horse's injury, Fionna's sudden motion to spur her mount into action startled him. The little mare was fast as the wind, whickering in pain. And, then, they were thundering past him on an uneven gait down the road to Brunanburh, the one direction they hadn't placed a trap.

Galahad swore, kicking his mount to follow. He hadn't thought she'd be able to get past him so nimbly!

Fionna was already putting distance between them. Galahad narrowed his eyes against the grit her horse kicked up, his focus on her form before him. But then, seemingly out of nowhere, a black steed and rider appeared directly in Fionna's path.

Zephyr screamed in surprise, rearing and pawing the air. Fionna tumbled off her back and landed with a thud on the hard-packed road. She hissed in pain as her shoulder smacked the earth, rolling to her side to protect her own injury.

Arthur. How had his king known?

Galahad had little time to wonder. Arthur threw himself off his mount onto the ground and grabbed Fionna by the buckles of her leather armor, hauling her up to her feet. Blotches of red blossomed from Fionna's wound.

"Arthur!" Galahad shouted, fearing what his king might do in his rage.

Lancelot's mount skittered to a stop behind him and he was off his horse in a flash, his sword drawn. He leveled his weapon at Fionna, laying the sharp edge against the nape of her neck. Where was Percival? Galahad thought briefly, but his attention was pulled back to his two murder-bent fellows.

Galahad pulled his sword from its sheath too, not sure if he would have to use his blade on Fionna or to scare sense into the other men. "Easy all," he bellowed.

Fionna was blinking away her confusion from the fall, one half of her coated in dust from the road. She held up her hands in surrender to the men surrounding her, gritting back in pain.

Arthur pulled a knife from his belt, leveling the razor-sharp edge at the other side of her pale throat, his other hand still twisted in the buckles of her leather armor. And his face contorted with thunderous wrath.

"I yield," she said with a cough. She closed her eyes, and said with what almost seemed like relief, "I am outmaneuvered. Take the sword. Excalibur is yers."

Chapter Thirty-One

Percival

Percival felt strange. In his mind, he knew his other knights needed him—that there was no more important place to be than at the crossroads waiting for Fionna. He needed to see her again, to gauge the look on her face and try to understand why she had left. But there was an invisible tether pulling him away. The unseen line tied a fisherman's knot to his stomach, or so it seemed. The tether tugged at him, making the contents of his breakfast lurch skyward. Giving in to the stronger sensation, he spurred his chestnut horse, Kit, to the east—away from Arthur and his brothers and Fionna.

They plunged through silver birch and hemlock trees and soft ferns, the feeling growing ever stronger. He had thought Fionna was the most powerful pull he had ever felt, and he felt her still, but this was more urgent. The sensation commanded him to hurry. It was always unsettling when his Fisher King heritage asserted itself. Years would go by without so much as a twinge, making him question whether hiding in the forest wasn't all a dreadful joke played by his mother to ruin his childhood, and his adulthood at that. But then the magic would seize him, and he would remember long-lost words from his father. The pull was true. Undeniable. That's how the invisible tether felt now.

Percival cursed under his breath. He didn't want to be thinking about the Grail, or his father, or magic. He wanted to be thinking about Fionna, to be there to stop Arthur and Lancelot from doing something they would regret. When Galahad had pointed out the single set of hoof prints in the mud, Percival had felt his heart splinter. Not because he thought Fionna had betrayed them. Somehow, deep down, despite all evidence to the contrary, he knew she hadn't. He felt the truth in his bones. But he knew what her flight would do to Arthur. What her absence would mean for their future. Everything would change. And Percival wanted nothing to change. For the first time in a long time, with Fionna as their fifth, the world felt right. All of them together. Their quintet band of warriors was how their group was supposed to be.

Kit pushed through a dense patch of underbrush into a circle of trees. Percival reined him in. The hackles rose on the back of his neck, the breath stolen from his lungs.

It was a faerie circle. A single beam of light pierced through the dense tree canopy, spilling like liquid gold across a single pillar of ancient mossy stone. Excitement churned in his veins as he swung down onto the soft loamy soil.

Percival looked about, but he was alone, just him and the stone. He walked toward the large granite boulder slowly. The tumult of forest growth held no dominion here, the ground clear but for a carpet of tiny white flowers. A ring of mushrooms bounded the circle, their creamy white heads glowing in the ethereal light cast from above.

The circle looked as if the magic had not been disturbed in generations. Did anyone alive know that this relic existed? The stone was as tall as him, an oblong of dark gray granite. Though the stone's venerable form was covered in moss, Percival could see that something was etched onto the surface.

Slowly, with a shaking hand, Percival peeled the moss from the stone's face, baring the words written there. It was in Ogham, the runic language of the druids. And the faeries. Percival's mother had made him learn how to read the runes—just another part of her unconventional education. Half the time he believed her touched in the head.

He wiped away a wee bit of moss and squinted his eyes to better read the Ogham marks. His eyes then widened, a disbelieving laugh escaping him as he realized the rune's meaning.

"Across the wall and atop the rock hill, the blessed five shall drink their fill."

A riddle. But more than that. The runes were directions. To the Grail. Directions meant for five. Finally, the sídhe took pity on their mortal souls!

Chapter Thirty-Two

Fionna

I had never felt so broken as I did in that moment. The anger and hurt in the eyes of my knights tore at me with savage claws. Ripping away my resolve. Cutting to my core and draining the fight from me. Part of me was relieved they had found me. Excalibur belonged with Arthur. The thought of giving the sword to O'Lynn turned my stomach, no matter the reason.

And my reason—what would become of them now, after Arthur took out his rightful vengeance on me? The thought of my father's face when O'Lynn gloated about sending me to my death was too much to bear.

"Just kill me," I said, voice hoarse. Closing my eyes, I leaned forward incrementally, feeling the bite of Arthur's and Lancelot's blades against my neck. I relished the feeling. The sting brought me back to myself in some small way, returned my power to me.

"Unstrap the sword from her, Galahad." Arthur's

tone was foreign—cold. It belonged to a cruel man, a bitter and twisted man. To think this was what I had done to my sweet and sincere king filled me with the hot flush of shame.

I opened my eyes as Galahad stepped in close, reaching around me to unstrap Excalibur from my back. I drank in the sight of his chiseled face so close to mine. I then breathed in his scent of cedarwood and leather, holding back a whimper at the comfort his nearness brought me. Never again. Never again would I feel the burning passion he ignited, nor the bright burst of laughter Percival chiseled out from my hard resolve. Never would I feel the warm sunshine of Arthur's favor that bolstered my confidence, or the sharp bite of Lancelot's edge drawing sparks against my own. I had told myself I would be strong, but I was nothing without them. These knights were like my limbs. How I had functioned so well before them, I knew not. But after them, without them, I was no longer whole.

Galahad stepped back, Excalibur held tightly to his chest. I felt the space between us as though it were a physical thing.

"Why?" Lancelot asked. I turned my head slightly in surprise. Of all of them, I expected least from him. But in his face, through the careful shield of his piercing eyes, I saw a hurt just as deep as Arthur's or Galahad's. Dear goddess. Was there no bottom to the depths of my betrayal?

"Where is Percival? Is he all right?" I asked, finding myself desperate to know that he was well. I felt his absence keenly. The five of us should all be present, when the five of us ended.

"You have lost your privilege to ask questions." The ice of Arthur's tone frosted my bleeding heart. "Or to care about my knights."

I chanced a glance at Galahad, who gave me a quiet encouraging nod. Relief welled in me. Percival was all right at least.

"I believe Lancelot asked you a question. I would know the reason for your betrayal, before the end," Arthur said.

Before the end. Before they killed me. I sighed, weariness settling into every aching bone.

"I was sent here by Donal O'Lynn, chieftain of the Uí Tuírtri clann. The very same clann who raided yer shores and killed Lord Bronn," I began. I saw the anger blackening their faces and hurried on. "He is my enemy. His clann and mine have fought for generations. In our last battle, he captured my father and sister. I paid him a generous ransom, but he refused any coin. The only price he would accept in exchange for my family's freedom was the sword of a Welsh king. Excalibur. So, I sailed to Wales to take yer blade. I didn't know . . ." I stumbled over the words, tears threatening to fall anew. "Didn't know what I would find here. How I would come to feel for ye."

The men were silent, the muscles in Arthur's jaw working furiously.

"How do we know you speak truth?" Arthur asked.

I shrugged helplessly. Lancelot and Arthur's blades had slackened slightly, but still rested on my collarbones. "Ye could verify my story if ye went to Ulster, but I have no proof on my person."

"Why does this chieftain want Excalibur?" Lancelot asked, his eyes narrowed to slitted chips of ice.

"I don't know," I answered. "He shared that he had a new acquaintance who had told him about the sword's power, that is all. Not even a name of the acquaintance . . ."

The men exchanged glances. "Could be Morgana, or the Saxons, or another Briton king," Lancelot said. "You have no shortage of enemies."

Arthur nodded.

A desperate piece of me wanted to beg for my life, but I didn't know how I could go on, torn between love and duty. Between my knights and my family. So, I settled for trying to tell them what they had meant to me.

"I know ye have no reason to believe me, but I will say the words anyway. These days with ye have been the strangest and best of my life. I didn't know when I came to Caerleon how I would come to feel for each of ye. I have never experienced such a powerful connection to any man, let alone . . ."

Let alone four. The confession sounded insane, even in my tumbling thoughts. I plunged ahead, anyway.

"Let . . . Let alone each of ye." I paused as a tight sob broke free, then choked out, "Taking Excalibur broke my heart. If ye believe nothing else, believe that. The sword belongs with ye, Arthur. The sword belongs in Caerleon. And I think, somehow, I do too. I know I've ruined every opportunity, though."

I closed my eyes as more tears squeezed through. Disbelieving. How did it all come to this? "I just couldn't abandon my family. Without the sword, they'll be tortured and killed. My sister..." I struggled to keep my voice even. Opening my eyes, I swallowed against the knot in my throat and half-whispered, "Who knows what O'Lynn's men will do to her. I couldn't abandon them, no matter what my heart was telling me."

"Why didn't you tell us?" Arthur asked. The anguish in his green eyes twisted me like a knife in my gut. "We could have helped you."

I let out a hollow laugh. "Tell ye that the only reason I had come to Caerleon was to betray ye? I know ye are a generous king, Arthur, but I think even yer generosity doesn't extend that far."

"I might have surprised you," he said softly. "For you, my generosity would have extended to the ends of the earth."

I closed my eyes again at that. I didn't want to know that there could have been another way. I didn't want to hear his heart in his words.

"And now?" I asked, opening them, looking at my knights though blurry, tear-stained eyes. "What now?" Perhaps I asked the question to make the decision easier on them. Because I knew they were stalling. I could sense they didn't want to do what they must.

Arthur stepped back abruptly, turning from me, sheathing his knife. Lancelot stepped in closer, his blade still strong and sure against my neck. Our eyes met. In some ways, I think Lancelot and I understood each other the best. We knew what it was to make a fool decision, to betray your king. Yet, he was still standing here at Arthur's side. And I would pay for my mistake with my life.

Arthur turned, nodding, taking Excalibur from Galahad. The big knight laid a hand on Arthur's shoulder and squeezed.

My heart thundered in my chest as Arthur buckled Excalibur's scabbard around his waist, as he drew the blade. His movements seemed as slow as a dream, a nightmare that would not end—I wasn't sure if he was stalling further, or whether the last few moments at one's end moved more slowly.

I fought the weakness in my knees, the roiling of my gut, drawing myself up proudly. Arthur bowed his head at me, and I dipped mine in return, as much as Lancelot's blade would allow. I knew Arthur would strike clean and true.

The moment stilled as we all seemed to take in a breath. Centering ourselves. Preparing. It was then that the thundering roll of hoofbeats came into my awareness—so deafening I was shocked I hadn't noticed the clattering sound before. I supposed facing one's own death was like that—the moment drowned out all else.

"Arthur!" Percival crashed through the nearby trees, emerging onto the road, reigning his horse to a stop. He launched himself off his chestnut horse, running toward our strange little standoff, pushing away Lancelot's blade to pull me into a fierce hug.

I collapsed into him, weakened by my freshly bleeding wound. His warmth and smell of sunshine and sage infused me with comfort, soothing the terror and sorrow within me. "I missed ye, dove," he murmured into my ear, burying his nose into my neck.

I let out an incredulous, sorrow-filled laugh. Percival had returned. And he had brought me a nickname.

Chapter Thirty-Three

Arthur

Arthur was never so relieved for Percival to ruin his plans. His terror had felt like riding for a cliff, able to see the horror but unable to pull away, until the young knight startled them out of sure disaster. The thought of killing Fionna was too much to bear, but Arthur couldn't see another way, no matter how hard he longed for one. When a subject betrays their king, the punishment is death. Great ancestors, how he longed for a better world between kings and men, where mercy was valued over blood sacrifices.

Fionna was crying now, shaking against Percival like a leaf in a gale. Percival was shushing her, stroking her hair.

Arthur turned away. It was one thing when Fionna was standing strong and tall. A warrior. But that facade crumbled to reveal the frightened woman beneath. The woman he loved. And it was he who had caused her such terror. What was wrong with him? Even knowing what she had done, that she had tried to ruin him, he didn't want to live without her. Her reason for taking Excalibur had been noble—understandable even. His heart told him she wasn't being false. That she hadn't wanted to take the sword. That there *was* something between them, and she felt the connection too. But could his heart be trusted?

"Percival, where in the gods' name have you been?" Lancelot asked, his sword still hanging loosely in his hand. His knight was on edge, and the guarded tone was a good reminder for him. Fionna may seem harmless right now, but their fifth knight was anything but.

Percival pulled back gently from Fionna, who wiped her eyes and her nose, a rosy blush of embarrassment coloring her cheeks. Then the lad's face grew alive with excitement. "I found a clue to the Grail."

That startled Arthur back to himself. "What?"

"I was going to go with ye, Arthur, to lay in wait for Fionna. But I felt the tug of magic—so strong I couldn't ignore the tethering pull. I followed the urge into the wood. Magic led me to a faerie circle where an ancient rock sat, carved with words in Ogham. A clue to the Grail!"

Lancelot narrowed his eyes. "A clue? Here? Why on the Mother Goddess's green Earth would a fae stone possess a clue to the Grail along the River Dee?"

"Ye doubt magic, crabapple?" Percival shot back, a cheeky grin in place. "Have ye forgotten yerself, oh wise foster son of the faeries?" The young knight tilted his head toward Arthur and added, "Obviously, some fae still favor our king."

"What did the stone say?" Arthur asked, trying not to let hope overtake him. He could use a little good news right now, and a touch of favor by the Túatha dé Danann would qualify. But he'd been disappointed before.

Percival cleared his throat and winked at Lancelot. "Across the wall and atop the hill, the blessed five shall drink their fill."

Arthur processed the words, disbelieving. "Five?" he asked.

Percival nodded meaningfully at him, gently squeezing Fionna's shoulder. She was still tucked against him. "Five."

Arthur exchanged glances with Galahad and Lancelot. Galahad looked hopeful, and Lancelot sighed, shoving his sword into his scabbard.

"Can you show us this faerie circle Percival?" Arthur asked.

"Of course!"

They rode through the woods after Percival, Fionna on Galahad's horse, leaning against the man. They tied her hands to be safe and had hobbled her lame horse. A stitch or two had snapped open and dark crimson bloomed down the exposed areas of her arm and shoulder where her armor didn't cover. The wound appeared to have stopped bleeding, thankfully. By bringing her along, she would have no chance of outrunning them, injury and lame horse or no. Arthur didn't want to take any chances.

The circle was just as Percival shared. The feel of magic was thick in the air like a humid summer day.

Arthur dismounted, nodding to Galahad, who helped Fionna off his horse.

Together they walked to stand before the stone as light streamed from above to illuminate the rough-hewn letters.

Percival pointed to each rune and explained their meaning, since neither Arthur or any other present could read Ogham. Very few could, the runic language of the gods was used only by the druids and the Túatha dé Danann. For all the wrong Percival's mother wrought—a former druidess in training before she married the Fisher King—at least she served the lad right in this way.

"Across the wall," Galahad said, repeating the riddle. "Could be Hadrian's Wall, no? So, the Grail is to the north, in the Scoti kingdom of Alba?"

Arthur nodded, gnawing the inside of his lip. "Atop a rock hill."

"The city of Castellum Puellarum is built atop a rock hill," Percival suggested. "That's where I would start."

"If Castellum Puellarum is good enough for the heir to the Fisher King," Arthur replied, "Then it is good enough for me."

They fell silent, none wanting to broach the

next subject. None knowing how. Once again, Arthur was grateful when Percival barreled ahead with youthful tactlessness, giving little heed for the sensitivity of the situation.

"Fionna has to come with us. I dinnae care what she did. She's one of us. She's our fifth."

Arthur risked a glance at Fionna. She was staring vacantly at the stone, lost in her own thoughts.

"You're certain of this?" he asked carefully.

"We won't find the Grail without her," Percival said. "I know it in my bones. Just look at this." He motioned to the stone and the circle around them. "We never would have found this if Fionna hadn't fled. She led us right here."

"You led us here," Lancelot corrected.

"But we wouldn't have been close enough to feel the magic's pull without her, ye ken."

"Excalibur *did* choose her," Galahad pointed out.

"Yes, before she tried to steal it," Lancelot countered again.

Arthur tried to set aside his feelings, to view the situation dispassionately. Merlin had foreseen that a fifth knight would join them, whose blood would be the key to breaking the faerie curse on Excalibur and over all Caerleon. Fionna had broken the curse on Excalibur. There was no denying that. And now the stone suggested they needed her as well. He would welcome the devil himself under his roof, it meant healing Caerleon. Would it be so bad to allow Fionna to stay with them?

"Lancelot, a word," Arthur said, pulling his sword brother aside and away from the circle's bright, cloying feel. Arthur took a steadying breath. "I do not trust my judgment when it comes to her. What would your counsel be?"

Lancelot let out a dark laugh. "You're trusting *my* judgment when it comes to women?"

"As a fellow son of a king, as my second-in-command, as my *friend*, I'm trusting your judgment when it comes to my kingdom. I think we need her, if we have any hope of freeing Caerleon from this dark curse. But . . . I fear this idea is just my heart telling me so."

Lancelot closed his eyes, as if warring with something, though what, Arthur couldn't say. His eyelids snapped open and he leveled a gaze at Arthur. "Your judgment isn't worth shit when it comes to her, but you're right this time. Percival is right. Merlin is right. The bloody rock is right. We need her. The Fates have a funny way of bringing souls together, and for better or worse, Fionna *is ours* now."

"And we are hers," Arthur replied softly.

Lancelot nodded and clapped Arthur on the shoulder.

"But the punishment for betraying a king must be death. How could I deviate from that law? And what kind of precedent would I set, if I pardoned her?"

"As for the punishment, don't forget you *are* king. *You* make the rules. You could make her shine your boots every day for the rest of your life, if you wished."

Arthur frowned. "That wouldn't be very fitting for a lady."

Lancelot rolled his eyes. "You know what I mean. As for precedent, no one knows about Fionna's little misadventure but us five. Let's keep it that way."

"You're right." Lancelot spoke sense. For the first time in weeks, Lancelot seemed himself again—his eyes clear and bright, his shoulders pulled back proudly.

Arthur's mouth twisted as he tried to hold in a smile. "You're really loving not being the fuck up anymore, aren't you?"

Lancelot grinned, letting out a delighted laugh. "You have no idea."

Arthur laughed too, and they moved back toward the circle.

"But Arthur," Lancelot slowed him, his voice lowering. "We watch her. All of us. We must stay on our guard."

Arthur gave a curt nod. Wise counsel. Fionna would need to earn their trust, if she wanted their good opinion back. He didn't know what would pass between them now, if anything could. She had lied about so much. But not everything, he thought. He believed that what he and Fionna had shared the night before was real. Their connection had felt real—more real than anything he had ever experienced. He stabbed fingers through his hair in disbelief. Had their time together only been last night? It now seemed a lifetime ago.

The tension was thick as Arthur and Lancelot rejoined the other knights around the standing stone. Arthur took the moment to drink in the sight of Fionna—regal and lovely and fierce. Her tears had left trails through the dust on her face, but she stood proud, once again composed, ready to face his decision. His heart and soul longed for her still, despite her betrayal, perhaps stronger than ever. He couldn't let her pass from his life like nothing more than a surreal dream. He couldn't be the one to rob this world of her. He wouldn't. The worried expressions on Percival and Galahad's faces showed they prayed that he wouldn't either.

"Well," Arthur began. "Seems the Fates have bound us together with bonds so tight that even treachery cannot tear them asunder. For what it's worth, I believe your story, Fionna, about why you stole Excalibur. They do not justify theft, but I understand. I will pardon you for your crime, on one condition." He paused a beat and met her silver eyes. "Help us find the Grail."

Chapter Thirty-Four

Fionna

rthur's words rang in my ears, foreign and strange. Hope surged in me like a tempest. Surely . . . surely, he couldn't be saying what I thought he was.

"Fionna?" Arthur asked, the warm green of his eyes filled with concern. His merciful gaze stunned me. Battle I understood. Strength, and competition, and kill or be killed. But forgiveness?—it took my breath away. A gift as tender and delicate as a newborn lamb. And one freely given. I wondered again, for the hundredth time, about what a strange manner of man King Arthur Pendragon was. Strange and unexpected and wonderful.

They were waiting for me to speak. I struggled to find my voice. I was still shaky after having stared into the dark of the abyss. "Ye would forgive me?" I asked, still not daring to believe his pardon could be true. That everything could go back to how it was . . . surely, this was a cruel dream and I would awake with Aideen in my arms and my father snoring like an old, grizzled bear nearby. And my knights? They would remain pure and whole and I would be spotless in their eyes, as before. The possibility of such a gift, of forgiveness, carved a gaping hole in my chest and I peered up, afraid to see truth.

Arthur blinked shyly at me, in that boyish way of his, before standing tall as king once more. "I believe you were acting under duress from one of my enemies. You cannot be entirely faulted for your actions." He swallowed and I watched as his Adam's apple bobbed. "And . . . and we need you. You've seen the curse. How the dark magic is poisoning Caerleon. We need your help to find the Grail. Help us find this fae relic and you're forgiven."

"But—" I began, wanting to foolishly protest that I knew nothing that could help them find the mythical bowl.

"Just yer presence will aid us lass," Percival said. "Trust me."

"Will you stay?" Galahad asked, his words breathless with hope.

I looked between them, my heart squeezing painfully as I took in each of their wary faces. Arthur, the sweet verdant warmth of summer; Percival, the playful swirl of ochre leaves in autumn; Lancelot, hard and cold as ice, but with a promise of a thaw. And Galahad. The explosion of life in the spring, exuberant and sensual. How had they so quickly worked their way into the marrow of my bones, the aether of my soul? They were my sun and night and stars, my seasons turning. I could no sooner leave these men than I could leave my own body.

"I will help ye find the Grail. I'll stay." I nodded heartily, all pretenses of a stoic warrior gone. I found I no longer cared. They had seen the real me—raw and imperfect and flawed. And still they welcomed me with open arms. My knees gave out beneath me, but Galahad was there on one side, Percival on the other.

Lancelot stepped forward and pulled a knife from his sheath, slicing the bonds at my wrists. And Arthur. He stepped close and I reached for him, unsure, afraid he would shy from me. But he didn't. He stepped into my arms and I clung to him—breathed in his scent of grass and summer that I feared I would never smell again.

There, in the deep of the forest, with my knights around me, I was overcome by a certainty stronger than anything I had ever felt. Whatever came next, we'd be able to face it.

Together.

Epilogue

Morgana

Perched atop a mossy stone, the crow burned with anger as she watched the Little Dragon King kiss the witch's forehead. The fool human man reeked of cloying pheromones and bruising shame. Did the man even realize he was enchanted still? Compelled by the lily dangling from her throat? Two other weak human men shared turns pulling the witch into an embrace, and the crow nearly cawed with disgust.

Almost, but . . .

A pulse thundered, singing to hers. The crow angled her head in search of the mortal heartbeat she knew intimately. There. The fourth man, who stood apart from the others to emotionally parry the witch's and necklace's charms. The one with glacial eyes and hair as black as her feathers. The one who had made a mockery of her love.

Clíodna be cursed!

Calling upon the forest's dark shadows and the prayers of warmongering men, the crow vaporized into a woman's form. A cool summer breeze swirled around Morgana in a fury of leaves and twigs. Her hair danced like obsidian snakes as her dark magic faded into the rotting forest floor and tree shadows.

"You are weakest of all," she whispered for the breeze's ears alone.

With a flutter of her hand she pushed the wind, warmed with guilt, toward Lancelot. The wildflowers and grass shuddered as her breath passed by. And when her words found their target, they caressed his face and toyed with the curls in his hair.

A muscle in his jaw worked as a flush colored his cheeks, his gaze chilled to ice. Lancelot turned stiffly from her half-brother and his idiots and strode over to his horse. He leaned his forehead against the beast's sleek withers.

A smile twisted her lips as his pulse changed tunes and began thundering with fear instead of desire. The war drums in his chest would demand a fight soon enough. Or some other drastic reaction. She cared not. She was not cowed by him. He deserved to know this torture. She would have loved him for all eternity. Morgana would have traded her immortality to rule a kingdom of man, if Lancelot remained by her side. Or she would have carried him into the Otherworld when his mortal days ended. Now he could rot like the farmlands and the forest beneath her slippers.

The witch may be in Arthur's good graces again, but he hadn't won. Caerleon was her and her sisters' birthright. The honor price for their father's death and mother's defiling. And for their mother's disappearance when Uther Pendragon died at the hands of his enemies—the Saxons. The very tribes who had slain her own father.

She dug her sharp nails into a maple tree until it wept sap. Excalibur would be hers, even if the witch failed in her blind mission. What did the Romans once say? A kingdom divided is easily conquered?

Lancelot tightened the straps on his saddlebag and then looked out into the forest near where she stood. Morgana stepped into golden light, revealing herself to him. They locked eyes.

Her lips curled back in wicked promise and his lips sneered into a cold vow of his own. She laughed, and leaves rustled and fluttered. *I am not done with you yet, little knight*, she thought. Then, the breeze glittered into swollen darkness filled with the sounds of wailing and gnashing of teeth.

The crow flew from the moss-covered stone into the dank shadows of the forest. In a sharp swoop, she turned toward the Irish Sea to hunt for a vessel pushed by Lir's currents to his misty green Isle and the shores of Ulster.

The Dark Fates had a new course.

To Be
Continued

Author Thanks

Thank you, Readers for giving our Arthurian Legend reverse harem tale a try. We hope you enjoyed Fionna and her brave knights! Please leave a review on Amazon, Goodreads, or wherever else online you talk books. Reviews will help other readers find our book and is a wonderful way to thank an author for entertaining you.

Writing a book takes a village! And, in this case . . . an international one :-)

Our hearty thanks to Gareth Thomson of North Lanarkshire, Scotland for helping us craft Percival's lyrical language. We had so much fun pouring over the list of words and slang you so wonderfully provided us.

And, our eternal gratitude to fellow author Dierdre Reidy of Dublin, Ireland for reading a beta copy of The First Knight to provide feedback on the Irish elements in our story, including the language.

We also appreciate Deborah Woods of Norway for her insight into Scandinavian culture to help shape Galahad into the loveable Norseman that he is, and Katie Kent of Seattle, U.S. for assisting us with our druid research (as she's in druidic bardic studies) as well as lending us the book, "Arthurian Magic" by John &

Caitlin Matthews.

An audiobook is also in the works and will be narrated by Sunil Patel of London, England and a female narrator (to be announced).

All right . . . time to get back to writing :-)

Happy reading!

Claire Luana & Jesikah Sundin

Historical Notes

Once upon a time, a starry-eyed college student majoring in geophysics, with high aspirations of becoming a technical writer for the National Oceanic and Atmospheric Administration (NOAA), decided to take classes that fed her equal love of the humanities. And so, she enrolled in an Arthurian Legend class and instantly fell in love with Arthurian Cycle stories and fairy tales (even more than she already had).

Hey there. This is Jesikah, one half of the Wonder-Twin duo known as MoonTree Books (aka Claire Luana & Jesikah Sundin). With our powers combined, we became badass mistresses of fairy tale fiction. Okay, we already were . . . *winks* But, we each have strengths that beautifully meld together in our partnership. Claire is truly magical when it comes to zero drafting and micro-outlining. And my powers manifest best in macro-outlining and research. We both write in ways that border on the poetic and pay hawk-eye attention to characterization. But I digress. Back to the title of this post: Historical Notes.

I. Love. Research. And I love historical factoids.

I also have a love for origin stories. And the Arthurian Legend is a tale with origins as misty and mysterious as the gateway to the Otherworld. Most of the Arthurian narratives we know today stem from *The History of British Kings* by Geoffrey of Monmouth, a 12th century Welsh cleric who was obsessed with King Arthur and Merlin stories. Medieval tales aside, history buffs do know this: the Arthurian Legend is of Celtic origins and was hijacked by the French courts after the Norman invasion. The Normans, like the Romans (ha! They kinda rhyme), knew the key to assimilating people groups was to kill their gods. So, they killed their gods by re-writing and assimilating their fables and myths first. King Arthur began as a Bran the Blessed archetype (from the Welsh *Mabinogion*) and was transformed into a biblical King David archetype by the Christian Normans. The Normans even changed the grail from a cauldron-like serving dish, common in Celtic homes, to the cup of Christ.

As I dug deeper into myth origins, I grew frustrated with the druids and medieval monks. The druids were historians and lore keepers for the Celts, whether Gaels or Britons. But—a big BUT—the druids and Celts were orators. It was against their religion to write things down. There were a few heretics in the bunch and so we do have Ogham runes carved into standing stones and a few stone tablets. But not many and certainly not enough to piece together historical details we can confirm absolutely. And with nothing written down, it was easy for medieval monasteries to re-write Celtic history as a propaganda campaign for the Holy Roman Church. And, thus, paganism dissolved into the Otherworld's mist and Christianity became the new state religion.

Despite these unfortunate drawbacks, I did learn a few interesting things about Celtic culture (from the continent and the Isles). The majority of their gods were water born (more on this in a bit). And they were branched out in Star Wars fashion. You either followed the Light side or the Dark side. The Light side were known as the Children of Danu (aka the Túatha dé Danann) and the Dark side were the Children of Domnu (aka the Formorians), as illustrated in *The Ulster Cycle* from Ireland.

The first mention of a "King Arthur" is in the *Historia Brittonum* dated 826 A.D., often attributed to Nennius, a 9th century Celtic monk and historian, who mentioned a "King Arthur" of Caerleon, Wales, also known as the Roman City of the Legion. Camelot is fantasy, which is why dozens of cities throughout Great Britain claim to be Camelot. Some historians even believe Arthur was Ambrosius Aurelianus, a Roman-British war leader from the 5th century who is famed for winning a major battle against the Anglo-Saxons. Me? I don't think Arthur existed. Not as an actual person in history. Rather, he was the equivalent of a super hero to deliver hope and rally the masses. We have The Avengers and they had Arthur Pendragon. That age was fraught with never-ending wars, invasions, territory expansion and border re-assignments, and old gods vs new gods. The people needed a hero to believe in, someone who would unite the masses and bring peace. Arthur was the post-Roman British mythological man for the job.

Another interesting factoid I learned about Celtic culture was their obsession with water sacrifices. When we modern people think of human sacrifices, we often think of a stone table and a bloody mess. But, actually, human sacrifices for the Celts were drownings. Their gods were born from and dwelled in water. And humans weren't the only things sacrificed to the water. Archeologists have found hoards of swords, shields, helmets, spears, and daggers in lakes, ponds, river beds, and even in the oceans around Celtic regions. Lady of the Lake anyone? Why a goddess would lift a sword out of the water makes sense when put in the context of Celtic culture. And Excalibur's inscription? Even more so. "Take me up, cast me away."

But my favorite part of the research? Learning how the Celts were more progressive than modern society with regard to certain social issues. They believed that women were 100% equal to the men, legally and socially. Women in Celtic cultures didn't need a man's approval or permission for . . . *anything*. And, the women practiced polyandry (multiple husbands). So, for those who are trying to piece together how an Arthurian Legend story works with Reverse Harem? This is how. Polyandry was a fairly common practice from what historians are beginning to uncover.

We set our tale in the mid-11th century. By this time, druids had appeared to have died out for nearly 800 years. Forgive our creative license, but Arthurian Legend just wouldn't be the same without Merlin. Also, the official term "knight" was first noted in the late 11th century, after the Norman invasion. Until then, they were just known as noble-titled warriors. And, finally, castles didn't appear until the 12th century, also thanks in part to the Normans. Wooden fortresses and manors were all that existed until then. Still, we used the term "Castle of the Maidens" as that is integral to Arthurian lore and even has Celtic ties.

There's far more, which I will delve into after book two. Especially information on who "Gwenevere" actually was in the myth origins of Arthurian Legend.

If you've read *The Biodome Chronicles*, then you'll recognize my ending: all errors that may exist while trying to represent Celtic and Welsh culture, mythology, geography, and Arthurian Legend elements are entirely mine. I am a storyteller, weaving together information that builds and forms worlds in our imaginations. In the famous words of Nennius, a ninth-century Celtic monk, "I have made a heap of all that I could find."

Your *Knights of Caerleon* lore keeper,

Jesikah Sundin

Interview By Our Readers

When not keyboard deep into writing stories for others to enjoy, we both like to have fun with our readers. Authors are often interviewed by blog sites and promotional companies. But we are rarely interviewed directly by our readers. And so, we decided to change this :-) At the end of August 2018, we opened up our social media for our readers to ask us anything. Seriously . . . anything.

And here are their questions:

1) Kyra Roy from Bothell wants to know: how much tea/coffee do you consume in a single writing session? And what's the ratio of caffeine to words written? lol :D

Jesikah: Uuuhhh *hides face* I can personally consume 1-1.5 pots of coffee per daily writing session. While caffeine aggro, I can push out 1500-2000 words :-P If I'm coffee zen, then it's a more leisurely number around 500-1000 words.

Claire: At least one cup of tea per chapter written. I gave up coffee a few months ago *sobs* so I stick to the leafy stuff now!

2) Chani from Seattle, WA, USA wants to know: boxers or briefs?

Jesikah: Boxer briefs :D *says like Austin Powers* Yeah, baby!

Claire: Um, briefs...(runs away from conversation)

3) Tammie Lou from Wyoming wants to know: when it comes to characters, what is your favorite one and why do you chose this one?

Jesikah: I love bad boy characters. Not the alpha, dominating, toxic masculinity type, but more like the artsy punk boys with snarky, intelligent humor. Dark and broody on the outside, vulnerable and heart-of-gold on the inside. *le sigh* I could write and read these types of characters foreverrrr . . . But, in the The Fifth Knight? This would translate to a combination of Galahad and Lancelot.

Claire: My favorite character in The Fifth Knight

is definitely Fionna, she's such a bad-ass and was super fun to write! I have fun writing characters with big bold personalities that are unapologetic about who they are. I like to write more subtle characters too, but it's just a lot harder.

4) Nicole from Monroe, WA, USA wants know: What's your favorite thing to throw at someone?

Jesikah: I like to throw Claire at people. She's fierce!!! And, I only have to throw her once for people to get a clue. Okay, seriously . . . sometimes I need to throw her twice. But if I'm really honest? I like to throw compliments at people. We need more kindness in the world.

Claire: I don't know, I'm so disoriented from Jesikah throwing me at everything...haha! No, for real, I have terrible hand eye coordination so I try not to throw things at people because I will totally miss.

5) Rebecca Bingham from Worthington Ohio wants to know: what are your tricks for getting past writer's block.

Jesikah: I like to take walks and allow nature to bring my stress levels down. I often find acute stress likes to dampen my writing sessions. But sometimes I don't have a firm grip on my story or character yet. If that's the problem, then I take a writing break and read--anything. The brain is wired for story and sometimes it just needs a little recharge in a world not of my own making.

Claire: I get two kinds of writer's block. One is where I've been working too much and am grumpy about having to write instead of doing something more fun, and the other is where I don't know where my story is going next. The first one is best solved by taking a break, or sometimes I dictate the scene on my phone, because it feels more leisurely to be writing laying on my couch with my doggies. The second I solve by spending some time either plotting out what is coming next in more detail, or imagining the scene playing out in my head until I know what to write.

6) Mary Schaal from Yuma AZ wants to know: What's the silliest crush on a star that you ever had?

Jesikah: I was IN LOVE with Edward Furlong in the early 90's and had his pictures from Teen Beat and Tiger Bop all over my walls. I think I was twelve when I saw Terminator 2 and he was a thirteen-year-old John Connor--a punk hacker boy who cried over a lethal android. I was done. DONE. I just knew we would get married one day. So, yeah, that didn't happen. But I did marry a man in the tech industry who loves to watch cyberpunk as much as me.

Claire: In high school I was nuts over Vin Diesel. (Hides face). The Fast and the Furious baby!

7) Jessica Jett from Kentucky wants to know: how this collaboration came about? Were you fans of each other's works first?

Jesikah: Well, I had been stalking Claire for nearly a year when I finally got the guts to ask her if she wanted to meet, because that's not creepy at all *fangirl* And when I say "stalking," I mean that I had read her book Moonburner and loved it and followed her on social media. We live 45 minutes from each other so a meet-up was possible. Then when we met? All my nerves dissolved. She is such a wonderful person. It didn't take much for me soon after to ask if she wanted to be my table mate at various conventions I attend as a vendor each year. And, thus, MoonTree Books was born. *Claire and Jesikah's words ride off into the sunset together*

Claire: I was just thinking I couldn't remember what prompted us to first meet, but I see Jesikah was the mastermind there :) After I met Jesikah I read her first book Legacy and fell in love with the intricacy of the world and characters she created. We shared a table at two conventions on June and spent a lot of time together talking story and trends. We joked about the idea for this story, not even intending to write anything together. But by the next day it had stayed on both our minds and we were like: we HAVE to write this book. It has all come together very serendipitously!

8) Jennifer from Snohomish wants to know: how you would spend your dream literary world day. You get to have it set in any literary world, and meet three literary characters from any books. Where would you go and who would you meet?

Jesikah: I want to spend a day in Cabeswater with Blue, Gansey, and Ronan from Maggie Stiefvater's The Raven Cycle. We would hunt the Blue Mountain's magical forest in Virginia for the remains of a Welsh king, researching together, laughing, and getting into all sorts of adventures. Plus, I want to pet Chainsaw, Ronin's baby raven.

Claire: OMG can I steal Jes's? Love that series. Ok well, I think I'd head over to Hogwarts to get a magic lesson from Hermione, Gandalf, and Aslan. Then afterwards we'd head down to Hogsmead to drink some butterbeers.

9) Chani from Seattle, WA, USA wants to know: dogs or cats?

Jesikah: Oh! That is so tough. I have to say both. I truly adore both. But, here's a fun fact: From age five through nineteen, I had an English Springer Spaniel named Guinevere :D Her first doggie boyfriend's name happened to be Arthur. She had the most beautiful puppies. I still miss her <3

Claire: Dogz for life! I have two: a Cavalier King Charles Spaniel named Guinness and a Brittany Spaniel named Jameson. Plus I'm allergic to cats (sniff) so me and cats have always had to stay at arm's length.

10) Bob Schaal from Yuma AZ wants to know: What's your favorite word that you use in your writing?

Jesikah: Ha! Hmmm . . . Well, I'm not sure what my favorite word is, but I do tend to lean toward old-timey words. I would probably say the word "susurration" <3

Claire: Ohmygosh that's so hard! My other new series is about magic sweets and I've really been enjoying using candy and food metaphors. Using caramel or caramelize to describe something like a sunset is pretty fun (and yummy).

11) Nicole from Monroe, WA, USA wants know: If you could live in any tree, which tree would you live in? How would you live in it?

Jesikah: An oak tree that looks like it came straight out of a fable. I would build a house mid-story that circles the trunk. One day, my husband and I plan to stay at the famous Tree Houses near Issaquah, WA. It's a dream of mine . . . Okay, I just read Claire's answer. Put our answers together you get Willow Oak, a character from my series, The Biodome Chronicles. This was not planned people, lol. I answered the questions first, haha!

Claire: I love Willow trees, they are so graceful. So maybe I'd have a little cabin amongst the boughs of a willow.

12) Tammie Lou from Wyoming wants to know: What is your favorite location for writing?

Jesikah: The forest *heart eyes* But, since I need battery power, I would say any location near a window and a coffee pot.

Claire: I like writing anywhere that is not my office at home (which is where I do most my writing). It feels like a novelty to go write at a coffee shop or at the park or at a library!

13) Chani from Seattle, WA, USA wants to know: how you do background research for the background and settings for books. Do you read up on historical papers/interview experts?

Jesikah: Oh man . . . I am a worldbuilding nut. Research is my thang. I like to interview people in the real-world regions I'm setting my stories and then I read, read, read. I also create a team of experts for me to lean on for questions and for review. I've been fortunate enough to always find individuals who are willing to read scenes and/or my work-in progress for accuracy.

Claire: Google. I leave the hardcore researching to Jes! I have read a book to do research for my past books, but for the most part I do my research online.

14) Erik from Mt. Vernon , WA, USA wants to know: If you were a beverage, what would you be... and why? And don't just tell us what you love, tell us what we can consume (without teeth) that would perfectly encapsulate your very essence. The

liquid core of your being! Your rehydrating quintessence!

Jesikah: I am an Irish Coffee, sweet creamy personality with a bitter inner-cynic, the billowing hot steam my love of gray skies and foggy days, with a touch of dizzying long-winded intellect that only my Irish roots could spin into story form or lament. Or it's the whiskey. Probably the whiskey and Bailey's.

Claire: Wow, this is tough. I guess I would be a berry smoothie with spinach and a touch of lemon. Overall it's sweet and pleasant and something a lot of people would enjoy, but there's some substance and serious nutritional value there to reflect my love of learning and my serious side, plus a squeeze of lemon to represent my stubborn streak :)

15) Nicole from Monroe, WA, USA wants know: what's your favorite cupcake, and how do you eat it??

Jesikah: My favorite is any kind Claire doesn't give me. She writes about poisoned cupcakes!!! *side-eyes Claire* But, if she offered me a chai spice cupcake with cream cheese frosting, I might give in and risk death. Who am I kidding? My last words would be, "Omg, this is SO good." And when eating, I just dive in. There is no decorum when eating a cupcake, probably because I'm a mom. If I don't eat it fast, my kids will want a bite!

Claire: Yes the non-poisoned kinds are good :) **Cupcake** Royale in Seattle has a lavender cupcake that I really adore. I try to maximize the bites that have both frosting and cake in them, but I have to end on a piece with frosting, so if I take a break from the frosting to eat the bottom part in the middle, I will!

Thank you, Readers! We adore hanging out with you online. You've filled this adventure with giggles and fantastic conversations from the very first page of ths series :-)

Claire Luana & Jesikah Sundin

More Books

Claire Luana & Jesikah Sundin

THE KNIGHTS OF CAERLEON
The Fifth Knight, book 1
The Third Curse, book 2
The First Gwenevere, book 3

Claire Luana

MOONBURNER CYCLE
Moonburner, book 1
Sunburner, book 2
Starburner, book 3
Burning Fate, prequel

THE CONFECTIONER'S GUILD
The Confectioner's Guild, book 1
The Confectioner's Truth, book 2
The Confectioner's Coup, book 3
The Confectioner's Exile, prequel

Jesikah Sundin

THE BIODOME CHRONICLES
Legacy, book 1
Elements, book 2
Transitions: Novella Collection, book 2.5
Gamemaster, book 3

CLAIRE LUANA grew up reading everything she could get her hands on and writing every chance she could. Eventually, adulthood won out, and she turned her writing talents to more scholarly pursuits, going to work as a commercial litigation attorney.

While continuing to practice law, Claire decided to return to her roots and try her hand once again at creative writing. She has written and published the Moonburner Cycle and the forthcoming Confectioner Chronicles, a trilogy about magical food. She is currently working on the Knights of Caerleon trilogy, an Arthurian Legend fantasy romance series, which she is co-writing with Jesikah Sundin. She lives in Seattle, Washington with her husband and two dogs. In her (little) remaining spare time, she loves to hike, travel, binge-watch CW shows, and of course, fall into a good book.

www.claireluana.com

JESIKAH SUNDIN is a multi-award winning Ecopunk SciFi and Forest Fantasy writer mom of three nerdlets and devoted wife to a gamer geek. In addition to her family, she shares her home in Monroe, Washington with a red-footed tortoise and a collection of seatbelt purses. She is addicted to coffee, laughing, and Dr. Martens shoes ... Oh! And the forest is her happy place.

www.jesikahsundin.com
www.jesikahsundin.com/moontreebooks

24823718R00166

Made in the USA
Lexington, KY
19 December 2018